Too Late
for
Angels

ALSO BY

Mignon F. Ballard

AUGUSTA GOODNIGHT MYSTERIES

The Angel Whispered Danger

Shadow of an Angel

An Angel to Die For

Angel at Troublesome Creek

The War in Sallie's Station

Minerva Cries Murder

Final Curtain

The Widow's Woods

Deadly Promise

Cry at Dusk

Raven Rock

Aunt Matilda's Ghost

Too Late for Angels

for

Angels

An Augusta Goodnight Mystery
(with Recipes)

MIGNON F. BALLARD

ST. MARTIN'S MINOTAUR
NEW YORK

m

Ballard

www.minotaurbooks.com

Library of Congress Cataloging-in-Publication Data

Ballard, Mignon Franklin.
    Too late for angels / Mignon F. Ballard—1st St. Martin's Minotaur ed.
        p. cm.
    ISBN 0-312-33186-X
    EAN 978-0312-33186-3
    1. Goodnight, Augusta (Fictitious character)—Fiction. 2. Women detectives—South Carolina—Fiction. 3. Guardian angels—Fiction. 4. South Carolina—Fiction. 5. Widows—Fiction. I. Title.

PS3552.A466T66 2005
813'.54—dc22

                                                        2004057823

First Edition: March 2005

10 9 8 7 6 5 4 3 2 1

For Clare

Acknowledgments

With thanks as usual to Laura Langlie for her patience and assistance; to my editor, Hope Dellon, for her keen editorial guidance; and to friends and attorneys, Bob Sullivan and David White, for sharing their valuable time and knowledge. Augusta says, "Bless you!"

Too Late

for

Angels

CHAPTER ONE

"Where's Mama? Is she here?"

The woman who stood on her porch would never see sixty again, Lucy Nan Pilgrim thought. Then she smiled. This was one of Ellis's pranks. Her friend had teased her about advertising a room to rent in yesterday's paper. "No telling what kind of loonies you'll attract," she'd warned.

"I'm looking for my mama." The woman spoke again, this time in a tiny, childlike voice almost plaintive in its urgency.

Lucy stepped closer, keeping a firm grip on the doorknob. There was no one about except for a car at the stop sign on the corner. She watched as it moved on. "I'm afraid she's not here," she said softly.

"Where is she?"

"I'm sorry. I don't know." Lucy smiled. The poor woman was clearly distraught. Now a lone tear began a start-and-stop path down her rose-tinged cheek. "I believe you have the wrong house," Lucy said.

"No, I don't!" The stranger straightened, grasping the strap of her pocketbook in one hand while smoothing the collar of her blue cotton dress with the other. "This is my house—Mama's house. She's here. I know she's here!"

She looked past Lucy and frowned, her gaze taking in the grandfather clock in the corner, the Windsor chair across from it. Both had come from Lucy's grandmother, to her mother, to her.

"Mama!" she hollered again, and pushed past her to stand looking about with such a frantic expression, Lucy began to fear for her own safety. The woman's boldness had taken her by surprise and she wasn't prepared to deal with her.

"Mama, I'm home!"

"No, wait . . . don't go back there!" Too late. Her desperate visitor had already started down the hallway that led to the back of the house. Now she turned and smiled. "Why, I'll bet she's in the kitchen—in the kitchen with Martha."

Oh, Lordy! Why is this happening to me? And who in tarnation is Martha? The woman seemed harmless enough and looked to be at least seventy, a good fifteen years older than Lucy, but she was obviously delusional. And what if she had a knife or something in that huge pocketbook she carried?

Since the stranger seemed to have reverted to her childhood, maybe she should use the maternal approach, Lucy thought.

"Why don't we sit down and have a glass of lemonade while I see if I can find her?" she called out sweetly. She was sure she still had that can of frozen concentrate stuck back somewhere in the freezer.

But the visitor stood transfixed in the kitchen doorway, still smoothing the collar of her dress. Although her clothing seemed to be of good quality, the woman's dress was wrinkled and the front spotted with stains, but her hair looked as if she'd made a recent visit to a beauty parlor and still smelled faintly of apricot shampoo. Now and then she fingered the two large rings she wore on her left hand, slipping them off and on. One was set with a glassy red stone about the size of a marble. The other was green and rectangular. Both looked fake.

"The big table's gone," she said. "Where's the big table? Where's Martha?" Stepping forward, she reached out to touch the back of an oak-stained captain's chair, one of six Lucy had bought at an estate sale. "This isn't my chair," she whimpered. "Mine has a pretty pillow on it."

Lucy Nan Pilgrim took a deep breath and tried not to sigh out loud. She wouldn't have been a bit surprised if the three bears returned from their woodsy walk at any moment.

"You look tired," she said. "And I'll bet you're thirsty, too. This chair might not be the same as yours, but I think you'll find it comfortable. Let's sit and rest for a minute, have something cold to drink."

She was relieved when the woman accepted the offered chair, plopping her bulging purse on the floor at her feet. "Do you have any cookies?" she asked. "I had breakfast last night, and again this morning, but I would like a cookie. Martha keeps them in the pantry—in a bunny jar."

"A bunny jar?"

She giggled, holding a frail hand over her mouth. "Not a *real* bunny! It just looks like one. And I'd like two, please, if they're molasses."

The best she could do was peanut butter—the kind with a chocolate kiss in the middle. Lucy baked them for her grandson, Teddy, and hid them in the freezer from his sugar-free mother. It was a delicious secret the two of them shared, and Lucy took a certain wicked pleasure out of putting at least one thing over on her rigid daughter-in-law.

Lucy watched as the woman carefully removed the chocolates from her cookies and set them aside before nibbling the edges as daintily as any kitten. She waited until the childlike

3

stranger was on her second glass of lemonade before making a move for the phone.

Her visitor took a bite of chocolate, then popped the whole thing into her mouth. "You're not leaving me? Don't go!" She licked her fingers between words.

"I'm not. No, of course I won't." Oddly touched, Lucy returned to sit beside her. "I just thought I might call and try to find your mother." She felt as if she were speaking to five-year-old Teddy, assuring him she would be sleeping all night in the room next to his. "You are looking for your mother, aren't you?"

The woman drained the last of her lemonade and crunched a piece of ice. "She's probably at The Thursdays," she said, glancing about. "Martha will look after me."

"The Thursdays?" How did this stranger know about what was probably the oldest social organization for women in Stone's Throw, South Carolina? Her own grandmother had been a member; her mother, too. Lucy, who'd considered the whole idea a lot of tommyrot, had tried to decline the invitation when her time came—Roger had been a colicky infant at the time, just too sickly to leave with a sitter; she'd tut-tutted in an oh-so-disappointed voice. But The Thursday Morning Literary Society (which now met on Monday afternoons) wouldn't take no for an answer. Lucy had been a member for thirty years and the reluctant secretary for ten of them.

"Your mother was—is a Thursday?" Lucy asked, and received a nod in answer.

"A Thursday, yes. I *knew* she wasn't in California! Martha should be here now. I want Martha!"

Oh, please, don't cry! Lucy patted the woman's hand. "I know," she said, although of course she didn't know. And she had no idea what California had to do with it. "Tell me, what's your mother's name?"

This was met with a frown. "Her name? Why, her name's Mama."

"But she must have another name. What does your daddy call her?"

Now she began to pleat, then smooth, the collar of her dress. "I don't remember," she said finally.

"My name's Lucy. What's yours?"

"Shirley." This time there was no hesitation.

"Shirley. That's a pretty name. Shirley who? Can you tell me your last name?"

The woman stood, pushing back her chair. "I'd like to rest now. I think I'll go to my room. I want to see my dollhouse. Papa Zeke made it for me, you know."

Papa Zeke! This couldn't be happening! "Papa Zeke sounds nice," Lucy said, trying to remain unruffled. "What's he like?"

"White hair. He has white hair." The woman frowned as she shoved a strand of her own silver-streaked locks from her face. "I don't remember. . . . Oh, he gives me jelly beans! We count them." She smiled at Lucy. "I can count to a hundred."

"You can? That's wonderful! Can you count for me?" Lucy eyed the telephone on the other side of the kitchen. If she could just stall her, maybe—

"I'm tired. I don't want to count now." Shirley, or whatever her name was, was out the kitchen door and halfway down the hallway before Lucy could catch up with her.

"Will you show me your room?" Lucy asked, following her up the stairs. She was surprised that someone as old as Shirley could move that fast, and guessed where they were going before they reached the top of the stairs. She was right. The woman led her to the purple room at the front, the one that had belonged to Lucy's daughter. Julie had always loved purple and Lucy hadn't bothered to redecorate even after her daughter moved out after college.

"I'm afraid the dollhouse isn't here," she said as they stood in the doorway.

"Where is it?"

"It's . . . well, it's being painted." Lucy smiled. "Just like new. Won't that be nice?"

"What color?"

Lucy Nan didn't know. Her friend Ellis had shown her the dollhouse when she redecorated it for her granddaughter's fourth birthday, but for the life of her, Lucy couldn't remember the color. "The same," she said finally.

Shirley seemed to accept this, just as she accepted as her own the purple room with the flea-market furniture Lucy had collected piece by piece. Now, sitting on the side of the bed, she untied her shoes and slipped them off, letting them drop to the floor. The gray leather oxfords were sadly in need of cleaning and her hose had ladders wide enough to climb. Probably tracked that sticky whitish mud all over the house, Lucy thought, and she had been too overwhelmed to notice.

"Tell Martha I want my blanket," she said, falling back against the pillow.

Bossy old soul, whoever she is, Lucy thought. She took a flower-sprigged throw from the window seat and gently tucked it around her guest. The woman's eyes were closed and her breathing deep and even. As Lucy stood looking down at her, she seemed to smile in her sleep.

Satisfied, finally, that she could safely leave her there, Lucy tiptoed from the room, paused for a couple of deep breaths, and made a beeline for the telephone in the hallway.

"Ellis? Thank heavens I caught you! You'll never believe who's asleep in Julie's old room."

"Look here, Lucy Nan, you know good and well I'm expecting close to a hundred people here for that drop-in tomorrow night. This had better be good!"

Lucy was glad Ellis couldn't see her expression. She had almost forgotten her friend was hosting a bash for her husband's nephew and his fiancée, and that she, Lucy Nan Pilgrim, of unsound mind and runaway mouth, had promised to make six dozen cheese straws.

"What was your cousin's name—the one who disappeared?" she asked.

"Who?" Ellis gave one of her impatient little snorts. "What on earth are you talking about, Lucy Nan?"

"You know—that little girl—the one they think was kidnapped or drowned or something back before we were born. Her family lived in this house."

"You mean poor little Florence?"

"Yeah, that's the one! Didn't she just up and disappear or something when she was about five?"

"Wandered out of the yard one day—never did find her. They looked everywhere—even dragged the river. Everybody always got teary when they talked about poor little Florence. Why?"

"I think she's back." Lucy spoke in a whisper, looking over her shoulder.

"*What?*"

"I said, I think she's back. Came here this afternoon looking for her mother. Said she wanted to see the dollhouse Papa Zeke made for her. Ellis, you're the only person I know who called her grandfather Papa Zeke."

"Until now," Ellis said, and paused. "This isn't one of your rotten little jokes, is it, Lucy Nan? Look, I *told* you I wasn't the one who recommended you as social chairman of the garden club this year—get over it!"

"If I were any more serious I'd be crying," Lucy told her. "And what am I supposed to do with her? She could wake up at any minute." Cradling the cordless receiver, Lucy padded quietly into the unoccupied room across the hall and pulled the door shut behind her.

"Don't ask me! I have my hands full as it is."

"Some help you are! She's *your* relative."

"Maybe. I mean, how do we know? What else did she say?" Ellis asked.

"She said her mother was a Thursday and asked for somebody named Martha. I thought she was going to cry."

"*Martha?* You're kidding!"

"Do I seem amused?" Lucy glanced out the window to see if just by chance anyone had come looking for the stranger sleeping across the hall. They hadn't. "Just who is this Martha?" she said.

"If I were Catholic, I'd cross myself," Ellis said. "Don't you remember Marty? Cooked for just about everybody in our family. I couldn't say Martha, so I always called her Marty. Lord, Mama said she wouldn't have known a tureen from a teapot when she first married if Martha hadn't taken her under her wing."

Lucy could hear her friend opening and shutting drawers, clanking silverware. "Looks like I'm gonna be short on forks— would you bring yours when you come, Lucy Nan? And you won't forget the cheese straws, will you?"

"Ellis Saxon! I can't believe you're worrying about silverware and cheese straws with your long-lost kin snoozing in this very house." Lucy opened the door a crack and took a quick peek into the hallway. Empty, thank goodness! "So . . . our Sleeping Beauty must've known Martha, too," she said.

"Had to if she's who you think she is. Marty—Martha cooked for Aunt Eva, little Florence's mama, for years. Lord, you haven't *lived* unless you've tasted her tipsy trifle!" Ellis smacked her lips. "She died when I was about twelve, I think . . . wonder if I have that recipe somewhere . . . "

"Maybe *Shirley* will remember how to make it." If words could cut through phone lines, Ellis Saxon would need a tourniquet. Lucy closed her eyes and tried to remember all the positive things her friend had done for her, beginning with that Girl Scout camping trip in the fifth grade when the tent had leaked on her sleeping bag and Ellis let her climb in with her.

"Shirley? Who's Shirley?" More clanking and dish-rattling. "I think twelve more forks should be enough."

"Calls herself Shirley. She doesn't seem to know her last name—obviously suffering from dementia." Lucy spoke in a whisper. "It's sad, Ellis. She's like a child, and she seems to think she's come home. I don't know what to do. Is there anybody I should call?"

"Just me, I guess. My luck for being an only child. Bennett's on the golf course, but he oughta get home before long. It'll be too dark to see in a couple of hours. He'll know somebody who should be able to tell us where to go from here."

Ellis's husband was an oral surgeon with a practice in Stone's Throw, as well as offices in several other surrounding South Carolina towns, and his vast list of patients put him in touch with people in a variety of professions, including some of the top legal names in the state.

"I guess we could use some legal advice," Lucy said, "but how can we be sure Shirley is really poor little Florence?"

"Nettie McGinnis!" Ellis practically shrieked.

"What about her?"

"She's lived right next door all her life, and she's seventy if she's a day. Nettie must have known Florence growing up. She might be able to help if you can pry her away from her soaps." Ellis rat-a-tapped a fingernail against the receiver, a sign that she was thinking. "What about ID? Does she have a billfold or anything?"

"A pocketbook—crammed full, from the looks of it," Lucy told her. "She left it in the kitchen."

"Look and see, then, and let me know what you find. I'm gonna

9

throw together that crab dip everybody likes, then pick up the petits fours from Do-Lollie's. Do you think you can hold the fort till then? I mean, she's not dangerous or anything, is she? I'll get there as soon as I can.

"And, Lucy Nan, about those cheese straws—do go easy on the red pepper this time."

CHAPTER TWO

Lucy, is anything wrong?" Nettie McGinnis had to speak loud enough to overpower the wailing in the background. "Here. Let me turn this thing down. Poor Sharlotta—that no-good husband has up and left her again! You'd think she'd learn, wouldn't you?"

Lucy smiled. And you'd think Nettie would learn it would take the scriptwriters a couple of years at least to decide on poor Sharlotta's fate.

"No, no, I'm fine," she said. "There's just something I wanted to ask you. Can you spare me a minute this afternoon?" She didn't dare risk telling her neighbor about Shirley/Florence turning up without some sort of preparation. The woman might have a heart attack or something.

"Well, hon, my show's just about over. Give me a minute or two to powder my nose and chase down my shoes," Nettie said, turning up the set again.

Lucy guessed by the sound of her that Nettie would have to chase down her teeth as well. The last time she'd offered her neighbor a ride to The Thursdays it had taken over thirty minutes to find them.

The mystery woman was still sleeping soundly when Lucy risked a glance in the purple room before creeping back downstairs. The lumpy brown handbag sat under the kitchen table where Shirley had left it. Feeling like a thief in the night, Lucy lifted it to the table and opened it, halfway expecting Shirley to sneak up on her from behind.

The bag was a well-known brand of good-quality leather, but was beginning to show signs of wear. She didn't know what she expected to find in there, but it surely wasn't this. The woman's large purse was filled to the brim with cellophane-wrapped snacks. Packages of crackers, cookies, peanuts, and a couple of smashed chocolate bars tumbled onto the table along with a crumpled pink-flowered handkerchief, a powder puff wrapped in tissue, a broken comb and three hairpins. In a small zippered compartment she found sixty-eight dollars in bills folded around forty-three cents in change. A cylindrical object that had slipped through a tear in the lining turned out to be a tube of pale pink lipstick that had been used almost to the nub.

After giving the bag a thorough check-over and a couple of shakes for good measure, Lucy put everything back as carefully as she could. If Shirley had any identifying papers, she—or somebody—didn't want them found.

Lucy took butter out to soften and put sharp cheddar in the food processor. Might as well start on the cheese straws while waiting for that woman to waken. She wished Nettie would hurry and come. But would her neighbor be able to recognize her old playmate after this length of time?

What had it been like living in this house over sixty years ago? she wondered. The basic floor plan hadn't changed much except for the bedroom they'd made by enclosing one end of the big back porch. But of course everything else was different—the colors, the furniture, and she and Charlie had remodeled the kitchen when they bought the place over twenty years ago. If

Shirley/Florence thought she had stepped into the 1940s-era home she'd known as a child, it wasn't surprising she was confused. Not only had the decor changed, but the people she had known and loved were gone.

Lucy remembered Papa Zeke, Ellis's grandfather, who had built this house in 1917 and lived here until he died, sharing it with Florence's parents. He'd outlived both of them. And she remembered little Florence's dollhouse, kept like a shrine in the room that would someday become Julie's. She and Ellis were not allowed to play with it.

After Papa Zeke died, the house came to Ellis's father, who sold it to the Methodist Church for a parsonage. Later, when the congregation opted to build a more modern home on the outskirts of town, Lucy and her husband finally got a chance to own the rambling cream-colored brick with too many fireplaces and not enough closets that Lucy had always admired.

"I don't know why you'd want to live there," Ellis had said. "The ceilings are too high, it has way too many rooms, and it's right there on Heritage Avenue. Why, Papa Zeke used to say that on Sundays the church traffic alone would make a preacher lose his religion. Called it Hallelujah Hill."

But Lucy loved the drafty old house from its musty dirt-floored basement to the cobwebbed attic, where now and then she still discovered delightful long-stored treasures like the high school yearbook from 1926 and a child's battered scooter with a fold-down seat. She loved the worn brick walkway that meandered between the magnolia that covered most of the front yard and the big ballerina-like spruce she and Ellis had always called the tutu tree. But Lucy claimed as her own the gazebo Charlie had built for her in a shady corner of the backyard. Her New Dawn rose climbed there in May, filling the air with its delicate pink scent, and now, in October, golden leaves from the crooked old black walnut tree carpeted the gray wooden floor. Lately, though, she sometimes wondered if the house had become too big for her. There had been times since Charlie died, and especially after Julie left, when Lucy Nan Pilgrim felt her days were as empty as her life had become. Her part-time job at Bud's Blooms, a local flower shop, had ceased to exist when Bud Fincher, the owner, retired the year before and sold the small brick building near the center of town to a dry cleaning establishment. And although Lucy was proud of Weigelia Jones, the student she had tutored for two years in the adult literacy program, she missed their Wednesday afternoons together since Weigelia had graduated last spring.

Her family had moved into this house when Julie was three and Roger ten, and they spent eighteen happy years there until Charlie died three years ago from injuries suffered in a traffic accident. Julie, who was just beginning her senior year at the university, had left in her closet at home a pair of shoes she planned to wear to a dance, and her father was making a detour from his business trip to deliver them when an eighteen-wheeler went out of control on the interstate. She had never been able to forgive herself.

How Lucy missed Charlie! Missed the feel of his arms around her, the way he would look through the house for her and call her name as soon as he came home, the touch and the smell of him. She even missed having to pick up his towels off the bathroom floor.

Now Lucy sifted flour and salt, then blended in butter and cheese. Julie had never been quite the same since her father's death, she thought. But just now she didn't want to think about her daughter, who hadn't been home since that last disastrous visit in August when she'd announced she was moving in with that doofus Buddy Boy Bubba, or whatever his name was. Here it was almost time for Halloween, and Thanksgiving with all its rich smells and colors would soon descend upon her household. Julie had never missed a Thanksgiving at home before. Her daughter's leaving had left another void. The world seemed hollow without the sound of Julie's voice, her offbeat sense of humor. Lately she hadn't even returned her mother's phone calls, and e-mails were ignored. The big house felt empty now without someone there to talk to. How comforting it would be, Lucy thought, to have someone compatible to share it.

Lucy Nan Pilgrim set the pastry blender aside, plunged in with both fists and squeezed the sticky dough, kneading it with her fingers.

The cheese straws were golden brown and cooling when she heard her neighbor's familiar rap at the door.

"Oo-wee! It's getting cold out there!" Nettie McGinnis, having found her teeth—much to Lucy's relief—clutched her coat together and refused to relinquish the wrap. "Something sure smells good."

"Cheese straws for Ellis's 'do' tomorrow. Come on back to the kitchen and we'll have some. I just put water on to boil."

"What's this you have to tell me?" Nettie asked, teasing the steaming water with her tea bag. "Good, juicy gossip, I hope."

"Better than that," Lucy said, and told her about the woman sleeping upstairs.

"Do-law! Oh, now . . . wait just a minute! How could that be?" Nettie held on to her cup with both hands and carefully set it back in the saucer. "Why, she's been gone over sixty years! Sixty-five years, to be exact, because I was eight years old when Florence disappeared and I turned seventy-three my last birthday."

"But you remember her? I mean, you must've played together."

"Well, I was three years older, but of course I remember her. I'll never forget the day it happened. I wanted to help them look for her but my parents wouldn't let me out of the house—or even out of their sight for the longest time after that." Nettie draped her coat over the back of her chair. "Wouldn't that be something if it *really* is Florence? What's she look like, Lucy?"

15

Lucy pushed back her chair. "Come on and see for yourself."

"Where is she? I thought you said she was sleeping?" Nettie picked up a cheese straw and broke it in two, letting the pieces fall onto the plate.

"Upstairs in Julie's room, and if her chest wasn't moving up and down, I'd swear the woman was dead. She hasn't stirred once." Lucy glanced at the clock. "And it's been almost two hours."

Her slumbering guest hadn't moved from her last position when the two women quietly opened the bedroom door and crept in to gaze down upon her. She slept on her side with her mouth partly open, the coverlet pulled to her chin. Her cheeks were lightly rouged, Lucy noticed, and a dusting of silvery eye shadow lingered on her eyelids. A small reddish mark near her hairline resembled a scar.

Nettie leaned over for a better look, her glasses sliding down her nose, then stood back and shook her head, frowning. "No way," she whispered, following Lucy out into the hallway.

"How can you be sure? After all, you said yourself it's been sixty-five years."

"Lips are too full. Florence had a thinner mouth, and her hair's too light. You can see she was a blonde. I remember Florence as being a brunette—a lot darker than this Shirley. Whoever she is, that shade of lipstick doesn't suit her. She does remind me of somebody, though. Can't think who."

Lucy shrugged. "People change. How could you know for sure after all this time?" She realized now how much she *wanted* this woman to be Florence. Maybe it wouldn't be the perfect ending to a heartbreaking saga, but at least they would finally know what happened to poor little Florence.

"There is one way you can be sure—other than DNA, of course." Nettie hesitated on the stairs. "Florence had a bad scar on her leg from that time she jumped off the roof of the toolshed."

"Why'd she do that?"

Nettie looked kind of sheepish. "Playing Peter Pan. Well . . . I was Peter Pan and she was supposed to be Wendy. I never thought the child would actually believe she could fly! Somebody had left a shovel on the ground and Florence got an awful gash from it. Had to have a bunch of stitches and a tetanus shot. Doc Loudermilk sewed her up, and you remember how fond he was of the bottle."

"That's awful!" Lucy said.

"It took a long time to heal and never did look right."

Downstairs in the kitchen Nettie struggled into her heavy coat. "I wasn't allowed to go to see *The Wizard of Oz* because Mama said I shouldn't have let Florence climb up there, and I'd looked forward to it all week!"

Lucy helped her neighbor into her coat. "I wish I could think of a way to get a look at that scar. Where is it?"

"Upper leg. Left one, I think, but I can't be sure. It kind of zigzagged. Maybe if you offered a change of clothes. Doesn't look like she brought any. She can't wear what she has on forever."

Lucy nodded. "True. I'll offer to launder the dress she's wearing— that is if she ever wakes up!"

"What if the scar's not there? What then? What are you going to do about her?"

"I don't know. Scars heal—even bad ones sometimes. Anyway, I'll let Ellis worry about it when she gets here. She's her cousin."

"Huh!" Nettie said. She helped herself to some more cheese straws before buttoning her coat. "Weather's getting nasty," she observed, wrapping her head in a green plaid muffler. "Cold as a well digger's butt out there! I reckon Ronald and Virginia are baking themselves on one of those pretty white Hawaiian beaches about now. Law, don't some people have all the luck?"

Lucy agreed that they did, but said that if anybody deserved a break it was a couple of underpaid teachers. Ronald and Virginia Brent, longtime members of Stone's Throw Presbyterian, where Lucy and Nettie belonged, had recently won a lottery prize of several million dollars and had immediately put their house on the market and taken off for destinations unknown to anybody but the immediate family, and possibly their travel agent.

"They probably want to escape all the gimme people," Lucy said. "It was in all the papers—even made the TV news."

"Do-law, I couldn't believe it!" Nettie said. "Turned on the television one night and there they were—Ronald and Virginia—standing in front of that statue of the Confederate soldier right here in our own Rutledge Park. Oh, well, they'll come home sooner or later," she added, making her way to the door. "All that sunshine and palm trees could get old after a while."

Lucy was going to say she wasn't so sure about that when she heard a loud clanging out front that made both of them jump.

"Now, what in the dickens was that?" Nettie asked as the two of them hurried to see what had caused the ruckus. "Sounded like two skeletons making love on a tin roof!"

"It came from somewhere out front. I hope there hasn't been an accident!" Lucy ran to the door to discover her garbage cans crushed against the sycamore by the curb and trash scattered all over the street. "Oh, hell! Some idiot has just run into my garbage cans—and just look at that mess! I'll swear, Nettie, it looks like they did it on purpose. They'd have to go out of their way to hit them."

"Did you see anybody?" Nettie stepped onto the porch, scanning the empty street.

"They were gone before we got out here—and a good thing, too! That plastic bin was practically new, and it looks like they've flattened the metal can. I hope it didn't hurt the tree."

It was almost dark by the time Lucy, with Nettie's help, finished shoveling the scattered debris into large plastic bags. The sycamore, she saw to her relief, had escaped with only minor scrapes.

"Oh, Lord! I almost forgot about Shirley/Florence up there," Lucy said after they had swept up the last of the broken glass. "She's probably awake by now and wondering what happened to Martha."

"Well, if that noise didn't wake her, she must be in a coma," Nettie told her. She frowned. "I thought you said you were expecting Ellis. I hate to leave you here alone."

"She had some errands, but she should be here any minute. You run on home now before you freeze out here. I'll be fine . . . and, Nettie, thanks again."

Except for a light in the kitchen, the house was dark when Lucy went inside, and she felt a bit uneasy as she stepped into the shadowy hallway, pausing to listen for footsteps upstairs. Everything was quiet except for the pinging of the furnace and the ticking of the grandfather clock in the corner.

The tall clock cast a deep shadow and Lucy thought for a minute that someone was standing beside it, then realized she was looking at the half-open doorway that led into the back hall.

I refuse to be frightened in my own home! Lucy switched on a lamp, took a deep breath and started upstairs. If the woman was still asleep, she would just have to wake her. This had gone on long enough.

Still, she was glad to hear the sound of a car in the driveway, then Ellis's familiar voice calling to her from the back of the house.

"Lucy Nan! It's me! Sorry I'm so late. Umm, those cheese

straws smell yummy!" Never one to use the front door, Ellis had come through the back porch and into the kitchen. Now she threw her wrap across a kitchen chair and met Lucy in the hallway. "Is she still here? Where is she?"

"Upstairs, I hope." Lucy told her what had happened in front of her house. "Nettie and I just now finished cleaning up the disgusting litter. She must be still asleep. I haven't heard a sound."

"You think somebody deliberately ran into your trash cans?"

"Either that or they had an early start on their evening libations. Took us over an hour to scoop up the mess."

"Speaking of . . . this must be the day for strange happenings. Have you heard about Calpernia Hemphill?"

"What about her?" The two of them stood in the downstairs hallway speaking in whispers.

"Dead. They found her body out at their place in the country—Bertram's Folly. You know—where Calpernia was going to have that theater workshop. Looks like she fell from the top of that crazy tower."

Back in the early nineteen hundreds, a fellow named Bertram with too much money and too little sense had decided to build a castle on a property several miles outside of town. Unfortunately, he ran out of money and then out of town before his creditors could pin him down. Calpernia Hemphill and her husband, Poag, had purchased the acreage for a weekend retreat when they first came to Stone's Throw and had built a small cottage there.

Lucy drew in her breath. The very thought of anyone falling from such a place made her legs go weak. "But Calpernia's afraid of heights," she said, "and everybody knows that old tower's not safe. What was she doing up there?"

"She was supposed to meet the director of the workshop at the Folly this morning. He was the one who found her. Heard her little dogs barking in the cottage and nobody ever came to the door, so he started looking around. He almost didn't see her because she fell right smack in the middle of a bunch of pokeberry bushes as high as your head," Ellis said. "I heard some of the stones had crumbled away at the top."

"Poor Poag!" Lucy leaned against the banister. "Didn't he just leave for a European tour with his choral group from the college? What a blow!"

Ellis nodded solemnly. "They had a farewell performance at Sarah Bedford last night. Calpernia saw them off afterward." She shook her head. "If only she'd gone with them."

"When do they think it happened?" Lucy asked.

"Sometime this morning. Had to. They say there were breakfast dishes in the sink at the cottage. Besides, it was almost eleven when the chorus left here for the airport last night," Ellis said. "Poag must be halfway around the world by now."

Lucy made the appropriate noises. Poag Hemphill, the college's talented choral director, was a tireless worker for many charities, a wonderful dancer and a pretty good bridge player, and she had always enjoyed his company, but she had never cared much for Calpernia. Too flashy, and the world wasn't big enough for that woman's ego—yet she wouldn't have wished her that end. "Stone's Throw won't be the same without her," she said. And Lord, wasn't that the truth?

"So, what did Nettie say—about this woman here?" Ellis asked as they started upstairs. "Does she think she might be Florence?"

"Says her lips are too full," Lucy said. "But Florence had a scar—a bad one on her thigh—that might help us decide if she's who we think she might be. She had to have stitches and Nettie said Doc Loudermilk botched it up."

"Huh! I'm not surprised," Ellis said. "Mama said he left a sponge in our milkman." She giggled. "Poor man was always thirsty."

"Maybe we can get her to take a shower, offer a change of clothes," Lucy whispered as they approached the door of Julie's old room.

She could feel Ellis's hand on her shoulder as she opened the door. Would the mysterious Shirley turn out to be Ellis's long-lost cousin Florence?

But they would have to wait to find out because the woman who called herself Shirley was no longer there.

"I don't know about you, but I'm having a glass of wine," Lucy said after they had searched the house from basement to attic and hollered themselves hoarse. Ellis had even telephoned Nettie to see if the woman had wandered next door.

Ellis swirled chardonnay in her glass. "Where on earth could she have gone?"

"Beats me, but it must have happened when I was outside cleaning up the spilled garbage," Lucy said. "Her pocketbook's missing and it was right here in the kitchen. She had to have slipped out the back way or I would've seen her."

"Must've had more on the ball than we thought," Ellis said. "Just needed a place to sleep for a while, I guess. Sure put one over on you."

"Then she had to be some good actress, and she knew all about poor little Florence and Papa Zeke." Lucy made a face. She didn't like being made a fool of and if she ever had an opportunity to see this Shirley again, she would tell her so in no uncertain terms.

But of course that would never happen because somebody from the police department called a few minutes later to tell them a woman had been found in the parking lot behind the Methodist Church with a sales receipt bearing Lucy Pilgrim's signature crumpled in her coat pocket. She was discovered at the bottom of a steep flight of steps with her neck broken. Her handbag was found a few feet away, but her money and rings were missing.

CHAPTER THREE

Lucy noticed her hair first. She had seen hair that color in vintage paintings: rich as honey, but lighter, with a soft metallic luster she imagined old gold would have. The woman who stood on the porch wore a long cape of deep emerald with a lining of shimmering plum that seemed to change like a holograph in the cold morning sun.

"I came about the room," she said, and her voice was so calm and reassuring after the disaster of the day before that Lucy had a strange impulse to unload all her troubles at her feet.

"You are Lucy Nan Pilgrim?" She took a torn fragment of newspaper from her worn tapestry bag. "And this *is* one-oh-eight Heritage Avenue? Oh, I do hope the room's not taken! Living here would be such a convenience—not that it matters, of course." And with a slight shiver she drew her cape more closely about her.

"Oh . . . sorry, you must be freezing. Please come in." As Lucy stood aside to let her pass, she detected the unmistakable scent of strawberries. Strange for this time of year, but then there's no accounting for some people's taste in cologne, she thought.

"Thank you. There is a bit of a chill in the air. I just can't seem to get adjusted to cold weather since—well, I do hope the room is adequately heated."

The very nerve! As if she'd be automatically accepted as a boarder. "If you wear long underwear, a toboggan cap and fur-lined mittens, you should be fine," Lucy said without the slightest change of expression.

The woman's laughter not only surprised her, but for a moment Lucy Nan Pilgrim forgot she was even annoyed.

"Then I suppose I'd better put in an order to L.L.Beet," her visitor said, extending a slender pink hand. "Augusta Goodnight— and I've come to stay for a while—that is, if you'll have me."

Lucy had walked around all morning feeling as though she were dragging a gigantic black sack of troubles with every step. Now, no matter how hard she fought it, she felt the corners of her mouth begin to turn up in a smile that just wouldn't stop. "Bean," she said, allowing a tiny laugh to slide out with the word.

"I beg your pardon? Your name is Bean?" The woman seemed confused.

"No, no. The catalog company! It's L.L.*Bean*."

"Oh, well, I knew it was some kind of vegetable." With a smooth twist of her wrist, Augusta threw aside her cape and swirled it over the back of the Windsor chair without even looking to see where it landed.

"I suppose you'd like to see the room," Lucy said. "Actually, it's quite comfortable. My husband used it as an office for years." Turning the room into a guest room had forced Lucy finally to clear it of Charlie's old army-surplus desk and years' accumulation of papers.

"There's no need. I'm sure it will be fine." Her visitor slung the handles of her huge handbag over the newel in the hallway and rubbed her hands together. "I would love a cup of coffee, though, if it wouldn't be too much trouble. I've brought along some of my strawberry muffins."

Lucy tried her best not to gape when she saw the cloth-covered basket she was almost certain hadn't been there before. "I . . . I think there's still some in the pot," she managed to say, and found herself following the stranger into her own kitchen.

"There's just no place like a kitchen to get acquainted," the newcomer announced as she whisked the cloth from her steaming basket of muffins. "I remember when in many homes it was the only room that was heated, and the family sat together around the fire. I've always considered it the heart of the home."

Lucy, who was reaching for cups in the cabinet by the sink, found herself holding her breath. This woman was certainly younger than she was! Have I accidently pushed some kind of freak button? she wondered. Yesterday her long-lost visitor from never-never land had turned up dead in a parking lot. This one seemed to be from outer space, yet there was something so right about her, something good, and it wasn't just the beautiful hair and miraculous muffins. Now she found sugar and cream and watched as Augusta poured coffee. "About the room," Lucy began, and that was when the policeman came to the door.

Ed Tillman had gone all the way from kindergarten with Lucy's son, Roger, and knew his way around her house probably as well as he did his own, but it had been a long time since his last visit. When Lucy looked up and saw him on the back porch she almost expected to find him tossing a baseball in the air.

"Excuse me," she said to Augusta, and went to see what he wanted.

"Didn't want to mess up your front hall," Ed said with a grin, wiping his feet on the mat. "I hate to take up your time like this, but if you could clear up a few more things about yesterday . . . "

"Of course, if I can." Lucy kissed his cheek lightly. "Come in, Ed, how about some coffee? And I'd like you to meet . . . "

Lucy turned to introduce her visitor but Augusta Goodnight was gone. Her muffins, however, still filled the kitchen with their spicy strawberry scent.

That was strange—but then lately, what wasn't? Maybe she's in the bathroom, she thought, yet she hadn't heard her leave the room.

Ed declined the coffee but accepted a muffin, then followed it with another. "The woman who came to your house yesterday," he began. "About what time was it when you first noticed she was gone?"

"Probably after eight," Lucy told him. "Somebody knocked over my trash cans next to the street and it was getting dark when Nettie and I finally got the mess cleaned up. Ellis was with me when we found she was gone—she might remember the time."

"You didn't notice anyone else near the house then? Was your back door unlocked?"

"Are you suggesting somebody might have wandered in here and *taken her*? Dear God, Ed, I had enough trouble sleeping last night without your reminding me of that!"

He tried to smile. "Sorry, but we're trying to find out what she was doing in that parking lot. She didn't happen to mention meeting anyone, did she?"

"She was a pathetic old woman who thought she was still five years old. She was looking for her *mother*, for Pete's sake! Nothing she said made any sense. I told your detective that last night." Lucy took a sip of coffee and found it cold. The taste made her faintly nauseated. "Whoever she was, she didn't deserve to die like that. I can't imagine why anybody would do such a cruel thing!"

Ed nodded, not speaking, as he made notes on a small pad. As he grew older, Lucy noticed, Ed looked more and more like his dad, which was a good thing, she thought, because his mom always reminded her of some kind of cartoon character, only she hadn't been able to decide which one.

"Did you find out who she was?" she asked. "She seemed to think she had lived here as a child, talked about Papa Zeke—he was Ellis Saxon's granddaddy, you know. Do you think she might

26

really be Florence Calhoun, the little girl who disappeared over sixty years ago?"

"We're still looking into that," Ed said, pushing back his chair. "We'll probably be calling on you again until we get to the bottom of this. Hope you'll bear with us."

"But you're still not going to tell me anything, are you?"

"You keep your doors locked, now. Promise?" Ed said.

Lucy could tell by the look on his face that Ed Tillman knew more than he was letting on.

Could this Augusta Goodnight who seemed so interested in renting a room have something to do with the brutal death of the woman who called herself Shirley? And where was she now? Lucy started to mention her doubts to Ed as she walked with him to the door, but thought better of it. What a fool she would seem if her seraphic-looking visitor turned out to be as harmless as she seemed. In fact, Augusta made Lucy think of the grandmother she called Mimmer, who had died soon after Lucy married. Mimmer's gentleness and strength had brought the family through the Depression, several wars, plus numerous calamities, and her wacky sense of humor sprang forth at the most unexpected moments. Lucy smiled, thinking of the Sunday when she was about ten. She had been sitting next to her grandmother in the sedate congregation of Stone's Throw Presbyterian Church during the singing of the old hymn "All Hail the Power of Jesus' Name." But where the stanza read *Let angels prostrate fall*, Lucy had belted out *prostate* instead! Her grandmother, unable to control her amusement, had rushed laughing from the sanctuary with a bulletin held over her face.

But this woman was not her warm, witty grandmother. She was a stranger who could be ransacking the house this very minute or even waiting behind the door with a butcher knife. Lucy stepped outside to call Ed back when she happened to glance behind her into the kitchen—and there her visitor sat, just as pretty as you please, helping herself to a strawberry muffin.

"Where *were* you?" Lucy asked, whirling about.

"Why, right here." She edged the basket toward Lucy. "These are better while they're hot."

"But you weren't here. You were gone—and now you're back again! How do you *do* that?"

Augusta Goodnight smiled. "It comes with the territory. Why don't you sit down and I'll tell you about it?"

Still, Lucy kept her distance. "You're not a reporter, are you?" She had already had several annoying phone calls from the press.

"Now, what makes you think I'm a reporter?" She frowned slightly as she examined the dainty cup and saucer in front of her. "This pattern seems familiar. I believe Constance Ledbetter had the same one. She let her spoiled cats get up on the table, though, and they broke nearly every piece in the set."

Lucy didn't give a rat's ass about Constance Ledbetter, whoever she was, or her cats, and said so. "You must know we had a murder here in Stone's Throw yesterday. The victim was wearing my coat when she was killed and spent her last hours sleeping in this house."

Augusta's eyes grew darker and she shoved her cup away from her, sloshing coffee into the saucer. "No, I didn't know, and now it's too late. I'm sorry—so sorry. This is not a good way to begin."

Her eyes, Lucy noticed, that had been the same shade of green as the frothy dress she wore, were now the smoky color of Whisper Lake at twilight. A long necklace of dazzling stones winked violet and indigo against fabric that looked as if it had been hand-painted in watercolor.

"Too late for what? And just what were you planning to begin?" she said, gripping her hands to keep them from trembling.

Augusta seemed not to hear her. "This woman who was killed," she asked, "do you know who she was?"

"We're—they're not sure yet." Lucy closed her eyes and felt tears welling under her lids. "She was like a child . . . it was horrible! She was wearing my coat—must've taken it from the closet in Julie's room—and it had a sales receipt in the pocket. When the police called, it took me a while to realize who they were talking about. Somebody shoved her down those steep steps just for what little money she had and those fake rings. Poor soul! And this happened right after Calpernia Hemphill fell from that stupid tower! Bless her heart, I suppose she couldn't help being such a complete ass." *What a rotten thing to say—and with Calpernia lying dead as a doornail! Shame on you, Lucy Nan Pilgrim!*

Augusta leaned closer and the fragrance of her made Lucy think of the honeysuckle that had climbed the fence behind Mimmer's house. Once she had tried to collect the nectar in a tiny tea-set cup. Now Augusta reached out and touched her hands and the trembling went away.

"Who are you?" Lucy asked. "And what are you doing here?"

"That's what I've come to talk to you about," Augusta said. "I'm a guardian angel, Lucy Nan Pilgrim, and it looks as though I've come not a minute too soon."

Lucy wasn't as shocked by what the woman said as she was by the fact that it didn't surprise her. Augusta Goodnight sat looking at her in all seriousness. A stray lock of her bright hair had tumbled onto her forehead and she absently shoved it back into place, then folded her hands in her lap, almost losing them in the depths of her wide, floppy sleeves. As Lucy watched, the glittering necklace began to change from deep blue to lavender to gold. She could hardly take her eyes from it. Now a faint suggestion of a smile began to play at the corners of Augusta's mouth.

"You're enjoying this, aren't you?" Lucy said.

The woman raised an elegant eyebrow. "Enjoying what?"

"You know very well what. All this angel crap—your disappearing act, the instant muffins, and that awesome necklace. Where on earth did you get it?"

Augusta fingered the stones which now couldn't decide if they wanted to be turquoise or amethyst. "I didn't," she said, "get them on earth, I mean, and it really isn't necessary to use such vulgar language."

Lucy frowned. "Just what do you want from me?"

"It's not really what I want from you, but what I can do for you while I'm here—if you'll allow me to, of course." Augusta rose and poured coffee again for both of them. It had a comforting cinnamon smell, although Lucy didn't remember using spices in the brewing.

"So, we're back to the guardian angel thing. What makes you think I need a guardian angel?"

"Everyone needs a guardian angel," Augusta said. "Yours—her name is Sharon, by the way—just happened to have been transferred to another field."

"No kidding. I hope it wasn't a demotion."

"Certainly not! Actually, she was given a position in the weather department as a regulator of seasons. Someone has to do it, you see, so we don't have snow in July or too much rain during harvest time."

"Then somebody up there must be sleeping on the job," Lucy said, and reminded her of the catastrophic floods and droughts that seemed to plague the earth from time to time.

"All we can do is try," Augusta said. "And now that Sharon's on the job, let's hope things will improve."

"Why have I never seen this Sharon?"

"Most people don't," Augusta said, "unless, of course, there's a specific need."

"And I have a specific need?" Lucy smiled. "And what might that be?"

"I believe you did experience a feeling of loneliness, did you not? A longing for someone to talk to. And as you told me earlier, two women were found dead yesterday right here in Rolling Stone."

"That's Stone's Throw," Lucy told her. "You'd think an angel could at least get the name of the town right. Besides, what happened to those women had nothing to do with me. Calpernia Hemphill's death was probably an accident. She liked her booze, you know. As for what happened to poor Shirley/Florence—or whoever she was—I'm sure the police will take care of that. After all, what else can happen, for heaven's sake?"

Augusta pulled a purple-flowered apron from her large handbag and tied it around her waist, then took the dishes to the sink to wash. "For heaven's sake," she said, smiling. "That's exactly why I'm here."

CHAPTER FOUR

Zee St. Clair balanced a plate on her skinny knees and dabbed her lips with a napkin. The napkin was *paper* and had a picture of a scarecrow on it. Wouldn't Mimmer just flip if she knew? Lucy smiled thinking about it.

"These chess tarts are wonderful, Lucy Nan," Zee said, "and I haven't tasted sandwiches this good since Mama used to make them. I don't know how you found the time or the energy to do all this with all that's been going on."

"I tried to tell her that," Nettie McGinnis said, helping herself to the salted nuts. "The world won't end if The Thursdays postpone their meeting, I told her . . . but of course she wouldn't listen!" She shook her head at Lucy as her hostess passed the tray of sandwiches. "Oh, no, I couldn't . . . well, maybe just one more! What's in these, Lucy Nan? I don't remember your making them before."

"Let's see . . . raisins, nuts, a little of this and a little of that." Lucy had no idea what else, as Augusta had made the cooked sandwich filling with much chopping and stirring the night before and now sat sedately in the corner by the piano observing the meeting of The Thursday Morning Literary Society That Now Meets on

Monday Afternoons. It didn't surprise Lucy that no one seemed to notice she was there.

"I didn't do all the work," Lucy admitted with a sly glance at Augusta. "The tarts are from Do-Lollie's. She brought them by this morning. Besides, I'd rather be doing something than just sitting here worrying about things."

This was more or less directed at her cousin, Jo Nell Touchstone, who, in Lucy's opinion, had developed the habit of worrying into a fine art.

Idonia Mae Culpepper drained her teacup and set her plate aside. "Is Lollie back in town? I thought she was away on a buying trip?"

"Got back a couple of days ago—showed me a sample of some of the things she's getting in for Christmas," Lucy told her. "And in case any of you are interested," she added pointedly, "I'd be happy with most of her selections."

Lollie Pate's small gift shop and bakery was one of her favorite places to shop or just to browse, and everyone agreed that Stone's Throw was lucky to have a store where you could buy a wedding gift and tonight's dessert all in one stop.

"Isn't Ellis coming?" Claudia Pharr asked Lucy as she helped to collect the dishes. As the youngest and most recent member of The Thursdays, she seemed to think it was her duty. "When I saw her in the grocery store this morning, she told me she planned to be here."

"Had some errands to take care of," Lucy said. "I expect she's just running a little late." Although she wasn't yet worried about her friend's absence, she was a little concerned. Ellis was usually punctual and it wasn't at all like her to miss out on dessert.

"Do you think that woman—that Shirley—could possibly be Ellis's cousin?" Idonia asked when Lucy returned to the group. "Why, everyone thought she was dead all these years!"

"Well, whoever she is—or was—she's dead now," Jo Nell

reminded them. "But why would anybody want to kill a poor, harmless soul like that? And right here in Stone's Throw, too! I'll be locking my doors from now on."

"Sounds like a bunch of punks to me." Zee glanced out the living room window as if she expected to see a horde of thugs approaching. "You've seen that group that hangs around the Red Horse Café! Up to no good, the lot of them! They oughta close that place down."

"But what was she doing behind the Methodist Church at that hour?" Claudia asked. "Remember how cold it was that night? And it must've been pitch-dark by then." She shivered. "Gives me the creeps!"

Cousin Jo Nell reached across Claudia's lap to squeeze Lucy's hand. "I hope you're remembering to lock up tight, Lucy Nan. I don't even like to think of your being in this big old house alone. Why, anybody could break in!"

Thanks for the comforting thought! "I'm not exactly alone," Lucy said with an eye on Augusta. "I've taken in a roomer."

"I saw your ad in the *Weekly Wipe*," Nettie said, referring to the local newspaper, "but you didn't tell me the room was rented. Who is it? Anybody we know? How come I haven't seen them?"

"She travels a lot." Lucy made an effort not to look at Augusta. Nettie frowned. "I haven't seen a car. Doesn't she drive?"

"Flies, mostly," Lucy said, biting back a smile. "Why don't we get started on the discussion? I was up late last night reviewing *Taking Lottie Home*. It's been a while since I first read it."

"I love everything Terry Kay writes," Claudia said, but I think *To Dance with the White Dog* is my favorite."

"But isn't Ellis supposed to lead the discussion this time?" Cousin Jo Nell drew in her breath with a loud sucking sound. "You don't suppose anything's happened to Ellis, do you? With a murderer running around loose, there's no telling what—"

"Bosh! Could've been somebody she knew who killed that

woman," Nettie said. "After all, we don't know where she came from or where she's been. Wouldn't surprise me if she didn't have some sort of criminal record herself!"

"Why, Nettie McGinnis!" Lucy said. "You saw that poor, addled woman yourself. She was perfectly harmless—wouldn't hurt a soul. I don't know how you can say such a thing."

"For all we know, she might very well have been Florence Calhoun trying to find her way home after all these years." Zee sniffed. "Bless her heart!"

"Didn't look a bit like Florence to me," Nettie said. "She did remind me of somebody, though, but I can't quite put my finger on it." She patted Lucy's arm. "You did tell the police about the scar, didn't you, Lucy Nan?"

"Several times, but they haven't told me a blessed thing—except that she was wearing my coat."

"What scar?" the others chimed in, so of course Nettie had to explain. When she was about to come to the part about old Doc Loudermilk hitting the bottle, Lucy gave her a sharp jab with her elbow.

"What are you poking me for?" Nettie asked, before realizing belatedly that Idonia Mae was the late doctor's great-niece.

If Idonia Mae was aware of the situation, she graciously chose to ignore it. The rose brocade of the upholstered rocking chair where she sat clashed dreadfully with her flaming red hair, Lucy observed, but Idonia Mae always chose it because it was close to the fireplace and she seemed to be perpetually chilly. Actually, Lucy thought, the rocking chair didn't really go with anything else in the room, which was decorated more or less in shades of blue and yellow, but her mother had chosen the fabric shortly before she died and Lucy couldn't bring herself to change it.

Now Idonia Mae hitched her chair a little closer to the blaze. "Suppose it *was* little Florence," she began, "and somebody deliberately enticed her away from the house?"

"But why?" Lucy said. "Besides, I would've seen them or at least heard them. I was here the whole time."

"Not exactly," Nettie reminded her. "It took us almost an hour to clean up the mess out front when that idiot ran into your trash cans."

"Of course." Lucy darted a look at Augusta and saw a question in her eyes. "Somebody could have telephoned her, or even—God forbid—walked in and taken her while we were both outside!"

"If this is true, whoever it was must've been watching the house, *and* they knew you lived alone," Zee said. Then, apparently seeing Lucy's stricken expression, added, "But this is all hypothetical, of course. I'm still betting on the local riffraff."

"What's this about local riffraff? I'll swear, I can't be gone an hour without you-all talking about me behind my back!"

Ellis had entered from the back porch as usual, but Lucy didn't hear her until she announced her arrival from the hallway, and even with her friend's smiling and joking, she could tell by Ellis Saxon's expression that something was wrong.

Putting her novel aside, Jo Nell went to greet her. "Ellis! Am I glad to see you! I'll have to confess we were getting a little worried. I hope everything's all right."

"Just a minor delay, that's all," Ellis said, but Lucy noticed she didn't protest when Jo Nell led her to a seat. "To give Mr. Kay his due, I think we ought to hold off on the book discussion until next time," she added, sinking into the depths of the armchair by the window. "I don't mind telling you, it's been a most peculiar afternoon!"

Now Lucy *was* concerned. Ellis looked pale even beneath her gardening tan. "I saved you a plate," she said, rising. "Won't take a minute."

"Thanks, but I'm really not hungry. I'd love some tea, though, if it's still hot."

Lucy touched her shoulder. It took a lot to shake up Ellis Saxon, but something obviously had. "Be right back," she promised.

Everyone was quiet as Ellis spooned sugar into her cup. "Well, Lucy Nan . . . " she said, after taking a sip, "it looks like your Shirley was little Florence after all."

"Are they sure? How do you know?" Idonia adjusted her spectacles as if that would bring the subject into clearer focus.

"What happened?" Lucy asked. Thinking of the sad, childlike woman, she suddenly wanted to cry. "Ellis, where have you been?"

"To the police station—by request." Ellis smiled as she sipped her tea. "They offered to send a car for me, but I preferred to drive myself."

"What did they want? Was this just so they could tell you they've identified the . . . woman who was killed?" Lucy couldn't bring herself to call the victim a *body*. It sounded so cold and impersonal.

"It seemed they wanted to ask me some questions . . . " Ellis began.

"What kind of questions, for heaven's sake?" Jo Nell's voice rose. "Oh, Ellis! They weren't holding you against your will?"

Ellis laughed. "No, no! They were perfectly polite—didn't shine any bright lights in my face or anything like that. They just wanted to hear my account of the night it happened. I was over here soon after she left the house, you know. Lucy Nan and I looked all over the place for her. Remember, Nettie? We even phoned you. And they wanted to know about my kinship with Florence— things like that. Florence's daddy and mine were brothers, so I'm the closest relative she had left. She and I are—were—first cousins, but of course she disappeared way before I was born."

Nettie clicked her teeth. "I thought everybody knew that." She leaned forward. "I still can't believe that woman was the Florence I knew. Did they find the scar?"

Ellis nodded. "Right where you said it was, on the upper left leg."

"You didn't have to *look* at her, did you?" Claudia asked.

"Thank goodness that wasn't necessary," Ellis said, "but soon after they learned who she might be, they did ask me to swab for DNA. They don't have the results back on that yet, though." She held out her cup for more tea. "Actually, they don't need it. I gave them a sample of poor little Florence's baby hair."

"Her *what?*" Zee's eyes widened. "How on earth did you come by that?"

"It was in her baby book. I've had it for years," Ellis said. "I mean, who else would it come to? I never could bring myself to throw it away."

Ellis grinned. "Oh, don't look so distressed, y'all. If I'm arrested, maybe they'll let us hold our meetings in the city jail!"

"Why would they want to arrest *you?*" Jo Nell looked threatening. "Why, that's just ridiculous!"

Nettie looked at her old friend before she spoke. "Maybe you've forgotten, Jo Nell, that Ellis inherited the estate that would've gone to Florence—but you're right, it is ridiculous. I think you're imagining things, Ellis. This is Stone's Throw! Those people at the police department know you better than that!"

Ellis only shrugged. "Speaking of the police department, guess who else I saw there? Jay Warren-Winslow!"

"*J* who?" Idonia asked.

"Jay Warren-Winslow," Ellis said. "Don't you remember? He was written up in *The Messenger* not too long ago. It was all over the front page. He's the man Calpernia Hemphill hired to direct that theater workshop she was planning out at the Folly."

Claudia Pharr nodded. "The one who discovered her body! Ohmygosh! Do they think he might have pushed her?"

"Surely not," Lucy said. "It was an accident, wasn't it? I heard the mortar was loose and part of the wall gave way, although I can't imagine why she went up there."

"Probably had a wake-me-up toddy—or two," Nettie mumbled. "Calpernia was . . . well, *Calpernia*, but I can't think why anybody would want to kill her."

Zee looked from one to the other and her expression didn't change. "Oh, I think they'd have to get in line," she said, drawing herself up ruler-straight.

"Zee, for heaven's sake, the poor woman's dead—" Claudia began.

"Dead or not, she was a nasty piece of work!" Zee's usually strong voice broke. "I hold that woman fully responsible for Melanie's eating disorder. We almost lost her, you know."

Lucy remembered the incident several years ago, when Zee's daughter Melanie had been a drama major studying under Calpernia Hemphill at Sarah Bedford College. Melanie had been turned down for a leading role in a college production because Calpernia told her she was too fat. According to Zee, this led to her daughter's battle with bulimia and resulting ill health, and Lucy had always agreed that it was probably a contributing factor.

A long silence fell over the room until Idonia finally said, "I can understand why you feel that way, Zee, but—my goodness—Melanie looked fantastic the last time I saw her, and you told me yourself she was happy in her new position with that arts council in—where is it? North Carolina?" She gave Zee's hand a friendly squeeze.

Zee pulled her hand away as if it had been burned. "Sure, after all the worrying, the misery, the therapy—not to mention the expense!" Fumbling in her purse, she took out a handkerchief and blew her nose. "I'm sorry, I just can't help it," she said, turning away.

After a series of soothing noises, Claudia announced that Calpernia had introduced her to Jay Warren-Winslow in the Scuppernong Tea Room just the week before and that he seemed just-as-nice-as-you-please to her.

"Oh, I'm sure there's probably nothing to it," Ellis said, "but Paulette Morgan, the dispatcher over there, told me she'd heard they'd asked him to stick around town for a while."

"That Paulette's the biggest gossip in the world!" Idonia said. "Always has been—even as a teenager. I had her in my language-arts class in high school and I could always guess who started the rumors. Don't know how she keeps that job!"

Nettie frowned. "I wonder where he's staying. If Calpernia's director's not supposed to leave town, he has to live somewhere, and let's face it, there's not that much to choose from here in Stone's Throw."

"There's the Spring Lamb," Jo Nell said, referring to Opal and Virgil Henshaw's bed-and-breakfast, so named because of the large cement planters in the shape of a lamb crammed with plastic flowers on either side of the front door. "Oughta call it the Old Goat! I declare it's a shame the way that Virgil carries on with every woman who's still breathing who comes into his butcher shop. It's almost enough to make me become a vegetarian!"

"Poor fellow won't get much to eat at Opal's," Idonia chimed in. "That woman can cook a pancake so thin it's got only one side to it! Tight as Dick's hatband—she and Virgil both!"

Zee had gathered her things together as everyone prepared to leave and now she turned at the door. "Well, he'll be welcome to stay with me," she announced.

"Do you think Zee really meant what she said about that director staying with her?" Lucy asked Ellis after the others had left. The two were washing the dishes by hand, as Lucy had used her grandmother's fragile china and didn't dare put it in the dishwasher. For a while, Augusta had stood restlessly watching the two from the kitchen doorway, and Lucy knew she was itching to help but reluctant to show herself to Ellis. The next time she looked she was gone.

"I wouldn't doubt it," Ellis said. "She has that guest house they built for Zee's widowed mother at the back of her property. As far as I know, nobody's lived in it since she died." She wiped a dessert plate with the dish towel, repeating circles on its blossom-painted surface.

Lucy gently took the plate from her. "You've dried that plate three times, Ellis. I know something's on your mind. What is it? You don't really think the police are seriously considering you as a suspect, do you?"

Ellis picked up another dripping plate and began to repeat her ritual. "I wish I didn't," she said, "but Lucy Nan, I'll swear to God I think they are!" Her voice dropped to a whisper. "Can you believe they asked me not to leave town?"

If Ellis had kicked her in the stomach it couldn't have jolted her more, but Lucy tried to hide her reaction. "Have you talked with Bennett about it?" she asked.

, "Not yet. He's out of town on some sort of dental convention and I hate to worry him unnecessarily." Ellis shrugged. "I'm probably making too much of this."

Lucy wanted to tell her not to worry, that everything would be fine, but the words stuck in her throat. She had an awful feeling there were going to be troubled times ahead.

Lucy rinsed the last cup and drained the water from the sink. "What about this Jay What's-his-name? Did they really tell him not to leave town or was that just one of Paulette's wild tales?"

Ellis shook her head. "Don't know, but he was there when I got there and still there when I left. Poor Poag! He's taking this pretty hard, I hear—and now to learn his wife might have been murdered! They've always been so close. I honestly don't know what he'll do."

"Calpernia was in our church circle, you know, even though

she rarely came," Lucy said. "I told them I'd help serve at the funeral whenever they release the body."

"I'll help, too, of course. I'll bring my funeral cake." Ellis always brought the same thing when there was a death in town: a chocolate sheet cake slathered in fudge-nut icing. It was a shame, Lucy thought, that somebody had to die to get one.

Ellis hung up the damp dish towel and leaned against the sink, arms folded, then stood looking at Lucy.

"What?" Lucy asked. "Why are you staring at me like that?"

Ellis smiled. "I'm just waiting," she said.

"Waiting for what?"

"Waiting for you to tell me about that strange woman with the out-of-this-world hair who was at The Thursdays this afternoon. Everybody just seemed to ignore her. I'll swear, Lucy Nan, she looked just like an angel!"

CHAPTER FIVE

"You *saw* her? I mean . . . well . . . I guess I didn't notice she was there." Lucy Nan groped for words. How could she explain this? What was she supposed to do?

"What do you mean, you didn't notice she was there? How could you miss her? And I must say, I thought it rather odd—not to mention rude—how everyone ignored her," Ellis said. "Who is she, Lucy Nan?"

Lucy sighed aloud. "If you must know, she's the woman who rented my room. She's—"

"Augusta Goodnight. I'm Lucy Nan's guardian angel, Ellis, but I believe you might benefit from my services as well."

Augusta crossed the room smiling and extended her hand. At first, Ellis didn't seem to know whether she should take it or not, but after a glance at Lucy, she accepted the hand that was offered with what appeared to be a placating smile. "I expect I could use an angel—borrowed or not," Ellis said with a laugh. "What happened to mine?"

"I believe she's taking a refresher course, and since I'm going to be here anyway, I told her I'd fill in." Augusta glanced at the coffeepot to find it empty, but that didn't seem to bother her. "Would anyone else like a cup of coffee? I thought I'd put on a pot if that's all right?"

Today, Lucy noticed, the angel wore a cream-colored tunic sweater trimmed in burgundy and gold over a full-flowing skirt in a dainty floral print. The winking necklace of lavender and turquoise fell loosely to her waist. "There should be some sandwiches left," Augusta said.

But Ellis was still trying to deal with her earlier statement. "A refresher course?" she said numbly, turning to Lucy for help. "What kind of course would that be?"

Augusta filled the pot with water. "The syllabus includes praise and adoration, blessings and hope—good things we all need to be reminded of from time to time. I took it myself some time ago."

"Oh, please, give me a break!" Groaning, Ellis plopped into a kitchen chair.

"That's exactly what I intend to do if you'll let me," Augusta told her.

"Hasn't this gone far enough, Lucy Nan?" Ellis shook her head as if she were trying to empty her mind. "I honestly didn't think this day could get any weirder!"

"Guess again," Lucy said, and pulled up a chair beside her.

"I can't believe I'm sitting here having a conversation with someone who claims to be an angel," Ellis said after Augusta had explained her mission. "But if you're crazy, then I must be, too." She laughed. "Of course I've always known Lucy Nan was a little peculiar." She rose to put her cup in the sink, and turned to face them. "Nobody else saw you, did they? Today at the meeting you were there in plain view, yet I'm the only one who could see you—besides, Lucy Nan, of course. Why is that?"

"That happens to be my choice," Augusta told her. "There's a darkness here in Stone's Throw that has nothing to do with nightfall, and we're going to have to work through it together. I suggest we take the cow by the ears and begin now."

"Fine with me," Lucy said, ignoring Ellis's quizzical glance while trying not to smile. "But how?" She ran a finger along the top of the round oak table. It really did need polishing, she thought.

"First, I think we need to find out why anyone would want to kill your cousin." Augusta directed her attention to Ellis. "From all I've heard, she seemed a harmless, if somewhat disoriented, soul reliving—or trying to relive—her childhood days. But why now after all this time? And where has she been all these years?"

"Something must have jogged her memory," Lucy said. "Maybe something she saw or heard . . . "

"The lottery!" Ellis shouted. "It had to have been the lottery. When Ronald and Virginia Brent won all that money, Stone's Throw was plastered all over the newspapers—television, too."

From the bay window in her kitchen, Lucy watched dusk turn to darkness and hurried to latch the door to the back porch. "Did this woman—did Florence—have a family? Maybe they can tell us something."

"A husband," Ellis said. "Leonard. Leonard Fenwick. Calls himself Len. He's the one who reported her missing. Seems she slipped away from a shopping trip with a group from the assisted-living residence where she was staying—somewhere in Illinois, I think. The police put us in touch and I spoke with him this afternoon. That's one reason I was so late getting here. Anyway, he's due in late tomorrow."

"Here? He's coming here?" Lucy drew the curtains across the big window and tried not to think of someone out there watching. She had never worried about things like that before and it angered her that she should have to now.

"I'm meeting him at the Greenville-Spartanburg Airport, but

yes, he's coming here. After all, Florence was his wife and I'm the closest relative she had—besides, we have plenty of room." Ellis paused. "He wants her buried here beside her parents. This was her home, you know."

"Finally together after all these years. How sad!" Lucy looked about her at the large, cheerful kitchen with its colorful striped curtains and Mimmer's own rag rugs scattered about the hardwood floor. "I feel almost guilty for being happy here in the house she only knew in memory."

"Let's hope she was happy somewhere else," Augusta said. "We don't know that she wasn't."

Lucy turned to Ellis, who was now sitting in the chair where Florence had sat to have lemonade and cookies. Had it only been four days ago? It seemed like an eternity. "Did her husband say anything about the circumstances of her disappearance? Did he know the people who raised her?"

"Only that Florence—he called her Shirley—thought she was adopted. The people who raised her told her her parents were dead. She called them Uncle and Aunt, he said." Ellis's voice quivered and she stopped speaking and looked at them for a minute. "Are you sure you want to hear this?" she said, and Augusta answered by quietly taking her hand. Calmer now, Ellis continued. "Shirley told her husband the couple had lost a child, a little girl, before she came to live with them and kept her pictures all over the house. They had no other children."

"So they just helped themselves to somebody else's," Lucy said. "Can you imagine the torment her parents must've felt?" She felt rage rising within her, spewing like burning embers from her stomach into her chest, and it made her weak with grief for them.

"They never got over it," Ellis said. "How could they?"

"How did they bear it, not knowing, wondering every day if she was still alive?" Lucy remembered Julie as a toddler hiding behind a display in a crowded mall when she had turned her head for a fraction of a second, and the panic that ensued until her little daughter called out to her and laughed. In that frantic moment she would have torn the whole shopping center apart, brick by brick, if need be, to find her child. Lately, Lucy might have found herself tempted to trade her daughter for another model, but no matter how annoyed she became with either of her children, she loved them better than she did herself—as her mother had loved her, and her mother before her. As Augusta said, it came with the territory.

Augusta stood suddenly and turned away from them and was quiet so long that Ellis asked her if something was wrong.

"I was thinking of someone I haven't seen in a while," she said, trying to avoid their eyes. "Someone I care about and miss very much." Augusta bustled about putting away the dishes they had washed earlier, but Lucy could see her eyes were misty with tears.

"Oh, Augusta, is it a child?" Lucy spoke softly. "Did you lose a child?"

"Not a child, but so like one at times. Penelope was an apprentice, and I didn't really lose her." Augusta drew herself up so that if she had had wings, Lucy could imagine them in full spread. "She's been assigned her own charge now," she said. "A baby girl, I understand, and Penelope is beside herself with joy. So am I, of course, but I grew accustomed to her company. I try not to think of it, but there's a bit of an emptiness there."

"Welcome to the empty nest," Ellis said. "Will you see her again?"

"Oh, yes, from time to time when she needs direction." Augusta smiled. "And maybe when she doesn't."

"Nettie remembers the day Florence was taken," Lucy told them. "She said her parents wouldn't let her out of their sight for ages. If she'd been the one out playing alone that day, it could've been her instead."

"I doubt it," Ellis said. "I've seen Nettie's picture as a child. She

47

was what you might call average-looking, and besides, she would've been too old, but Florence was beautiful. Her baby book is full of photographs of a rosy-looking cherub with a head full of brown curls."

"Kind of like Shirley Temple," Lucy said. "Maybe that's why the people who took her called her Shirley."

"I wonder who else lived on this street at the time," Augusta said. "It seems odd that no one saw anything suspicious, even after the fact."

"The O'Brians used to live on the other side of this house," Ellis said. "Remember them, Lucy Nan? Had a son, Barrett, who played on the high school football team. I was still in grammar school at the time, but I had a big crush on him."

Lucy nodded. "Mr. O'Brian died not long after Charlie and I married, and I think his wife left here to be near a sister. They were living here, though, when Florence disappeared."

"But both of them are dead, and Barrett wouldn't have been born yet," Ellis reminded her. "Nettie would remember the old neighborhood, I'll bet. Seems like she told me that Boyd Henry Goodwin grew up in that house on the corner—never lived anywhere else."

Lucy smiled. "Funny, but I can't imagine Boyd Henry *growing up*. I always thought he came here fully grown with that little gray mustache, wearing a three-piece suit and playing the violin!"

"Except when he's out working in his garden," Ellis added, laughing.

Boyd Henry had been registrar at Sarah Bedford College for as long as they could remember until his retirement a few years ago, and he and several others from the college were often called upon to provide music for anything from weddings to funerals in the area. They called themselves The Fiddlesticks and met regularly in members' homes.

"Poag Hemphill's a member of The Fiddlesticks," Lucy said. "I wonder if they'll play at Calpernia's funeral. I still can't believe the police suspect she was murdered. I'll admit there have been times I might've wanted to push Calpernia off a tower, but I never thought somebody would actually do it."

"It surprises me that she climbed up there," Ellis said. "She told me once she was terrified of heights."

Augusta, who had been quietly working at her needlepoint while listening to the conversation, suddenly put her sewing aside. "That puts a different light on things," she began, then stopped at the sound of a car in the driveway behind the house. "Are you expecting someone?" she asked.

"Oh, that's just Roger—he's my son," Lucy explained. "I can tell by the way he drives. That's his 'I'm here and I'm in a hurry' sound."

The words were barely out of her mouth when the lock clicked on the back door and Roger Pilgrim more or less blew in, looking every bit the young professor in tweed sport coat with tie askew.

"What's this I hear about your taking in a roomer?" he asked, bypassing his mother for the refrigerator. "Did these tarts come from Do-Lollie's? I hope they're chess."

It never ceased to amaze Lucy that her son, who, with his wife, frowned on allowing their child to eat sweets, went straight to the good stuff when Jessica wasn't around.

Helping himself, he grazed Lucy's cheek with a kiss and greeted Ellis with a hug. "I hope you're talking some sense into her," he said to Ellis. "Taking in a stranger she knows absolutely nothing about—especially with all that's been going on." With plate and fork in hand, he sat down to eat. "Just who is this person, Mom? Do you know anything about her?"

"I promise you, she's a perfect angel," Lucy said with a glance at Ellis. "And don't worry, I doubt if you'll ever see her."

Although Augusta still sat at the table, she had laid her needlework aside and Ellis held it up for Roger to see. "This is something she's been working on. Heavenly stitching, don't you think?"

Roger frowned. "Well, it is pretty. Don't think I've ever seen colors like that . . . but that's beside the point—and what are you two giggling about?"

Lucy tousled the top of her son's neat head. It was a gesture of affection but she knew it annoyed him. "Just ignore us, and please rest assured my roomer won't murder me in my sleep. I really think she's going to be a blessing."

"A blessing, huh? I'll bet you don't even know where she's from." Finishing his tart, Roger went in search of something to wash it down.

"I believe Augusta's from Realms," Lucy said.

Roger poured milk into a glass. "Realms? Never heard of it. Realms where?"

"Of Glory," Ellis muttered under her breath, then pretended to cough to cover her laughter. Thankfully, Lucy thought, Roger didn't seem to hear her.

"I think you two have been into the wine," he said, shaking his head. "I'm glad you can be so lighthearted with two people found murdered here in less than a week. I'm afraid it's not going to be good for the college."

"I doubt if it was too great for Florence, either," Lucy reminded him. "But *two* people? Is it true, then, about Calpernia Hemphill? Do they really think somebody pushed her from that tower?"

"I don't know much more than you do," Roger said, rising to go, "but Connie Jacobs—she's secretary for Dean Ackerman—said her cousin who works at the police department told her there was some doubt about the way Calpernia fell."

Roger was almost to the door before he remembered the other reason for his visit. "Jessica asked me to find out if you'd mind chaperoning Teddy's kindergarten class to Bellawood Friday. I think they're going to pick cotton. She has a dentist's appointment that morning or she'd go herself. I really am getting to be the absent-minded professor. I almost forgot to ask you."

Lucy followed Roger to the door. "The absent-minded *associate* professor, and of course I'll be happy to go."

Bellawood, a living-history plantation on the outskirts of town, dated back to the antebellum period and was a popular resource for teachers in the area. Lucy always enjoyed visiting there. "Remember, Ellis, how we used to take a picnic to pick cotton on your daddy's farm?" she said. "He always gave us a dollar whether we earned it or not."

"He didn't see you!" Ellis said to Augusta after Roger left. "I still can't believe this is happening. That was fun!"

"You shouldn't tease him so," Augusta said, taking up her needlework. Her radiant hair shone so brightly she could probably sew in the dark, Lucy thought.

"I should be leaving, too," Ellis said, shrugging into her coat. "I have to get the guest room ready for Leonard Fenwick."

"What can I do to help?" Lucy asked.

"I think he wants to have the funeral as soon as possible—just a small graveside service with a few old friends. Heck, most everybody she knew as a child is dead! Anyway, I thought I'd have a luncheon before the service. I'll let you know when."

"Wait a minute before you go," Lucy said. "I've been meaning to give you a copy of those old pictures you wanted for your scrapbook—the ones we made out at the lake on my sixteenth birthday. I think they're in that chest in Julie's room."

While Ellis waited below with Augusta, Lucy hurried upstairs thinking of what she could bring to help out with Ellis's luncheon. Baked ham might be good, but somebody else usually brought that. Quiche would be easy to make, or maybe a frozen fruit salad . . . Lucy had taken only a few steps into Julie's old room before she noticed something was different, out of place. It wasn't anything major, but the drawer of the nightstand wasn't quite shut;

the corner of a pillowcase peeked from the top drawer of the bureau. And maybe she was imagining things, but it seemed as if the framed photograph of Julie's high school graduating class had been moved from its usual position on the dresser.

Her heart thundering, Lucy snatched the album from the bottom drawer and slowly backed from the room, then turned and hurried downstairs. "Have either of you been upstairs this afternoon?" she asked.

They hadn't, of course. Somehow that didn't surprise her.

"What is it?" Ellis asked. "Is something wrong?"

"I'm not sure," Lucy admitted, "but it looks like somebody's been upstairs, and I think they were looking for something."

CHAPTER SIX

"Well, she's done it!" Nettie McGinnis said.

"Who's done what?" Lucy asked. It was a little before noon and the two were walking the three blocks to Ellis's, where the luncheon was scheduled prior to Florence Fenwick's funeral service that afternoon.

Nettie carried a basket of homemade yeast rolls with a small jar of her muscadine jelly tucked inside. From her other arm swung an ancient pocketbook of peeling leather that bumped her plump hip with every step. Now she paused to adjust the strap. "Zee Saint Clair, who else? Said she was going do it, didn't she? And I'll be John Brown if she didn't! Now she's gone and invited that jaybird man to stay in her mama's guest house."

"Jaybird man? Oh, you mean that director Calpernia hired, Jay Warren-Winslow!" Lucy, carrying two foil-wrapped quiches on an enamel tray, stepped carefully around a puddle. She hoped nobody would notice the tray had a picture of a buxom barmaid with a great armload of foaming beer.

"That *criminal*, you mean. Why would the police question him if they didn't think he'd shoved Calpernia from that tower?"

"That doesn't necessarily mean he did it," Lucy said. "They haven't arrested him, have they?"

"Only a matter of time," Nettie muttered. "I reckon Zee's trying to prove a point, but for the life of me I can't figure out what it is!"

"By the way," Lucy asked, "did you happen to go upstairs the other day when the Thursdays met at my house?"

"Why would I do that? Last time I was up there was when you wanted me to look at that woman—the one they claim is Florence."

"Somebody did and I was hoping it was you," Lucy said. "I thought maybe the bathroom downstairs was occupied so you came up to use the one next to Julie's room and were looking for a towel or something." She told her about the drawers left slightly ajar.

"Do-law! I'd dry my hands on my shirttail before I'd go rummaging in somebody else's dresser drawers," Nettie said. "Besides, you've got two toilets downstairs. How many people do you think would have to pee at once?"

Lucy was still laughing as they approached Ellis's house and saw Lollie Pate's white van with its teacup logo pull up in front. Lollie waved to them as she got out, then took a square cardboard box from the back of the truck. "Would you mind taking this in for me?" she asked. "I left one of the college students in charge of the shop and I really should get back."

"I guess I could balance the tray on top," Lucy said. "It won't smash anything, will it?"

"It's just cookies—tea cakes. I thought Ellis might be able to use some."

"Lollie, you're not leaving, are you?" Ellis called to them from the porch as Lollie turned to go. "Do come in for a minute, won't you? Leonard's gone to the church but he should be back any second. You have time for a glass of sherry, don't you? Or maybe some Russian tea to warm you up." She shivered. "I'm afraid it's going to rain again."

"Oh dear, I hope not!" Lollie said, her hands going to her perfectly-coiffed blond hair. "I just did my hair and it won't do to get it wet." She glanced at the sky and then at her watch. "Well, maybe for a minute. I told Becky I wouldn't be long—she's part-time, you know. Only been with me a few weeks."

"Ellis, these flowers are perfectly beautiful!" Lucy said of the arrangement on the dining room table as they made their way to the kitchen. A large blue bowl of yellow roses, white Lisianthus and tiny blue asters was centered on the oval walnut table that had belonged to Ellis's parents, as had the house. The spacious room was now painted a deep gold with molding in a lighter shade of the same color; floor-length windows, covered only in yards of a sheer ivory fabric, let in the light. Lucy remembered the time when, as children, she and Ellis had spilled cherry Kool-Aid on this very same Oriental rug, then scrubbed frantically at it for over an hour before it blended in with the design. She had enjoyed many happy meals in this room, but this was not to be one of them, Lucy thought.

"Poag Hemphill sent that arrangement," Ellis told her as she found a platter for the tea cakes. "Lollie, these look delicious . . . Can you imagine being that thoughtful with his own wife lying somewhere in a morgue?"

Ellis gave Lucy a knife for the quiches, then poured sherry into small glasses and arranged them on a tray. "Be generous with your portions, Lucy Nan. We aren't expecting many for lunch. I invited Poag when I called to thank him, but he declined, of course—not surprising, under the circumstances."

"Calpernia's death is going to go hard on him, I'm afraid," Lucy said. "They did so many things together. Was it last year she directed some of the faculty in that funny *Womanless Wedding?* Poag played the mother of the bride—wore grapefruit in his bra! I laughed so hard, my stomach hurt."

"I think it was year before last," Ellis said. "He stole the show, didn't he? Crying and carrying on. I'll swear, he sounded just like my cousin Sadie!"

Lucy laughed. "He's a talented man, all right," she said, passing the sherry around. "And it was thoughtful of him to send flowers, especially since he didn't even know Florence."

"I don't imagine there are that many people left who remember Florence Calhoun," Lollie said, accepting a glass. "How sad."

"Did you invite Boyd Henry?" Nettie asked. "He lived across the street."

"As a matter of fact, I did," Ellis said, "but he's volunteering at Bellawood today." She shrugged. "You'd think he could take some time to pay his respects to an old neighbor, wouldn't you? Isn't he about Florence's age?"

"Boyd Henry was a few of years ahead of me in school," Nettie said. "He would've been about twelve when Florence disappeared. I remember he used to sell snow cones—had a cart and everything." She laughed. "I was so jealous!"

"Nettie tells me Zee has taken on a houseguest," Lucy mentioned to Ellis as they moved into the living room. Her cousin Jo Nell and a few others had joined them, and since Leonard Fenwick hadn't put in an appearance, she assumed he was still at the church.

"You mean that young director? Knowing Zee, I'm not surprised. I just hope she knows what she's doing." Ellis placed the tray of drinks on the coffee table and passed a dish of cheese straws. "Yours," she whispered aside to Lucy. "I froze what was left from the drop-in."

"If you're talking about that Jay Walter Winchell, I heard

Calpernia was going to back out of their agreement," Jo Nell said. "She found out he'd put a lot of stuff on his résumé that wasn't true at all."

"That's Jay Warren-Winslow," Nettie told her. "And where'd you hear all this?"

"Bernice Okey—you all know Bernice, been living next door to me for close on thirty years—her youngest daughter Diane was in one of Calpernia's classes at the college and Diane says everybody at Sarah Bedford knows about it." Jo Nell sniffed the sherry in her glass and took a testing sip. "The man's not what he was cracked up to be."

"Do they really think he might have deliberately pushed her from that tower?" Lollie asked, eyes wide. "I assumed she just fell. The mortar was crumbling, wasn't it? Why, you couldn't drag me up there! That old thing isn't safe." She paused to look around. "You don't suppose she *jumped*, do you? Let's face it, Calpernia's always been a little moody. Maybe she was depressed."

"If Calpernia Hemphill meant to do away with herself, she wouldn't have done it that way," Ellis told them. "She was terrified of heights."

"It does seem extreme to me that this fellow—this Jay Whatever—would kill Calpernia just to keep her quiet about his falsified résumé," Lucy said.

"I suppose if he thought it would ruin his career . . . " someone said. "Sometimes ambition can be a dangerous thing."

A car door slammed out front and everyone turned at the sound of male voices on the porch. "Good! Here're Leonard and Pete," Ellis said, referring to Pete Whittaker, the Presbyterian minister. "They've been at the church discussing last-minute funeral arrangements."

Leonard Fenwick was not at all what Lucy had expected. Tall and tan with a distinguished-looking shock of graying hair, he looked to be a good ten years younger than his wife. Wearing tan slacks and a dark green polo shirt with some kind of club logo on the pocket, he carried a raincoat folded neatly over his arm. When he shook hands with her, Lucy noticed (how could she help it?) he wore a diamond-encrusted ring on the third finger of his right hand. His wedding-ring finger was bare.

"Do I have time to change before lunch?" he asked Ellis, and was told that of course he did. As soon as introductions were made, he lingered for a few minutes of polite chatter before going upstairs, leaving the rest of them to wonder among themselves about Florence's mysterious past.

"I suppose all this about your wife's other identity has come as quite a shock," Lucy said later as the two of them served themselves buffet-style in the dining room. "Did Florence—I mean Shirley—ever say anything about her earlier years? Did she remember anything?"

Leonard Fenwick helped himself from a large bowl of salad greens, carefully avoiding the cherry tomatoes, Lucy noticed. Now he nodded solemnly. "There were clues, but of course it didn't register with me then. When we were first married, she spoke now and then of a woman named Martha, who she seemed to remember as a cook or a nursemaid, but the Rhineharts—that's the couple who raised her—said they never had domestic help."

"What were they like, the Rhineharts?" Ellis appeared beside them to find a spot for a platter of stuffed eggs a neighbor had brought. "Did Florence really believe they were her uncle and aunt?"

"As far as I know, she did," he said. "Called them Aunt Alma and Uncle Fred. She was fond of them, I think, but I got the idea they were extremely overprotective, which isn't surprising, I guess, since they lost their first child. They wouldn't hear of Shirley going away to school, but she did talk them into letting her attend a local branch of the university." Leonard bypassed the asparagus casserole for a Waldorf salad and moved to one of the card tables Ellis had scattered about. Lucy followed.

"I don't think Shirley was ever much of a student," he said, shaking out his napkin. "She dropped out after her sophomore year and went to work for a local department store—still lived at home, though. Her parents didn't want her to leave, and frankly, I don't think Shirley had the confidence to go out on her own. I always thought she depended on them too much."

Ellis and her husband Bennett soon joined them and for a while no one spoke except to say, "Please pass the salt," or "This salad dressing is delicious." Finally Bennett Saxon gave his fork a rest. "I don't think you ever told us how you and your wife met," he said, addressing Leonard.

"Actually it was at a company Christmas party at Grimball and Carnes," Leonard said. "That's the department store I mentioned. I was in accounting and Shirley was in housewares." He sprinkled artificial sweetener into his coffee and stirred until Lucy was afraid he'd wear the bottom out of the cup.

"So you've both worked there since then?" Ellis asked.

He held up a hand and smiled. "Oh, no! I left several years ago to open my own accounting firm, but Shirley stayed until she retired."

"How long has she been sick?" Lucy asked.

"To tell the truth, I didn't notice it at first," he said. "She's always been forgetful—had to remind her to screw on her head in the mornings!" Leonard smiled. "And maybe a little dotty, too, but then it got worse. Much worse. She's been under a doctor's care for three or four years now and in assisted living for two."

"I'm sorry to hear that," Bennett said. "It must have been difficult for both of you."

" 'Difficult' isn't the word!" Leonard broke open a roll. "Shirley didn't have the greatest insurance coverage and Medicare will only pay so much. The expenses are about to drain me dry."

His knife clattered across the plate and Leonard Fenwick wadded his napkin into a ball. "I'm sorry . . . I don't know what got into me . . . I hope you'll overlook that. It's just that I've been worried so not knowing where Shirley was—how she was. God only knows when was the last time I got a good night's sleep!"

"That's perfectly understandable," Ellis assured him. "Please don't give it another thought. I'm curious, though," she added, "as to how your wife knew to come here. After all these years, what made her want to come home?"

"It always bothered her that she couldn't visit her parents' graves," Leonard said. "The Rhineharts told her they died in a plane crash at sea. I suppose she was still looking for something—anything that had to do with her past . . . " His eyes wandered. "Would anyone else like dessert?"

Laying his napkin aside, he excused himself from the table to look over the array of cakes and pies on the buffet.

Lucy, whose eyes had filled with tears at the story of poor Shirley/Florence's sad plight, met Ellis's stunned gaze across the table. "Doesn't look like he's lost his appetite," she said.

"Well, his financial woes are over as far as poor little Florence is concerned," Ellis said to the man's departing back. "I hope he's satisfied."

"You two shouldn't be so hasty to judge," Bennett began in his see-how-impartial-I-am voice. "After all, we don't know what the man's been through."

"Bah!" Ellis said, making a face.

Later, at the cemetery, Lucy huddled under the canopy with Nettie as the woman they knew as Florence Calhoun Fenwick was laid to rest beside her parents in the family plot. Leonard, in a dark gray suit, sat beside Ellis and Bennett, leaning forward with his hands on his knees as if he waited for a race to begin. Now and then, Lucy noticed, he took out a handkerchief to wipe his glasses—probably because of the rain, she supposed.

The day was cold and suitably drab. Rain had commenced to fall as they walked up the winding path to the hillside plot, and the wind blew icy needles into the small group of mourners as Pete Whittaker began his eulogy. The minister was halfway through the Twenty-third Psalm when Ellis caught Lucy's eye and directed her attention to a lone figure standing under a dripping magnolia several yards away. Lucy squinted through the drizzle to see Augusta shivering behind a lichen-covered stone, looking thoroughly uncomfortable and not the least bit angelic. When she saw she had Lucy's attention, the angel stepped aside.

Behind her, half-hidden by a huge black umbrella and a billowing nandina bush, stood Boyd Henry Goodwin.

Why hadn't he joined the others? Lucy wondered. As soon as the service was over, she paid her brief respects to Leonard Fenwick and hurried in search of Boyd Henry. But the elusive Mr. Goodwin had disappeared.

CHAPTER SEVEN

hat's the second time Jessica's phoned me today!" Lucy said, hanging up the receiver.

"Jessica who?" Augusta backed up to the sitting room fireplace, steaming cup in hand. She had made tea as soon as they got back from Florence Fenwick's graveside service and the warming scent of honey and ginger was especially welcoming on a dreary afternoon.

"Jessica Pilgrim, my daughter-in-law—Roger's wife," Lucy explained. "I'm to bring my grandson Teddy back to the house for lunch after the class trip to Bellawood this week, and Jessica's afraid I might feed the child a grain of sugar—or, heaven forbid—a hamburger!"

"Does he have a medical condition or a weight problem?" Augusta asked.

"Good grief, no! The child's so skinny, if he were to turn sideways you wouldn't be able to see him. I'm all for carrots and raisins, but Jessica goes too far. Anything that tastes good is junk food—including my cookies."

Augusta put her cup on the mantel, held her hands to the blaze, and sighed with pleasure. The orchid stones of her necklace reflected the light from the fire, and steam rose from her filmy dress of silvery turquoise.

"Aren't you getting a little close to the flames?" Lucy asked, curling up in her favorite armchair. The room felt warm and toasty after she had shed her damp coat and shoes. "I do believe you're the most cold-natured person I know!"

"I expect it's because of that winter at Valley Forge," Augusta said. "Those poor men—feet bleeding from the cold! It chills me just thinking about it."

"I assume you mean *George Washington's* men," Lucy said. "Are you telling me you were *there?*"

Augusta gave what Lucy considered a smug little smile and settled down with her sewing. "That's exactly what I'm telling you," she said. "But of course I wasn't there alone. We just about had to empty the heavens to pull that one off!"

"At any rate, I'm glad you showed up at the cemetery today," Lucy told her, wondering if Augusta didn't sometimes exaggerate maybe just a tiny bit. "If I hadn't seen you standing there, I wouldn't have noticed Boyd Henry Goodwin. Wonder why he didn't join the rest of us? And where do you suppose he went so quickly?"

"Home, if he had any sense," Augusta said. "This kind of weather isn't conducive to lingering, but I do feel the poor man is troubled about something." Her slender fingers darted above the cloth making dainty stitches with thread like sunrise gold. "Didn't you tell me he lived on this street when Florence was a child?"

"Still does. Right there on the corner. Nettie said he used to sell snow cones in the neighborhood. They're made from shaved ice and flavoring," she explained. "Children love them."

Augusta silently examined her needlework. "Then perhaps he sold one to Florence the day she disappeared," she said.

"But wouldn't he have said something? If Boyd Henry saw

63

Florence that day, surely he would've told somebody," Lucy said.

"Not necessarily—not if there was a reason he shouldn't. It would be a good idea, I think, to seek this fellow out."

"That shouldn't be a problem since he volunteers at Bellawood and I'll be going there with Teddy's kindergarten class the day after tomorrow," Lucy said. "I can't imagine Boyd Henry Goodwin hiding any deep dark secrets, though. He's the shyest man I ever saw. Wouldn't say boo to a goose!"

Augusta said she didn't see why anybody would want to say boo to a goose, as it seemed most unkind to her. She set her sewing aside and went to stir up the fire. "I hope you're going to have nicer weather than this for your outing Friday," she said. "Maybe it will clear up by then."

"Even if it does, it'll be muddy in the cotton patch. I'd better go upstairs while I'm thinking about it and round up my old boots. I know they're in a closet somewhere."

Augusta was thumbing through a magazine when Lucy came back downstairs a few minutes later. "There seem to be some good recipes in here," she said, looking up. "If you don't mind, I'd like to try my hand at this Harvest Stew."

"Sounds good to me—go for it!" Lucy hesitated in the doorway. "By the way, you haven't seen my boots, have you? I could've sworn I left them in that closet in Julie's room.

"I haven't worn boots since I learned line dancing," Augusta said. "I passed mine along to Penelope." With magazine in hand, she started for the kitchen. "What did they look like?"

Lucy shrugged. "Big, brown and grungy, but they're warm, and they keep my feet dry—more or less . . .

" . . . Augusta, I have an awful feeling!"

"About what?" Augusta tied a voluminous apron splashed with bright blue cornflowers around her middle and disappeared into the pantry.

"I think Shirley/Florence took my boots and left these behind!"

Lucy held up a worn pair of gray leather oxfords spotted with dirty white clay. "I'm sure these were the shoes she was wearing when she came."

Augusta deposited her apronful of potatoes and onions in the sink and held out her hands for the shoes. "Nancy Estridge," she said.

"Say what? Who're you talking about?"

Augusta smiled. "Someone I used to know on an earlier visit—long gone now, I suppose. She called this crawdad clay."

"What? You mean the mud on her shoes?"

"Nancy called it crawdad clay because the crawdads liked to burrow there. It seems Florence planned to be prepared for cold weather," she said, examining them, "so she traded these for your boots—which means she knew she'd be going outside."

"I set her shoes beside the bed," Lucy said, "so she could find them when she woke up. The boots were in the closet along with that coat of mine she took. I'm almost sure somebody telephoned her while Nettie and I were cleaning up the trash on the street."

Augusta took several sheets of newspaper from a stack on the back porch and folded the shoes into a neat package.

"I suppose we should take these to the police," Lucy said. "They knew Florence was wearing my coat because of the receipt in the pocket, but they wouldn't have had any way of knowing her boots belonged to me. Do you think the shoes could be important?"

"They might. It wouldn't hurt to give them a call."

Tomorrow, Lucy thought later as she stowed away the shoes on the top shelf of her hall closet. It had been a long and rather tiring day and now she just wanted to relax with a bowl of whatever it was that smelled so good that Augusta had simmering on the stove. And thank heavens for the angel's company! The knowledge that someone had died wearing her coat and boots made Lucy Nan Pilgrim want to look over her shoulder.

The two of them were just finishing supper when the phone

rang and Lucy almost tripped over her feet in her rush to answer it. She had left another message with her daughter earlier that day and hoped it was Julie returning her call. It had been several weeks since they had spoken, and if there was such a thing as heartstrings, Lucy felt that Julie was snipping hers one by one.

"Lucy Nan, I hope I'm not calling you too late," her cousin Jo Nell bellowed, "but if you have that sandwich-spread recipe handy, I'd sure like to have it for my garden club meeting next week."

Grimacing, Lucy held the receiver away from her ear. "What sandwich spread?" she asked, trying to keep the disappointment out of her voice. Suddenly she just wanted to cry.

"Why, that yummy concoction you served to The Thursdays the other day. I can scribble it down right now if you've got a minute."

What had Augusta put in that sandwich spread? Lucy wished she'd paid closer attention. "Jo Nell, can I get back to you on that tomorrow? I can't put my hands on it right now."

"Well, of course . . . are you all right? You sound funny. You didn't take a cold from being out in that awful weather today, did you? I'll swear that wind howls across Cemetery Hill like it's trying to raise the dead! I went on home as soon as I could—no use risking pneumonia!"

"It was cold, but I'm fine," Lucy said, rolling her eyes at Augusta. "Had some hot tea as soon as I got home." She took the phone into the sitting room and made herself comfortable. "Did you notice Boyd Henry at the graveside service?" she asked her cousin. "He stayed way off to himself. I saw him under that old magnolia in the Dunlaps' lot looking like he was about to blow away with his big umbrella."

"Boyd Henry—he's kind of a loner," Jo Nell said. "He was a good many years ahead of us in school, still, I don't remember him playing with the others much. Guess he didn't have time with his after-school jobs and violin lessons. Always was a hard worker, though."

"Nettie says he sold snow cones," Lucy said.

"That's right, he did! I'd almost forgotten that. Had a little cart on wheels. Boyd Henry's daddy died when he was fairly young, and his mother had a hard time making ends meet. I expect that little snow cone business helped buy the groceries."

"I wonder if he sold one to Florence the day she disappeared," Lucy said, "but I'm sure someone thought to question him about that."

"From what I've heard, I doubt if Eva Calhoun—that's Florence's mama—would let her have one," Jo Nell said. "She was so afraid that child would get a germ! I was too young at the time to remember much about Florence, but Mama said the poor little thing had to wash her hands practically every time she touched anything, and wore fancy little dresses all the time. Can you imagine her mother letting Florence dribble cherry syrup on one of those?"

Lucy admitted that she couldn't, but that still didn't explain why Boyd Henry was so reluctant to mingle at the graveside.

"What did you think of Florence's Leonard?" Jo Nell wanted to know. "Didn't seem too broken up, if you ask me."

Lucy remembered Bennett Saxon's advice and said maybe the poor man was just overwhelmed by it all, but she didn't believe it for a minute.

The clock in the hall was striking nine when Lucy got off the telephone. She had only spoken briefly with her cousin, but what if Julie had tried to call? "Oh, the hell with it!" she muttered aloud. "She isn't going to call because she doesn't care!" She plopped down as hard as she could into the most uncomfortable chair in the sitting room, which happened to be the green-striped one they had inherited from Charlie's mother. The springs made a peculiar noise and sagged even lower.

Augusta settled across from her with a bowl of nuts and began to crack them one by one, filling a fruit jar with the shelled pecans. She didn't speak.

"Oh, go on!" Lucy said finally. "Just say it. I know what you're thinking!"

Augusta's eyes flew open wide. "How can you do that? Will you show me how?"

"Do what?"

"Know what I'm thinking."

Lucy groaned. "My own daughter hates me and it's all my fault! I've as good as shoved her out of my life." She told her about Julie's relationship with her current boyfriend. "For the life of me, I can't see the attraction!" she said. "I can hardly bear to be in the same room with him."

"Have you tried?" Augusta asked, nibbling a nut.

"I've haven't had much of a chance. Well, she's made her choice. I wash my hands of it!" Lucy picked up a pillow and squeezed it, wishing it were Buddy Boy's neck. Her heart hurt. It hurt all the way up to her head and down to her toes.

"Are you sure you want to burn your bridges to spite your face?" Augusta asked.

When the telephone rang at a little before eight the next morning, Lucy didn't dare to hope it might be Julie, which was a good thing because it was Idonia Mae Culpepper and she sounded as if she had been running. Lucy knew that couldn't be true because as far as she knew, Idonia had never run anywhere in her life.

"LucyNanhaveyouheardfromZee?" she asked, seemingly all in one breath.

"Zee?" Lucy repeated, since it was the only word she had understood.

"Zee, yes! Zee Saint Clair. She was supposed to fill in with my bridge group last night, but she never showed up."

"She probably just forgot. Did you call?" Lucy yawned. She hadn't had her second cup of coffee yet.

"Well, of course I called. And called. And called. She's not picking up. It's not like Zee to forget something like that. I'm worried, Lucy Nan. You know she has that director living in her guest cottage—the one they think killed Calpernia Hemphill. For all we know he might have cut her into little pieces and—"

"Oh, for heaven's sake, Idonia! Maybe she went out to eat or something. Have you tried to phone her this morning?"

"Well, not yet, but I'm going to. I didn't want to wake her."

"I didn't notice it bothering you to wake me," Lucy told her.

"Oh, I'm sorry. Did I?"

"No, but you might've. Actually I've already had my breakfast." Pancakes so light they could float, with the most divine strawberry syrup. "Why don't you wait a little while and try her again?"

"And if I can't reach her then, will you go with me?"

"Go where?" Lucy glanced in the kitchen where Augusta, drying the breakfast dishes, paused to admire her reflection in the bottom of a stainless-steel frying pan.

"To Zee's, of course. You surely don't expect me to go by myself, do you?"

And that was why, an hour later, Lucy found herself turning into the long tree-shaded driveway of Zee St. Clair's Victorian home, with Idonia sitting white-knuckled beside her. Except to comment that she hoped they weren't too late, Idonia hadn't said a word during the brief drive over. Now she leaned forward and shaded her eyes from the morning sun. "It's awfully quiet," Idonia said. "Don't you think it's unusually quiet, Lucy Nan?"

Lucy replied with a noncommittal grunt. Of course it was quiet! What did Idonia expect at nine-thirty in the morning?

"And look at all these trees! I don't know why Zee wants to live so far from the street. Why, anybody could come back here and burglarize her house or *worse* and no one would be the wiser." Idonia dropped her voice, as if anyone could hear. "I wonder if she's home. I don't see her car . . .

" . . . Zee really needs to cut back those rhododendrons. Look at that—they're just taking over her front walk."

Lucy drove slowly, trying to avoid the potholes in Zee's gravel drive. She didn't want to frighten Idonia even more by mentioning that Zee's copy of the morning newspaper was still in its tube at the street.

Her friend's garage door was shut and if Zee was at home, her car was probably inside, Lucy thought. It was not until she turned into the parking area behind the house that she saw the bright blue Toyota parked in front of the small guest cottage.

"That must be his car! *He's here!*" Idonia clutched at the dashboard. "Oh, dear God, what do you suppose he's done to Zee?"

"Idonia, if the man had done anything to Zee, he'd be miles away by now." Lucy switched off the engine and opened her door.

Idonia snatched at her sleeve. "Where are you going?"

"Why, to check on Zee, of course. Isn't that why we're here?" Lucy marched boldly up to the back door, hoping she wouldn't look inside to find Zee lying stone-cold dead on the linoleum. Maybe this wasn't such a good idea. She looked back to find Idonia following at a safe distance and was about ready to chicken out and go home when she heard voices inside.

Hearing their footsteps, Zee St. Clair, clad in a slinky, hot-pink lounging thingy, met them at the door.

"Well, you're just in time for breakfast! I'll put on another pot. Come in and meet Jay."

A young man turned from the stove where he was frying bacon and waved a spatula at them. "How do you like your eggs?" he asked.

He wore cutoff jeans and a baggy shirt with the sleeves rolled up. Jay Warren-Winslow was of slight build with a nondescript brownish beard, but he had a nice smile and the greenest eyes Lucy had ever seen. And as for Zee St. Clair, she looked happier than a pig in the sunshine.

CHAPTER EIGHT

"Well," Idonia said, "I never."

Lucy giggled. "Maybe not, but it sure looks like Zee has!"

"Why, Lucy Nan Pilgrim! Surely you don't think Zee and that Jay person have been behaving in an inappropriate manner! She's old enough to be his mother."

The two were driving home after what Lucy considered a most uncomfortable visit in the St. Clair kitchen, during which they sat at the table sipping coffee strong enough to get up and walk, and tried to avoid looking one another in the eye.

Lucy thought Zee would behave in an inappropriate manner in a New York minute under the right circumstances, but she wasn't sure that was the case—not yet, anyway. "To tell the truth, I think Zee's just enjoying the moment," she said. "She might be caught up in the idea of it, but I'll bet she'd run for dear life if that man took her seriously." She slowed as they drove past the red brick school where children chased one another during their mid-morning break. "I haven't seen Zee wear that hot-pink number since we used to drink whiskey sours by Ellis's pool. Remember? I had a yellow flowered one-piece job kinda like it—zipped up the back—a real problem when you had to go to the bathroom in a hurry." Lucy smiled, remembering happier times when Charlie was still alive and her friends entertained one another at dinner parties. She had given the yellow lounging pajamas away years ago when they got too tight to meet across the back. When was the last time she had entertained on such a scale? Surely it hadn't been as long ago as it seemed.

Zee had been most apologetic about forgetting about Idonia's bridge club. Jay had taken her to this quaint little restaurant in Charlotte, she'd said, and the bridge club just went completely out of her head. Lucy hoped her brains weren't leaking out as well.

"It might be perfectly harmless," Idonia said, "but it just doesn't *look* right, and Zee doesn't even seem to care. I still don't feel good about that man staying there. You heard what Jo Nell said: He padded his résumé with a bunch of lies and Calpernia found out about it. Ask your own son. Roger teaches in the history department, doesn't he? I heard it was common knowledge on campus at Sarah Bedford." Idonia sniffed. "It'll be a cold day in Hades before I ask Zee Saint Clair to fill in again. Can you believe that flimsy excuse she gave?"

"That she went out to dinner and forgot? Absolutely! Wouldn't you?"

Idonia was quiet for a minute. "No," she said finally. "I don't think I would. That Jay Warren-Winslow—his eyes are too close together to suit me. What do you reckon he's up to?"

"He *says* he just wants to show appreciation to Zee for taking him in," Lucy said, "and I can understand that. I just hope Zee doesn't make more of it. I'd hate to see her hurt."

"Maybe she's looking for husband number three," Idonia said. "After all, it's been at least three years since she dumped the last one—but she'd better watch her step this time."

"Well, at least he knows how to cook." Lucy waved to Ashley Butterfield, the organist at the Methodist Church, as she pulled out of the church parking lot. The day was crisp and sunny; flaming maple leaves framed a bright October sky, but the thought of that parking lot made her want to rush home and lock the doors behind her.

Idonia must have been thinking the same thing. "I don't know how Ashley can bear to park behind that church by herself, just like nothing's happened."

"She has to practice for Sunday," Lucy said. "Where else would she park? Besides, the staff's there during the daytime, but I know what you mean. The place gives me the willies, too. I wish they'd hurry and find who did that to Florence."

"I thought you might've heard something," Idonia said. As they neared her house, she began searching in her handbag for her house key. "Nettie says she's still not sure that woman they buried *was* Florence. Wouldn't that be awful, Lucy Nan, if it turns out they put some stranger in the Calhoun family plot?"

"Who else could it be? She knew her way around the house all right, knew the name of the cook—even said her mama was a Thursday. Why would anybody pretend to be Florence Calhoun?"

Idonia jangled her keys and snapped her handbag shut. "For the inheritance. Why else? Just think about it, Lucy Nan: The very house you're living in would've come to Florence Calhoun!"

Lucy did think about it. She remembered going to Papa Zeke's funeral when she and Ellis were fifteen. She knew that because they had the visitation in the new fellowship hall of the Presbyterian Church, which had just been completed that year. At his father's death, Ellis's dad had inherited the family home along with additional property and investments—which came to a sizable amount—now in the possession of Ellis.

"But that was so long ago!" Lucy turned into the driveway of Idonia's modest brick ranch house where shaggy gold chrysanthemums billowed along the sunny front walk. "Ellis's dad sold the house to the Methodist Church for a parsonage thirty years ago.

Why now? Besides, if Shirley Fenwick was just pretending to be Florence, her husband would have to be in on the scheme as well, wouldn't he?"

"You got a look at him, didn't you? Jo Nell says that man's about as tender as a judge's heart. We've not heard the last of Leonard Fenwick!"

If Leonard Fenwick had been involved in a plot to pass off his wife as the long-lost Florence Calhoun, did he also have a hand in her murder? Lucy wondered as she drove to the post office after dropping off Idonia. Ellis said the police had questioned some of that rough-looking bunch that hung out at the Red Horse Café—many of whom were no strangers to the inside of a jail—but so far nothing had come of it. Lucy could believe some of them might have been desperate enough to take what little money the poor woman had on her that night, and even the costume jewelry she wore. After all, in the dark, how were they to know the difference? But why did they think it necessary to kill her? Florence or no Florence, the woman didn't deserve what had happened to her, and the thought of anyone deliberately pushing her down the steep steps, then leaving her to die in the cold, made Lucy rigid with anger.

Leonard had said his wife had obviously planned her visit to Stone's Throw in advance of the shopping trip with the group from the residence where she lived, yet she had no luggage when she arrived at Lucy's front door. It would've been difficult to hide even a small suitcase from whomever accompanied them shopping, so it was possible she didn't bring any extra clothing. But how in the world did the woman get here? She might have taken the bus, although the people at the bus station in town didn't remember seeing her get off; perhaps someone gave her a ride. But who?

Idonia's question was still on her mind as Lucy parked in the lot beside the post office and gathered the letters she planned to mail. *Wouldn't it be awful if they put some stranger in the Calhoun family plot?* Drat Idonia! Leave it to her to plague a person with a worrisome notion like that! But obviously the police felt certain the woman they buried was Florence; after all, she did have the identifying scar. As for the rest of them, they would just have to wait for the results of the DNA tests. Lucy realized the labs were sometimes slow to confirm the results of these samples, but she wished they would put a rush order on this one.

Clouds streaked across the sun and the wind had picked up as Lucy came out of the post office and crossed the parking lot to her car.

"Blanche, Stella! You come back here! Lucy Nan, stop them! Don't let those naughty imps get past you!"

Lucy stopped in mid-stride to see two miniature white poodles tearing across the parking lot, leashes whipping along behind them, with Poag Hemphill, breathless and red-faced, in pursuit. Quickly she dropped her handbag and sprinted to scoop up the closest escapee, cuddling it as she stroked its woolly head, while Poag coaxed the other from underneath a minivan.

"Shame on you, Blanche! You, too, Stella!" Poag took a handkerchief from his jacket pocket and cleaned his glasses. "Thanks, Lucy Nan. I stopped for just a second back there to pick up some litter off the sidewalk and I guess I must've lost my grip on the leashes. If it hadn't been for you, they would've run right into the traffic!" He held out a small plastic bag half-filled with empty cigarette packages and soft-drink cans. "I know I shouldn't let it bother me so, but I can't understand people throwing trash right here on the street. It's unsightly and disgusting!"

Lucy agreed with him and set the little dog—Stella, she presumed—down beside its companion, keeping a firm grip on the leash. "I've been wanting to call you," she said, reaching out to touch his shoulder. "I was so sorry to hear about Calpernia, Poag. I know what it's like to lose someone you love, and I've had you on my mind since it happened."

He smiled, collecting both leashes. "I know. It's hard to know what to say, isn't it? It's been a week now since Cal's been gone and—well, frankly, I don't know how to act."

The dogs began to chase each other, winding their leashes around his legs, and he slowly extracted himself. "Walk with me a little way?" he asked, his voice muffled.

"Of course." Lucy smiled. "Not that I need the exercise!" She took his arm. "Poag, this has been a terrible shock to all of us—and to have it happen while you were away! I can only imagine what you've been through."

He cleared his throat. "It was a long trip home, Lucy Nan. A long trip home. Thank God we had a chance to spend at least a few minutes together before I left for that tour with the chorus—too damn few!"

Wind blew brown leaves across the walk as they turned the corner into Palmetto Street, and they walked silently for a minute. "People have been so kind," Poag said, as they waited to cross the street. "The other day the editor of *The Signal*—that's the campus newspaper, you know—brought me a photograph made of Cal and me saying our good-byes just before I boarded the bus the night I left. They were planning to run it in the next issue until . . . well . . . that happened.

"If only she'd come with me—but Cal didn't like to fly." He shook his head. "Well, I guess she's flying with the angels now."

Lucy rather doubted that but she hoped she looked suitably soulful.

"I still don't know what in hell Calpernia was doing up there," he said, taking her arm as they crossed the street. "I suppose you've heard they suspect foul play—seem to have zeroed in on that young director, but I honestly can't see him doing anything like that. He may have jazzed up his résumé—probably did—but we've had the fellow over to the house for dinner a couple of times, and, Lucy Nan, he just doesn't seem the type."

"So, do you think Calpernia might have fallen?"

"I'd like to think that, considering the alternative. Cal wasn't fond of heights, but she was really committed to the idea of developing a permanent theater workshop out there—and you know how impulsive she was. I wouldn't be surprised if she didn't suddenly decide to climb to the top of that idiotic Folly just to get the lay of the land."

Poag paused to let the dogs sniff at the base of a dogwood tree. "Oh, I know Cal wasn't always popular with some of the people here," he said, "but not to that extent." His hand trembled as he untangled one of the poodles from the leash. "No, damn it! Not to that extent!"

He looked so utterly miserable that Lucy wanted to fold him into her arms right there in front of the Baptist Church and soothe away the hurt as she did for Teddy, and for her children before him, but she knew in her heart the kind of hurt Poag Hemphill was experiencing couldn't be easily soothed. "When was the last time you sat down and had a decent meal?" she asked, taking his hand.

He avoided her gaze. "Oh, neighbors have brought enough food to feed an army, and several friends invited me over, but to tell the truth, I don't have much of an appetite." He shrugged. "I've just been eating whenever I feel the need."

"I've plenty of soup left from yesterday and it won't take a minute to stir up some corn bread. You need some nourishing food inside you, Poag. Come back to the house with me for lunch." *But first leave Stella and Blanche at home!* Lucy had seen what one of them had rolled in and she didn't care to have it smeared on her freshly cleaned carpet.

"Oh, Lucy Nan, you are a dear! My poor deprived stomach rumbles at the thought, but I really must get these two back home. I have to meet with Albert Evans this afternoon to make plans for Calpernia's service. They're finally letting her go."

It would be a busy week for Evans & Sons Funeral Home, who had just put poor Shirley/Florence away. "Do you know yet when it will be?" she asked.

"Saturday afternoon at three. We'll have the visitation afterward. There should be a notice in tomorrow's paper."

One of the dogs scrambled to chase after a squirrel and Poag picked up the poodle and tucked it under his arm. "I just want to get it over with," he said bleakly. "Is that awful, Lucy Nan?"

"Of course not! I don't blame you. And naturally our circle will take care of dinner. Do you expect many relatives from out of town?"

"I'll have to let you know. Cal's only sister lives in Orlando. She's due in tomorrow—and my sister Myra will be here of course with her husband and two daughters. I'm looking for them this afternoon." Poag shifted the dog to glance at his watch. "I'll get back to you as soon as I have a more definite number, but right now I'd plan on about twenty or so. There'll be plenty of room at our—at my place." He smiled. "Cal would want the wine to flow and we can't do that at the church. I want our friends to celebrate her life in a positive way—I just wish she could be here to enjoy it."

They parted at the corner. Poag, a dog under each arm, walked briskly in the direction of Sarah Bedford campus, and Lucy hurried back to her car, wondering if anyone had notified their circle chairman about the need for food. She turned once to glance at the man's departing back. Although his pace was quick, his head was bowed and his usually straight shoulders now slumped forward.

Poag Hemphill was not a large man but he kept himself in shape with tennis and swimming, and he and Calpernia often bicycled together. Their comfortable bungalow near the campus had been a gathering place for students as well as friends. He was going to need them now, Lucy thought as she stood looking after him. She knew from experience how devastating it was to lose one's mate, but at least she had Roger and his family, as well as Julie (well, sort of) in her life. Poag had inherited only Blanche and Stella.

"You'd better get started on your funeral cake," Lucy told Ellis when she found her munching pumpkin muffins in the kitchen with Augusta. A pot of soup simmered on the stove and the ingredients for corn bread waited on the table. "I thought I'd wait and let you show me how you make it," Augusta said, smoothing her apron. "Ellis said you like it a certain way."

"As long as it doesn't have sugar in it," Lucy said, measuring the cornmeal. "If I want something sweet, I'll eat cake."

"Did you ask Idonia if she noticed anybody going upstairs when The Thursdays met here the other day?" Ellis asked. "I just can't believe any of our friends would be rude enough to look in somebody else's dresser drawers."

"Or if they were, they'd be careful not to leave such obvious evidence," Lucy said. "Whoever it was must have been in a heck of a hurry. Idonia didn't notice a thing either, and she usually doesn't miss much.

"I saw Poag Hemphill this morning," she told them. "They're having the funeral Saturday afternoon."

"I know. Jo Nell called a while ago and enlisted both of us," Ellis said. Jo Nell was chairman of the Letitia Jane Whitmire Circle, named for an early worker in the church whose stern countenance still looked down on them from the walls of the Ladies' Parlor.

Ellis lifted the lid of the soup pot, took a deep breath, and said, "Ahh!

"So, how is Poag?" she asked.

"Not so good, but then who would be? I'm afraid he's in for a rough time," Lucy said. "Funny thing, though . . . he doesn't think Calpernia was murdered."

"I guess it would be hard to believe anyone would deliberately do away with somebody you care about," Ellis said. "Unless that somebody happened to be Calpernia. I'll have to admit, the woman's tempted me more than once! Remember how she used to blot her lipstick all over our good linen napkins, Lucy Nan? And Nettie said she told her she sang off-key—standing right there in the sanctuary in the middle of the Gloria Patri!"

Augusta looked up over her coffee cup. "Tsk, tsk!" she said. "Don't perspire over inconsequential matters."

"What about Zee?" Ellis reminded her after she finished laughing. "Her complaint wasn't exactly inconsequential."

What about Zee? Lucy wondered. *And what was she doing during the time Calpernia was killed?* And then she immediately felt ashamed for even thinking such a thing. This was the friend she'd known for most of her life. Zee St. Clair had her faults— and who didn't? But murder wasn't one of them. Was it?

"Speaking of Zee," she said, "wait until you hear about her breakfast guest!"

"I wish he'd teach Bennett how to cook," Ellis said, after she'd heard the details. "The man can't seem to learn how to make toast."

"I suppose your guest has left?" Lucy said.

Ellis frowned. "My guest? Oh, you mean Leonard? Left early this morning—and oh, I almost forgot; he left this behind. The police brought it by after the service yesterday, and I guess he didn't want it." She took a brown grocery bag from a chair by the door and brought out a worn leather purse. "Remember this?"

Lucy nodded. "It belonged to Florence." Just looking at the pathetic brown bag made her sad and she wondered why Ellis would bring it here to remind her.

"I think they overlooked something when they went through her purse," Ellis said. "I found this inside the lining." And she reached into the handbag and brought out a small scrap of blue paper.

"What is it?" Augusta asked, looking over Lucy's shoulder.

"A ticket stub," Ellis said. "Poor little Florence came here on a bus."

CHAPTER NINE

It has a date on it—or part of one," Lucy said, holding the paper to the light. "And what looks like the end of a word . . . somewhere in South Carolina."

"I believe it's Stone's Throw," Augusta said. "Look: ESTHROW, S.C. Whoever printed the name of the town ran the two words together." She looked at Ellis with her clear-eyed gaze. "Have the authorities seen this?"

Ellis shook her head. "First I want to do a little sleuthing on my own. After all, they had their chance."

"I missed it, too, when I looked through her purse the day she came," Lucy said. "A lipstick had slipped behind the lining, but I didn't see the ticket stub. Did the police give you back the lipstick, too?" she asked Ellis. "It was pale pink—practically used up . . ."

"It was in a box with some other things—mostly a lot of crushed snacks. Why?" Ellis frowned. "Why are you staring at me like that?"

"The lipstick! Why didn't I think of that before? Florence had on what I'd call a persimmon-color lipstick when she showed up here. It looked like she'd worn most of it off, but there was enough left for Nettie to notice it didn't match her dress or her complexion—of course with the way she was acting, nothing surprised me."

"So where's the other tube of lipstick?" Ellis said. "I'm almost sure I didn't see it in the box."

"It wasn't in her purse, either. I would've found that," Lucy said.

"Leonard said she probably left from somewhere in Chicago," Ellis said. "That's where the group was shopping when they discovered her missing from the mall. That would have been an awfully long bus trip. She'd have to travel through several states."

Augusta began to ladle up the steaming soup while Lucy took corn bread from the oven. "But where did she get off?" she asked.

"I think we should pay a visit to the bus station and see if we can jar their memory," Ellis said, tucking in a napkin. "But first, let's eat!"

The grizzled clerk with a gold tooth shook his head. "I been hearin' 'bout that pore woman all week, but I done told the police I don't recollect her gettin' off here. If she left Chicago on October eighteenth, she'da been here the next day—that is, if she didn't get off sooner." He nodded toward a woman at the counter beside him who appeared to be seriously studying something in a magazine. "Maedean will tell you the same thing. You remember the police wantin' to know 'bout that woman what was killed? Did you see her come through here?"

Maedean looked up from her reading material—one of those women's magazines, Lucy noted, whose cover always features some kind of miracle diet along with recipes like "Desserts to Kill for." "Nope, and I would'a remembered, too, because that's my mama's birthday and I was looking for my Aunt Myrtle to come in that day from Knoxville." She sipped from a mug of coffee. "Nobody got off the bus here that looked like that."

"Then she must have gotten off before the bus reached here," Augusta said when Lucy reached home. "Did you ask about the driver? Maybe he'll remember her?"

"I did. It wasn't the regular driver. The clerk said it was a substitute that day but he'd try and see if he could get in touch with him. I'm not holding my breath."

Augusta paused to wipe a streak of dirt from her face. Lucy had found her on the back steps repotting pansies. "You have too many in one planter. The poor little things can't breathe," Augusta told her, gently patting soil around the seedlings. "I should think the police could follow up on that," she said. "Did Ellis give them the ticket stub?"

"She's on her way there—or so she says. The police had returned my coat to Leonard, too, but I asked Ellis to pass it along to The Salvation Army." Lucy sat on the steps beside Augusta and fingered a velvety blossom. She never wanted to see that coat again.

The wind that had picked up earlier in the day was calm now and the two of them sat in a patch of sun on the weathered back steps. Augusta hummed as she worked and Lucy was content to sit and watch the last of the golden hickory leaves cling to the tree by the summerhouse. She and Charlie had sometimes picnicked there on mild autumn days, and Julie had entertained her little friends there with tea parties. It looked sad now and lonely. Lucy had always loved spending time in her special place, but after Charlie died, she rarely went there anymore.

Stop feeling sorry for yourself! she told herself. *Maybe it's time to look for another job outside the home, or for an adult who needs help learning to read!*

Lucy sniffed. Something smelled wonderful. "Are you baking strawberry bread or something?" she asked, "or is that some kind of perfume?"

Augusta had moved to a small circular flower bed in the center of the driveway where a pool of blue pansies nodded. The flowers looked larger and their colors more vibrant than they had earlier, Lucy thought.

The angel's dazzling necklace seemed to reflect the color of the pansies, winking from purple to violet to the blue of the October sky. "I suppose it's because I worked in the strawberry fields," she said, lightly touching a wilting leaf. The leaf perked up at once. "The scent seems to stay with me here."

"Strawberry fields? Where?"

"In heaven, of course. Can you imagine heaven without them? And now and then I was fortunate enough to be assigned to the flower gardens as well. What a heavenly duty that was! You should see, them, Lucy Nan: acres and acres of flowers of every color and variety. No perfume on earth can equal it!"

"That must be why you have such a magic touch," Lucy said as she rose to go inside.

Augusta laughed. "I suppose you could describe it that way." She put away her gardening tools and followed her into the house, still humming.

"What's that tune you keep humming? Is it a hymn or something? I don't think I've ever heard it."

"No, I doubt if you have. I learned it when I was here on assignment in the 1940s during what you refer to as World War Two. It's called 'Coming in on a Wing and a Prayer.' Rather catchy, don't you think? I can't seem to get it out of my head."

"That figures," Lucy said.

Bellawood, former home of Poindexter G. Potts, Confederate veteran and onetime governor of South Carolina, sat on a wooded knoll at the edge of once-fertile river-bottom acreage about ten miles south of Stone's Throw. Although during its working years it technically had been a plantation, the modest two-story house didn't look anything like Margaret Mitchell's Tara but was a simple clapboard farmhouse that was said to have been built in the mid-1850s. During the Victorian era, its owners added gingerbread trim to the wide front porch and tacked an ornate circular towerlike room onto one corner.

Lucy, bumping along the asphalt road in the school activities bus along with Teddy, his twenty-three kindergarten classmates, their teacher, and three other adult chaperones, cheered with the others when the bus turned onto the curving oak-lined lane that led to the farm.

"When do we get to pick cotton, Mama Lucy?" her grandson asked, bouncing in his seat.

"Soon, but first I think they want to show us what life was like here a long, long time ago," Lucy said, resisting the urge to hug him yet again. *Twice is enough for one bus trip, Lucy Nan! But oh, his smile is so like Charlie's!*

"You mean like when you were a little girl?"

Lucy laughed. "Well, a little before that."

The bus soon came to a stop in a spurt of gravel and twenty-four shouting children jumped to their feet and began clamoring to disembark until their teacher, Miss Linda, held up her hand for silence. Immediately the group became quiet and still. Lucy was amazed at such power. How did the woman do it? She stood with the other chaperones at the foot of the bus steps as the children filed past and followed Miss Linda into the small log building which had been erected as a replica of a school of that era. Harboring a fear of misplacing a child in her charge, Lucy counted them as they stepped down from the bus: *twenty-two, twenty-three, twenty-four, twenty* . . . Had she counted someone twice? No, another adult she hadn't noticed before paused to straighten her wide-brimmed straw hat before emerging from the bus. A mother of one of the children, probably. Lucy smiled and started to introduce herself when the woman raised her hand and waggled her fingers in recognition. It was Augusta.

"I hope you don't mind if I join you," she said, wrapping what seemed like an endless plum-colored shawl about her shoulders. "Oh, my! This place does take me back a bit!" Augusta hurried after the children and took her place at the back of the schoolroom. Lucy trailed after and stood beside her, looking about to see if anyone had noticed the angel's presence.

They hadn't. The children sat on rows of crude benches while a docent dressed in a drab brown dress that reached her shoe tops explained to them that this was a living-history plantation where they not only grew their own cotton, but raised sheep for wool and made it into cloth. "The clothing we wear here is all made from natural fibers," the teacher told them. "Even the dye that colored my dress came from the husks of walnuts, and the buttons are made from bone."

Lucy glanced at Augusta, who smiled and nodded as the teacher demonstrated the use of a slate and read from a book students might have used over a hundred years ago, and she knew she must be remembering children in another time.

"I wonder where Boyd Henry is," Lucy whispered aside to Augusta as they waited to enter the main house. "Nettie says he's a regular volunteer. I wish I could get him aside for a few minutes."

She was soon to have her chance. Boyd Henry Goodwin, in brown cotton britches held up with suspenders and a white linen shirt with loose floppy sleeves, waited for them in the wide entrance hall. A slight man, he always stood fence-post-straight as if to make up for his small stature. With his patrician nose and trim gray mustache, Boyd Henry didn't look at all like Lucy's idea of a nineteenth-century farmer. He welcomed the group heartily, though, and pointed out the room where the family would gather around the hearth at the end of the day. "They didn't have television, so the women would usually sew until it got too dark to see. Even little girls as young as some of you worked on samplers. You'll see a few of these in the upstairs hall."

He spoke with a smile, but there was something troubling about the expression in his eyes. "I'll bet he goes home and writes melancholy poetry," she said aside to Augusta.

"I'll beg your pardon. Did you say something?" Miss Linda asked as she steered a straying child back into the group.

Lucy could feel warmth creeping into her face. "Sorry, no. Just talking to myself." She lingered behind as the others tramped up the wide oak staircase to the second floor. The treads, Lucy noticed, sagged slightly in the middle and were worn from the footsteps of generations long gone. Although it was cared for on a regular basis, the old house smelled musty. The wide floorboards were dark-stained and drab, and except for a few pieces, the furniture was plain and serviceable. A portrait of Bella Potts, for whom the plantation was named, hung over a large walnut chest in the entrance hall. Her dark hair was parted in the middle and pulled tightly back from a broad face. Small brown eyes made her seem shrewd and exacting. She looked, Lucy thought, as if she were itching to jump up and slug the portrait painter smack in the kisser. Ugly as homemade sin, Charlie would've said. Lucy smiled as she followed the children upstairs, letting her hand glide along the smooth old banister. You wouldn't want to mess with Bella!

The children crowded into a large bedroom where Boyd Henry let them take turns rocking a hand-carved cradle.

"How would you like to sleep on that?" Miss Linda asked, pointing to the trundle bed.

Teddy made a face. "But that's just ropes. They didn't sleep on ropes, did they, Mama Lucy?"

"A tick or mattress filled with straw or feathers went on top of this," Boyd Henry told them. "They didn't have springs like we do, and eventually the ropes would loosen and sag, so they would have to tighten them." He smiled. "That's where the expression 'Sleep tight' comes from."

Lucy thought about the children who had played with the lonely-looking china doll who sat in a little rocking chair by the fireplace with the high mantel. From the tall windows on either side she could look out on a green meadow where sheep grazed. In the yard below, a group of older children sang as they circled a large iron pot.

"What are they doing?" one of the children asked.

"Making candles," Boyd Henry said. "They dip the wicks in the melted wax until it builds up enough thickness for a candle. After you see what's in the kitchen, I believe Miss Linda has planned for you to try your hand at making one."

Lucy caught Augusta's eye as she helped to shepherd the children down the crooked narrow stairs that opened onto a hallway at the back of the house. Boyd Henry had gone ahead of them to alert the docent on duty in the kitchen, which was in a separate building behind the main house. *Was she ever going to find a chance to speak with him alone?*

Outside, Boyd Henry waited until the last of the kindergarten class had filed up the three wooden steps into the log cabin where food was being prepared over a large stone fireplace. "Smells good, doesn't it?" he said to Lucy, who had dropped behind the others. "Several students from the high school are learning how to make chicken stew today."

Lucy took a deep breath and wished they'd invite her to eat with them. Even from where she stood, the blend of wood smoke and chicken made her think ahead to lunchtime. "I'll have to remind my stomach it's not yet time to eat!" she said as he started back to his post.

"Thank you for being so patient with the children, Boyd Henry. It's hard to hold their interest at this age, but you managed very well."

"I enjoy it," he said, pausing only to nod her way.

Lucy glanced at the kitchen full of small children—her own grandson among them—and hoped they were well in hand. "I wonder if you could spare me a few minutes?" she said.

Lucy had lived on the same street with Boyd Henry Goodwin for almost twenty years and had known him all her life. A gifted musician, he sometimes played violin solos during appearances with the Fiddlesticks, and he was a tireless gardener, often laboring in his flower beds until it was too dark to see. In the spring his whole yard became the pride of the neighborhood, a festival of bloom with daffodils and tulips, but she had never taken the time to get really acquainted. Conversation, she found, didn't come easy to Boyd Henry. He gave her a puzzled frown, but at least he didn't say no.

She suffered through an awkward silence until he answered. "I have about ten minutes before the next group's due," he said finally. "We can sit here on the back steps."

"I'm sure you're aware that the woman they believe is Florence Calhoun came to my house on the day she was killed," Lucy began. She watched his face for any change of expression, but it was beginning to be apparent that Boyd Henry Goodwin didn't display a wide range of emotions. He nodded silently, his eyes on a large dog of dubious heritage lapping water from a pan in the shade of the smokehouse. It was obvious that the dog had just had puppies and Lucy could hear faint yapping coming from the smokehouse behind her.

"It seems she was taken by a childless couple," Lucy told him. "The whole time Florence was growing up, she believed her parents had died in a plane crash."

Boyd Henry shook his head and sighed.

"Nettie tells me you sold snow cones on our street when you were a boy, and I wondered if you might have seen her the day she disappeared. If a stranger had stopped and spoken to her, you would've noticed them, wouldn't you?"

"You're talking about something that happened over sixty years ago," he said. "I can't even remember what I had for supper last night. Besides, what good would it do her now? Florence is dead and buried."

"Nettie says she's not so sure that *was* Florence they buried," Lucy said. "And even if it was, we still don't know who killed her—or why."

Boyd Henry shook his head. "Nettie!" he began. "Why, she wouldn't—"

"Excuse me, Boyd Henry, but your next group is waiting!" Patricia Sellers stepped from her small office off the back porch. "Oh, hey, Lucy Nan! I didn't know you were going through docent training."

"I'm only here as a chaperone with Teddy's kindergarten class," Lucy explained. "And I guess Miss Linda's wondering where I am."

Patricia, who had graduated from high school with Roger, scheduled and promoted events for the plantation. "Our twins will be in her class next year, so I hope she's prepared," she said. Patricia laughed as she patted her round stomach. "Now we're working on number three." She gestured toward the mother dog as three fat puppies waddled out to try and suckle while she drank.

"Poor Shag! I know how she feels. Her babies just won't leave her alone," Patricia said. "They're old enough to be weaned, but there's eight in the litter and I don't know where we're going to find homes for them all."

"Does the dog belong to somebody here?"

Patricia shrugged. "She does now. Took up with us back in the summer, and I like having her around, but we can't take care of the rest."

"I hope Teddy doesn't see them," Lucy said. "Jessica's allergic to animal hair." She chatted with Patricia a few minutes longer before hurrying to catch up with Teddy's class as they left the kitchen. Boyd Henry hadn't been receptive to her questions, but maybe she would find him more approachable before they left for the day.

Lucy was relieved to learn that the woman in charge of candle-making had removed the warm wax from the fire before allowing the children to dip their wicks into a strange-colored mixture of old candles that had been melted down. She and the other chaperones helped each child tie a piece of string to a stick. As they circled the pot singing "Here we go round the mulberry bush," each in turn dipped the dangling string into the wax until everyone had a lumpy, misshapen candle which they then plunged into water and set aside to cool.

After a bathroom break, the children sat in the shade of a huge blackjack oak for a snack of juice and crackers before going to the field to pick cotton. As they rested, Lucy noticed Boyd Henry returning to the house after conducting his last tour. Hoping to finish their conversation, she called after him and followed him into the house, but the docent was nowhere in sight.

Determined, Lucy stood at the foot of the stairs and hollered, "Mr. Goodwin!" Still no answer, but she was almost certain she heard muted footsteps overhead. Surely he heard me, Lucy thought, and called to him once more.

"It seems Boyd Henry has given you the slip again," Augusta said beside her.

"It looks that way," Lucy said. "He's so shy I've probably frightened him away. I hope he doesn't think I'm accusing him of anything, but I guess he's not going to give me a chance to explain."

That was why a few minutes later she was surprised to find him standing almost hidden by sumac at the edge of the cotton field as they picked.

Teddy, dragging a huge burlap sack twice as big as he was, called to her across the row of brownish stalks, "Mama Lucy, what's that man doing over there behind that red bush?"

Lucy helped another child pull cotton from the boll and put it into her sack. "What man, Teddy?"

"The man who told us about the house. Why is he looking at us like that?"

"That's Mr. Goodwin, honey. I guess he's just taking a break." Lucy gave the man a friendly wave. The next time she looked, he was gone.

Chapter Ten

"I'm hot! Can we quit now?" Karen, the little girl Lucy was helping, let her sack fall to the ground.

Lucy glanced at Miss Linda. They had only been picking for about fifteen minutes, but the sun was hot and some of the children were complaining of being tired. She thought of all the children who had picked these fields because they had no choice.

"I want to see the puppies," another child said.

"What puppies?" their teacher asked.

"They were in one of those little buildings back there. I saw them when we went to the bathroom. They're so cute! Couldn't we pet them? Please? Please?"

"I thought you wanted to pick cotton," their teacher said. She held open her sack. "Let's see how much we have if we put it all together. Who knows what happens to the cotton after it's picked?"

"They make it into cloth," Teddy said. "My mama doesn't like to wear anything but cotton. She says that other stuff makes her itch."

"But first they have to get the seeds out," their teacher explained. "Now that's done at the gin, but they used to have to do it by hand and it took a long, long time—"

"I gotta pee—real bad!" A small boy wearing an Atlanta Braves shirt that was almost bigger than he was, grabbed himself in a conspicuous place and jumped up and down until one of the other chaperones led him away.

Miss Linda smiled through gritted teeth. " . . . and then it was spun into thread before they wove it into cloth," she continued. She held out the collected cotton for all to see. "What do you think they might make from what we've picked today?"

Lucy heard someone laugh behind her and turned to find Augusta there. "There might be enough for a hankie," the angel said, "for someone with a very small nose."

"Why are you laughing, Mama Lucy?" Teddy wanted to know.

"I just thought of a funny joke," Lucy said, frantically searching for something suitable she *hadn't* heard from one of The Thursdays. "Why did they throw Cinderella off the baseball team?" she asked.

"Why?" Teddy wanted to know.

"Because . . . she ran away from the ball!"

In a grassy area behind the house the children tried rolling large hoops by controlling them with a stick while others learned a game called graces which involved catching wooden throwing rings with dowel-like catching wands. Teddy wasn't interested in either. He wanted to see the puppies.

"Don't get too attached," Lucy warned her grandson as he cuddled a fat black-and-white puppy with a brown patch over one eye. "You know your mother's allergic." Teddy laughed as the little dog licked his cheek. The puppy's feet, Lucy noticed, looked like plump furry pillows. This dog was going to be huge when it was grown. She didn't envy whoever ended up having to feed it.

Patricia Sellers, on her way back from another bathroom break, paused to rest on the large stone that served as a doorstep to the smokehouse. Inside the building the mother dog, Shag, rested in the cool shade on the smooth dirt floor that smelled of salted pork and wood smoke. Several hams hung from rafters overhead.

"Shag won't mind if the children pet the puppies, will she?" Lucy asked.

Patricia laughed. "Heavens no; as long as they don't hurt them, I'm sure she's glad of a break. We just have to be careful they don't slip through the gate to the other side of the fence where Ben Maxwell's repairing furniture. One of the puppies got away from us the other day and turned over a can of stain."

Lucy had met Ben Maxwell briefly the year before when he made a cherry hutch for Ellis's family room, and thought his furniture so beautiful she wanted to throw out all she owned and let him replace every piece. Unfortunately, she couldn't afford even one. And it was a good thing he was a talented craftsman, Lucy remembered thinking, as he wasn't going to reel in customers with his sparkling personality. The whole time she had spent in his shop that day he had barely managed to growl out a sentence or two.

He became practically loquacious a little later that morning when the puppy wiggled out of Teddy's arms as Miss Linda shepherded her charges into line prior to boarding the bus for home. Patricia had asked Lucy if she knew anyone who might be interested in assuming her duties at Bellawood when she went on maternity leave, and as the two of them discussed possible applicants, one of the children unlatched the forbidden gate and rode it open.

"Stop! Come back!" Lucy shouted, chasing after Teddy, who chased after the puppy with the big feet. Now they were joined by three or four more of the puppy's brothers and sisters, at least half of the kindergarten class, the pregnant event-planner and a panting, red-faced mother who would probably never chaperone again. The woman muttered under her breath as she ran and Lucy was close enough to hear she wasn't quoting scripture.

Lucy had heard about people who threw up their hands when overwhelmed, but Ben Maxwell was the first person she saw who actually did it.

"Lord love a duck!" he shouted, waving his arms at the horde of yelping puppies. "Get these animals out of here!"

One of the dogs scurried under a bench, followed by at least three children who fought to pick it up. The bench teetered, sending a scattering of nails to the floor. The workshop smelled strongly of sawdust and turpentine and somebody behind her sneezed. Augusta.

"Here, here! This is no place for little ones!" Ben snatched the disappearing shirttail of one of the small invaders and pulled him from underneath the bench, whereupon the offending child began to wail. The puppies, sensing disaster, joined in.

"Who's responsible for these children?" the man demanded, running a large hand through his hair. Ben Maxwell's hair was thick and reddish-brown with streaks of gray, Lucy noticed, and curls of wood shavings were caught in his beard. He set aside the plane he had been using on what looked like a walnut secretary Lucy could only dream of owning and looked for all the world like a Highlander ready for a fray. "Would you please get them out before somebody gets hurt? Get them out *now!*"

The rest of the children, frightened by his loud voice, now joined in the tearful chorus. "I'm sorry," their teacher said, trying to comfort her flock while herding them toward the door. "I'm afraid the puppies got away from them, and—"

"We're doing the best we can," Lucy told him, wading through shavings to reach two sniffling five-year-olds. "Your yelling at them doesn't help."

"My eye and Betty Martin! There are sharp tools about. You wouldn't want to see them hurt, would you?" The man bent and scooped up a squirming puppy which he practically shoved at Lucy. He was tall, she noticed, maybe a little taller even than her Charlie had been, and his eyes were a blue so intense they seemed to burn . . . but she wasn't here to think about his eyes.

"I don't know what Betty Martin—whoever she is—has to do with it, but we'll get out of your way as soon as we can." Lucy cradled the puppy in one arm while calming the small boy in the Braves shirt with the other. She wanted desperately to kick this impatient grouch in the shins, but since she was supposed to be a chaperone, that might be frowned upon. Lucy almost smiled. Maybe one of the children would do it. Teddy, she saw, was still crawling along the wood-littered floor after the dog with big feet. She opened her mouth to call to him when the puppy he was pursuing turned and trotted sedately out the door, followed by the others. Augusta smiled and waved to her from the dooryard, then turned and led her tail-wagging charges through the gate.

"Well, I'll be—" For a minute Ben Maxwell was speechless, as were the rest of them. "I've never seen anything like that!"

The children, suddenly silent, filed after them, leaving the tall bearded man in the plaid shirt standing dumbfounded and alone.

Teddy didn't have to ask twice to go to his favorite place for lunch. Lucy, whose nerves were wearing thin from their experience at Bellawood, was only too glad to indulge her grandson in a grilled cheese sandwich (on whole wheat, of course) with ice cream to follow at Benny Jack's diner. Jessica would flip when she found out as she suspected Benny Jack bribed the sanitation inspector in order to get a passing rating, but as far as Lucy knew, nobody had died from eating at Benny Jack's yet. She only wished he served wine, as she could do with a glass about now. Sitting in the small dark booth at the back of the diner, Lucy taught Teddy how to blow the paper from his drinking straw and send it sailing across the table, and then the two of them played ticktacktoe on a paper napkin until it was time to go.

"That man acted funny, didn't he, Mama Lucy?" Teddy asked as Lucy drove him home.

"What man, honey?"

"That man at Bellawood. The one who was following us around."

"You mean Mr. Goodwin, the man who showed us through the house?"

"Yeah. He was there while we were picking cotton, and you know when we were playing with the puppies and all? Well, I saw him watching us out the window. What you reckon he wanted, Mama Lucy?"

"Maybe he was just interested," Lucy said. *Or maybe he wanted to tell us something.* She'd like to find out what it was—but first, she was going to put her feet up and relax.

Thank goodness Jessica wasn't in the mood to chat after her visit with the dentist. She didn't even ask what they had for lunch, so Lucy escaped quickly after seeing Teddy inside. The day had turned cooler by mid-afternoon and she wondered if Augusta had laid a fire in the sitting room fireplace. A cup of tea would be nice with some of those lemon ginger cookies Augusta had made the day before.

But as soon as she saw the angel's face, Lucy knew something was rotten—and it wasn't in Denmark!

Lucy tossed her jacket on a chair. "What's wrong, Augusta? You look like you've seen a ghost . . . but then in your job, you must be used to that."

Augusta didn't smile. In fact, she seemed to have abandoned

her usual serene demeanor. "Just come and see," she said, beckoning Lucy into the living room. "I shouldn't have gone with you! Something told me to stay here. I'm afraid someone has been here while we were gone and torn the place apart. It looks as if they were searching for something."

"I'll say!" Lucy stood in the doorway staring at the disarray: sofa cushions pulled to the floor, drawers left open; even a corner of the carpet was folded back as if someone had looked under it.

"We should get out of here and call the police right now!" Lucy said, after the realization hit her. "Whoever did this might still be inside."

"No one's here. I've looked." The angel's face was flushed as she sank onto a chair. "I imagine they were here much earlier— probably soon after we left for Bellawood. I came here straight from the bus and found it like this." Augusta fingered her necklace, now a glitter of silver and midnight blue, and pulled her shawl closer about her. "If only I had been here!" she said.

"What could you have done?" Lucy hurried to check the drawers in the dining room buffet. Thank goodness the silver seemed to be all there.

"But I would have known who's responsible." Augusta followed her into the kitchen, where cooking utensils littered the floor. Open cabinet doors revealed dishes that had been disturbed, and the broken pieces of a saucer were scattered on the countertop. The pattern had strawberries on it and was one of the few dishes remaining of a set Lucy had purchased a piece at a time from the A&P when she and Charlie were first married. She remembered how excited she had been each time she was able to bring home a new piece, and the sight of it lying shattered there by some unknown intruder's hands made her want to cry. Yet another reminder of her years with Charlie was gone from her life.

The shoes! Lucy remembered Florence's clay-covered shoes she had hurriedly stored in the hall closet. What if someone had been looking for the shoes? Her heart raced as she jerked open the door. *The paper-wrapped shoes were still there!*

They found the upstairs much the same, with closets open and clothes left in jumbles on the floor. Even the beds were stripped, and in the bathrooms the contents of jars had been emptied into the sink.

"What on earth were they looking for? Whatever it is, it must be something important." Lucy found it hard to breathe. She leaned against the doorframe in the room that had been Roger's. "I wonder if they found it."

"Whatever it is, it was something small if they were looking for it in a jar of hand cream," Augusta said. "Did you look to see if all your jewelry is accounted for?"

Lucy rushed downstairs to see. *All her jewelry* included her engagement diamond, a small sapphire ring that had belonged to her mother, a pair of pearl earrings Charlie had given her on their twentieth anniversary, and a gold locket she'd inherited from Mimmer. She still wore her engagement and wedding rings and the rest were in the small brown velvet box in her underwear drawer, although it was obvious someone had searched through her lingerie.

Lucy's face burned. The fact that a stranger had gone through her undergarments angered her even more than the knowledge that they had ransacked her house. She picked up the phone to call the police. If she could get her hands on whoever did this, they would be the ones who would need protection!

Ed Tillman looked about him with his hands on his hips while his partner, Sheila Eastwood, checked the downstairs area. "And you say this is the second time this has happened?" he said. "Why didn't you call us earlier?"

"It was hardly noticeable the first time," Lucy said, trying to avoid incriminating The Thursdays. "A lot of people were in the house that day, and I just thought somebody was being curious. Besides, nothing was taken."

He frowned. "Who do you mean by a lot of people?"

"Well . . . my book club . . . you know, The Thursdays. But none of them would do a thing like that. The back door was unlocked and we were in the front of the house all afternoon. It could've been anybody."

"I thought I told you to keep your doors locked." He sighed. "Miss Lucy Nan, be honest with me. Was your house locked while you were gone today?"

She nodded. "Of course. After what's been happening around here? Are you kidding?"

"Then how did this person get in? Any signs of breaking and entering?"

"Not that I could see." Lucy grabbed a kitchen chair for support. "Oh, Lordy, Ed! I just had the most horrible thought! What if somebody has a key?"

"I think I've found how they got in," Sheila said, coming back into the room. "Your downstairs bathroom window was open and the screen is unlatched. Whoever was in here just climbed in your window."

"The one off my bedroom?" Lucy felt as if she'd swallowed an ice cube and it stuck there in her throat. *How long had that window been open?*

"We'll try to get some prints, of course," Ed said, "but I doubt if anything will turn up. Do you have any idea what they were looking for?"

She shook her head. "Not a clue, but it has to have something to do with Florence Calhoun's being here. Maybe somebody thinks she left something valuable behind."

"Did she have anything like that with her when she came?" Sheila asked.

"Just the things you saw that were in her purse. I didn't notice anything else except those rings she wore, and I'm almost sure they were fake. She certainly didn't leave them here."

"But she could've had something else? Something on her person?" Ed said.

"Well, yes, I guess she could've. I didn't search the woman, Ed."

"You can rest assured we'll check this house from top to bottom to be sure everything's locked up tight. And I wish you'd do me a favor and ask somebody to stay with you tonight. Or, better still, why not spend the night with Roger and Jessica? I'd feel better if someone were with you—for tonight, anyway." Ed Tillman sat across from her at the kitchen table just as he had many times as a boy. "I want you to promise you'll be more careful and let me know immediately if you notice anything even faintly suspicious. Whoever entered your house today knew exactly when you'd be away. I think they planned it ahead of time."

CHAPTER ELEVEN

ut who?" Ellis said. "Who knew you were going to Bella-wood with Teddy's class this morning?"

"Who didn't?" Lucy had finally put away the last baking pan and refolded the clothes in her dresser drawers, but she still had a long way to go in straightening the disorder in her household. It was eight o'clock at night and Ed Tillman and his crew had just left after finding no fingerprints that didn't belong there and very little evidence except for a smudged footprint in the soil beneath her bathroom window.

Ellis had phoned earlier while Ed and Sheila were checking windows to make sure the house was secure. "Do you have a few minutes to talk? I have something to tell you," she began.

"Likewise," Lucy said, and told her what had happened. "In fact, I was going to ask you if you'd mind staying over tonight. Ed seems to think I need a chaperone."

"Why don't you come here? Bennett's out of town. We can stay up late and raise hell."

"It looks like I'll be up late anyway, and the hell-raising's already been done. You should see this mess, Ellis! It's going to take hours to put everything away—even with Augusta's help."

"I'll pick up a pizza," Ellis said. "Does Augusta like pepperoni?"

Augusta did, it seemed, as she put away three pieces and washed them down with a glass of red wine.

"Do you have any idea what this person was looking for?" Ellis asked as the three of them relaxed later in front of the sitting room fire.

"It must be something they think Florence—if it *was* Florence—left here," Lucy said. "I can't imagine what it might've been."

Augusta drew her needlework from the large tapestry bag she carried and began weaving the threads with quicksilver fingers. "She wasn't wearing her rings when they found her," she said. "Do you think she might have hidden them here?"

"Surely you don't believe they were *real?*" Lucy shook her head. "Those stones were huge, Augusta—gaudy as anything you'd ever see in a dime store. They didn't suit her at all. I'm talking tacky here. And even if they were genuine, what was Florence doing with them? I didn't get the idea they had that kind of money."

Ellis stood to warm herself by the fire. "I just assumed that whoever killed her took the jewelry."

"They might have. We just don't know." Augusta smoothed out her handiwork, a pastoral scene in rich colors of emerald, gold and azure, and tucked it back inside her bag. And we still don't know if they found what they were looking for today."

"Where else would they look?" Lucy said. "Seems to me they didn't miss a thing."

"What about the attic?" Ellis asked.

"I keep that door locked," Lucy said. "I don't like Teddy going up there. The stairs are steep and it's cold and dirty." She yawned, stretching. "Relax! It's okay. Ed and Sheila have already looked up there. It hasn't been disturbed." She wiggled her toes toward the fire. "This has been a day and a half! For a while I thought it would never end!"

Suddenly Lucy sat forward. "Oh my gosh, I almost forgot! The casserole! I haven't made the vegetable casserole for Calpernia's funeral tomorrow. There was a message on my answering machine from Claudia Pharr about bringing enough for ten!"

"She got me, too," Ellis said. "Told me several others were bringing dessert, so I made that green bean thing—the one with the onion rings on top." She frowned. "Do you think people are tired of my funeral cake?"

Lucy rose to her feet—which ached; in fact just about every bone in her body seemed to have aged about ten years. "If I hurry, I can throw together that marinated bean salad," she began. "But that's not really a casserole. Besides, you said you were bringing green beans—"

Augusta put a hand on her arm. "There's something all ready in the refrigerator," she said. "I could see you were running short of time, so I doubled that squash recipe of your grandmother's— the one with cheese and eggs. I believe it turned out quite well. I hope you won't mind, Lucy Nan."

"Mind? Are you kidding?" Lucy threw her arms around Augusta, who flushed. "You really are an angel!"

"Well, of course," Augusta said, then turned to Ellis. "I believe Lucy said you had some news to share?"

Ellis nodded, turning to warm her other side. "Right. In all the excitement, I almost forgot. Guess who came to see me this afternoon?"

"Let me see . . . I'll bet it was Mel Gibson!" Lucy said.

"Oh, him? He was here yesterday. Guess again."

"Okay. Mickey Mouse? The Great Pumpkin? Ellis Saxon, you know I hate it when you want me to guess!" Lucy tossed a pillow at Ellis and missed. "Will you please just get to the point?"

"Boyd Henry Goodwin." Ellis announced the name and waited, as if she expected applause. "Called and asked if it would be all right if he came by for a minute, so of course I said yes—only he didn't stay just a minute. Lordy, I thought the man would never leave!"

"What did he want?" Augusta asked.

"I think he wanted to get something off his chest," Ellis said. "He told me he saw poor little Florence the day she disappeared. She bought a snow cone from him."

"Surely he told that to the police!" Lucy said.

"But he didn't. Boyd Henry said he wasn't supposed to be selling snow cones that day. His mother thought he was having a violin lesson over at the college, but Boyd Henry was trying to earn enough money so he could go to Columbia on a class trip, so he skipped his lesson that day." Ellis sat on the arm of Augusta's chair and sighed. "Poor Boyd Henry! Not only was he disobeying his mother, but Florence wasn't allowed to eat snow cones. Her mother wouldn't give her a nickel to buy one, but a lady in a green dress did."

"Lady in a green—you mean the woman who *kidnapped* Florence?" Lucy remembered how evasive Boyd Henry had been at Bellawood that morning. No wonder he hadn't wanted to talk about the day little Florence disappeared.

"Probably," Ellis continued. "Boyd Henry remembers seeing her get out of a car and approach Florence. They spoke for a minute or two, then the woman got back into the car. A man was driving, he said."

Augusta didn't seem surprised. "What then?" she wanted to know. "Did they drive away?"

Ellis shrugged. "Boyd Henry didn't remember. He said he didn't think too much about it because Florence was such a pretty little girl, people were always making a fuss over her. And the woman seemed nice—although he admits he didn't get a good look at her or the man."

"So he didn't actually see them *take* her." Augusta fingered her necklace.

"He said he thought they had driven away by the time Florence started home," Ellis said. "Boyd Henry decided to take his cart to the other end of town where there were a lot of children. He says he didn't think any more about it until later that afternoon when he learned Florence had turned up missing."

Augusta was silent for a minute. "If the child wasn't supposed to have the snow cone, she would probably eat it before going back home. The couple could have circled the block and waited for her."

"And she never saw her family again." Lucy felt an ache in her throat for the unsuspecting child. "I can't believe Boyd Henry's been holding that back all this time! I tried to speak with him at Bellawood this morning, but he acted peculiar—like he didn't want to discuss it. Now I know why, but I wonder why he came to you?"

"I guess because I'm the closest kin she had left." Ellis frowned. "What an awful thing to be burdened with! And I got the feeling there was something else on his mind. He practically drank the coffeepot dry, and kept hanging around until I thought I was going to have to ask him to stay for supper. It was dark by the time he left."

"I wonder what it was," Augusta said. "Did he give you any idea?"

"I think it probably has something to do with the way Florence died," Ellis told her. "He kept talking about the dreadful—that was how he described it: *dreadful*—thing that happened to Florence, and who would have believed somebody would attack anyone in the church parking lot *right across the street from his own house!*"

"He probably feels guilty," Lucy said. "He damn well should!" She heard Augusta's slight snort at the curse word but ignored it.

"That, too," Ellis said, "but I believe he might've seen something that night—the night she was killed. You know how he works out in his yard till all hours. And then he said something about vile deeds and poison weeds—like he was quoting a poem or something. 'There's a poison creeping through this town,' he told me." Ellis shuddered. "I'll tell you right now, it just plain gave me the willies."

Lucy checked both windows in the room just to be sure Ed and Sheila hadn't missed them. Good. Locked tight. "He is a peculiar old sort," she said, "but surely you don't think Boyd Henry had anything to do with Florence's death . . . do you?"

"After all that's been going on here, I don't know what I think anymore, except that I'm about to fall asleep on my feet." Ellis yawned. "Where do you want me to crash?"

"The bed's made up in Roger's old room, if that's okay. Augusta's right across the hall," Lucy said.

"You're going to sleep downstairs *all by yourself?* I could curl up right here on the sofa," Ellis offered.

"Good grief, Ellis, I've been sleeping down here by myself for over three years now since Charlie died. I'll be fine." She waved her arms. "Now, shoo—both of you!"

Neither of them argued, Lucy noticed, and she was relieved. Although she was glad of the company, it had been a long and trying day and the thought of her bed with its plump pillows and downy comforter was inviting. If anyone were to break in her window tonight, Lucy thought, she'd probably sleep right through it.

That was what she thought. Lucy couldn't have been asleep for more than an hour when she heard a board creak just outside her door. The noise brought her wide awake and she sat up in bed and listened. She was accustomed to the settling-down noises old houses make at night, but this wasn't a settling-down noise. This was a footstep. She was reaching for the phone beside her bed when there came another.

"Lucy Nan? Are you asleep?"

Ellis!

"Well, I *was*." She switched on a lamp. "Is anything wrong?"

Ellis crept into the room and closed the door softly behind her. "I'm not sure, but it sounds like something's going on up there."

"Up where?"

"In Augusta's room. Sounds like somebody whimpering. Do angels whimper?"

"Not that I know of." Lucy wrapped herself in the faded flannel robe that had been Charlie's. It brought him close and she liked to think it still smelled of him. She grinned. "Maybe she's snoring."

"It's not that kind of noise. I hated to bother her if she's upset about something personal, but she could be in trouble. I didn't know what to do." Ellis stuck close to Lucy as they went upstairs together.

"There it is again!" Ellis whispered as they stood in the upstairs hallway. "Did you hear it?"

Lucy waited. The house was so quiet she could hear herself breathe. Then she heard it. Yes, it was definitely a whimper . . . and there was something else . . . a faint laugh. Did Augusta have company? She wasn't up on celestial relationships, but if Augusta had expected an overnight guest, she could have at least mentioned it beforehand.

Ellis must have been thinking the same thing because she clamped a hand to her mouth to suppress a laugh. Lucy paused as they moved closer, her hand on Ellis's arm. Someone was rocking in the big upholstered rocking chair that had belonged to Mimmer. Lucy's children had been rocked in that chair, as had she and her mother before her, and it had a comforting squeak. Now someone—Augusta, she assumed—was humming (rather tunelessly, Lucy thought), as she rocked. As the two of them stood outside Augusta's door, the angel began to sing: *"There's a church in the valley by the wildwood, no lovelier spot in the dale . . ."*

The notes were far from true but her singing was so sweet and pure, it didn't seem to matter. And then they heard a sharp yelp.

That did it! Lucy knocked on the door. "Augusta? Is everything all right in there?"

She was about to knock again when the door opened a few inches and Augusta stood there smiling. "I'm sorry," she said. "I hope I didn't wake you." Her face was flushed and she brushed aimlessly at the front of her dress. Lucy noticed she didn't step aside to let them in.

"We thought we heard someone—uh—crying," Lucy began. "Augusta, is there—"

"Crying? I don't believe so." Augusta started to close the door. "I do regret that I disturbed you. I'll try to be quieter . . . "

And that was when the puppy dashed between her legs.

"Where on earth did *you* come from?" Ellis asked, scooping the dog into her arms.

"I think I know." Lucy looked from Augusta to the puppy with the big feet. "Augusta Goodnight, you know this dog doesn't belong to us! How did you manage to get it home?"

Augusta sat in the rocking chair and pulled the puppy onto her lap. "I was going to tell you tomorrow," she said, "but I wanted her to get acquainted first. The poor baby misses her mother. They've never been apart before, you know." Cuddling the little dog to her breast, Augusta began to rock and hum.

"Well, she's going back tomorrow," Lucy told her. "I don't have time for a puppy in my life right now."

"I'm afraid Teddy will be disappointed." Augusta spoke in mid-hum.

"How can he be disappointed if he doesn't expect a pet?" Lucy asked.

Augusta stroked the puppy's floppy ear. "You could see, I'm sure, how the two of them bonded. Your grandson loves this little dog, and the puppy loves him. Since your daughter-in-law seems to be allergic to animals, the only solution is for the puppy to come here."

Lucy laughed in spite of herself. "How do you know the puppy loves Teddy?"

"I can sense these things, just as I know that child needs a pet—this pet," Augusta said. "Besides, she has no other home."

"He is adorable," Ellis chimed in, stooping to pet the dog, now sleeping in Augusta's lap.

"She," Augusta said. "And since she has such large feet, I think we should call her Clementine. Remember that old song?"

"I'm going to bed," Lucy said. "We'll deal with Clementine— or whatever her name is—tomorrow."

But she was already making a mental note to call Patricia Sellers in the morning to let her know she'd have one less puppy to worry about.

CHAPTER TWELVE

"If you send tuberoses to my funeral I'm gonna rise up and snatch you bald-headed," Ellis whispered from behind her printed program.

"I was thinking more in the line of skunk cabbage," Lucy said. "If you should happen to croak first, that is—which you probably will, since you're a good four months older than I am."

Stone's Throw Presbyterian Church was packed to overflowing the afternoon of Calpernia Hemphill's funeral, and the people who hadn't known to come early were already being crammed into the basement fellowship hall, where they would listen to the service over a speaker. It wouldn't be the same. Lucy was glad she and Ellis had made a point to get there with time to spare, even though the sickening smell of tuberoses was beginning to make her wish she hadn't eaten that leftover pizza for lunch.

At least they hadn't left the coffin open. She hated it when you had to sit through a funeral service staring the corpse in the face. Calpernia's coffin, which looked to be mahogany or some other kind of expensive hardwood, was covered in a blanket of red roses and baby's breath, and sprays and wreaths of every flower available filled the front of the church. Lucy spied the offending arrangement of tuberoses tucked between a display of yellow chrysanthemums and a tall vase of pink gladiolas. A huge wreath of white roses interspersed with stargazer lilies rested at the foot of the deceased. Probably from the faculty at the college, she thought, looking about. How many of these people came here to pay their respects to Calpernia's memory and offer comfort to her husband, she wondered, and how many were just out-and-out curious? Lucy supposed she could qualify for both categories. According to Roger, Calpernia wasn't well-liked by her contemporaries at Sarah Bedford and she had never been accepted among the townspeople either. But like Lucy and her friends, most of Stone's Throw's citizens managed to tolerate the woman—more or less. Obviously someone had decided on less.

The sanctuary was filled with the small restless sounds of too many people packed in too small a space. Someone behind her who had been coughing now crunched a cough drop. The smell of the menthol competed with Nettie McGinnis's lilac-scented cologne and the overpowering aroma of flowers. Lucy remembered the handkerchief Augusta had tucked into her coat pocket as she left the house and held it thankfully to her nose. It smelled faintly of strawberries.

The organist was into what was probably her third or fourth hymn. Lucy found it hard to keep track as they all seemed to merge together, but as the soft strains of "Softly and Tenderly" washed over her she felt tears sneak up on her unannounced. An eternity ago she had sat in this church for her own husband's funeral service. Thank goodness she remembered little about it, except that she hurt. She still hurt—especially now in the fall of the year, when winding trails beckoned in the surrounding woodlands now vibrant with color. She and Charlie had hiked together whenever they had the chance, and although she walked with others from time to time, it wasn't the same. Lucy had lost her partner.

Poor Poag! The loss was going to be painful for him as well. He and his wife had done just about everything together, and although Calpernia hadn't been one of Lucy's favorite people, she was sorry about her death and for the grieving partner she had left behind.

She glanced at her watch. Surely it was time for the pallbearers to be seated, followed by Calpernia's family. What could be keeping them?

"Ye gods and little fishes! Will you look at that?" Nettie, sitting on her right, gave her a sharp poke with an elbow. "Can you believe who just came in?"

Jay Warren-Winslow, in a dark suit that didn't fit, walked halfway down the aisle, followed by Zee St. Clair, and stood at the end of a pew until the people sitting there shifted about to make room for them. Lucy craned around Nettie's considerable bulk to see who was being inconvenienced and squelched a smile. It was Idonia Mae and Jo Nell and they didn't look happy about it.

The loud, exhaled breaths among those assembled would have provided enough air to send up a balloon, Lucy thought. Ellis rolled her eyes and made a face. "Tacky, tacky," she whispered. "I would've thought Zee had better sense than that. Can you imagine? Bringing that man in here like a trophy when everybody knows he was probably the one who—"

"Shh!" Nettie waved a program at them. "The Fiddlesticks are getting ready to play."

Lucy watched as four musicians took their places in the choir. Lawrence Delozier, who headed the music department at Sarah Bedford, sat beside his cello, bow in hand. Lawrence was barely over five feet tall and probably weighed less than she did. Why is it, Lucy wondered, the smallest people tended to play the largest instruments? Ashley Butterfield, the choir director from the Methodist Church, took her place at the piano, followed by Albert

Grady, the postmaster, with his violin, and his wife, Miranda, with hers. Where was Boyd Henry Goodwin?

With a nod from Ashley, the group began to play something from Bach—possibly a fugue. Lucy couldn't be sure, but it brought blessed relief from the depressing "Rock of Ages." She forgot about Boyd Henry's absence momentarily as Calpernia's family filed into the church. It was a small group, barely filling one pew. Poag Hemphill led them, head bowed, as if in a trance, and once, looking up at his wife's casket, almost stumbled. A plump middle-aged woman—probably Poag's sister—kept a hand on his arm as they walked down the aisle together, followed by a balding man Lucy supposed to be her husband, and two young girls. Lastly, a slight, shadowy woman in gray took her seat on the end.

Lucy frowned a question at Ellis, who mouthed in answer, "Calpernia's sister."

Lucy had never seen two sisters who looked less alike. Why, the woman was almost ghostlike! Calpernia, dead and laid out as she was, probably had more color about her than this poor soul.

The service didn't last long. Pete Whittaker, the minister, read several verses of scripture and delivered a brief eulogy praising Calpernia for her devotion to the arts as well as to the college and community; the congregation stood to sing a final hymn and recite The Lord's Prayer, after which The Fiddlesticks played something appropriately melancholy while the family followed the casket up the aisle and out the front door.

Nettie winked at Lucy as they made their way outside. "Was that *Calpernia* Pete was talking about? I hardly recognized her."

Ellis pointed out Ed Tillman and his mother Lydia, who had been sitting a few rows behind them. "I see the police are here to keep an eye on me," she said. "Guess Ed thinks I'll try to sneak out with the corpse or something."

"Don't be silly," Lucy said. "You know good and well Lydia Tillman works over at the college—art department, I think."

Ellis had a wicked gleam in her eye. "Not modeling, I hope," she whispered. "Have you ever noticed how she looks like Curly of The Three Stooges—only with hair?" She paused and turned as the young policeman and his mother stepped into the aisle behind them. "How are you, Lydia? And by the way, Ed, I'm heading straight to Poag's from here in case you need to know my whereabouts. I'll be helping to serve dinner . . . unless you think I might poison somebody."

"*Ellis Saxon!* For heaven's sake!" Lucy shook her head at Ed, who flushed, and Lydia, who frowned. "The emotional strain has been hard on her," she muttered, gripping her friend's arm. "Give him a break, Ellis! Ed probably doesn't even know what you're talking about."

"Oh, yes, he does! Who do you think informed me I wasn't to leave town?" Ellis looked over her shoulder. "He was polite about it, of course. Wiped his feet before he came in and took off his hat in the house." She sighed as they followed the crowd down the familiar brick steps and across the lawn to the parking lot. "They think I had something to do with that Shirley woman's death, Lucy Nan. How would you like it if the people you had known all your life suspected you of murder?"

Lucy opened her mouth to tell her friend that nobody in their right mind could possibly think she had anything to do with Shirley/Florence's death and that the police were just doing their job, when a clamor of voices distracted her.

Zee St. Clair and Jay Warren-Winslow clung together under the gnarled old holly tree at the corner of the building while Calpernia Hemphill's ghostlike sister confronted them, only she wasn't gray and lifeless anymore. The woman's cheeks glowed scorching red and a strand of her hair that had escaped its bun fell across her face as she shook her finger at the pair.

"How *dare* you! How can you show your face after what you did to my sister? What do you mean by showing up here to mock us as we tell our dear Calpernia good-bye?" The woman began to cry as Poag put an arm around her and attempted to lead her away. "He should be behind bars!" she said, sobbing.

Now the young director was the one who looked pale. His voice trembled as he spoke. "Please believe me, I would never do anything to harm Calpernia. I came here to pay my respects just like everyone else." He reached out to touch her, but the woman drew back as though he held a knife. "I'm sorry if my being here has upset you, but I had nothing to do with what happened to your sister."

Zee, who seemed little a little shaken up herself, drew herself up as tall as her slight frame would allow and directed her words to Poag. "I—we–certainly didn't intend to cause a disturbance, and I'm sorry, Poag, for your loss, but you're fixing the blame on the wrong person. Jay had—"

"Zee, please, what's done is done," Poag said, gently taking her hand. "I know you didn't mean any harm." Then, patting her arm, he turned away to ride to the cemetery behind the hearse.

Lucy stood looking after them until Ellis reminded her that they should hurry to Poag's so they could have the meal ready to serve when the family returned from the grave site.

Lucy nodded numbly. "I know," she said. "Just give me a minute. I want to speak to Zee."

Right now she yearned to shake Zee St. Clair until the silly woman's eyes crossed, but no matter how misled she might be, Zee was her friend and at the moment she looked as though she could use some support. Lucy, followed by a reluctant Ellis, walked over to where Zee still stood, looking rather lost, and put both arms around her.

She wasn't surprised when Zee began to cry. "Oh, Lord, Lucy Nan, what have I done? I wouldn't have upset poor Poag for anything—or Calpernia's sister either, but Jay was fond of Calpernia—why, I don't know—and felt like he should be here. I hated for him to come to the funeral alone."

"I'm sure that when things calm down, Poag will understand. They all will," Lucy told her. Ellis said she thought so, too, all the while signaling Lucy with her eyes that it was time to leave.

Jay, who wore his discomfort like a cloak, obviously thought it was time to go, too. "This will pass when they learn the truth," he said, although he didn't look too sure of it. "I'll fix you a drink when you get home and you can put your feet up. I expect you'll feel better when you've had a chance to rest."

"Rest? Rest from what?" Zee said. "And just how do you expect me to rest when everybody hates me? Jo Nell and Idonia wouldn't even speak today."

"They'll get over it, and so will you," Lucy told her, "and nobody hates you, Zee." *Except maybe Calpernia's spooky sister.*

Jay, who had given up on coaxing Zee away, had taken to pacing; now he stopped in mid-stride. "I think it might be better if I found another place to stay, Zee. I don't want to tarnish your reputation."

"Ha!" For the first time that afternoon, Zee St. Clair smiled. "You're too late for that claim, my friend. Besides, where would you stay? Opal Henshaw—runs that B and B she calls the Spring Lamb—came up to me after the service today and told me I needed to go right back inside and get on my knees and pray! I don't think *she'll* be welcoming you with open arms, Jay."

"Opal Henshaw's an ass," Ellis said. "You're just going to have to grit your teeth and ride it out like the rest of us, Jay Warren-Winslow."

Zee frowned. "What do you mean, the *rest* of us?"

"That little smarty-pants Ed Tillman asked me not to leave town until they find out who killed Shirley/Florence," Ellis said. "They think I did it, you know."

At that Zee looked up at the steeple towering above them and closed her eyes. "We could sure do with a guardian angel," she said.

"I almost swallowed my tongue when Zee said that about the angel," Ellis said later as they stored leftover food in Poag Hemphill's refrigerator. Most of the dinner crowd had drifted away except for a few lingering relatives and a handful of Poag's faculty friends.

Lucy laughed. "Me, too! I'll have to mention that to Augusta."

Ellis spooned rice casserole into a plastic container. "So what *is* she doing here?" she asked. "I thought angels knew everything. Isn't she supposed to help?"

"I'm sure she will in time," Lucy said. "She said it requires some thought."

"Huh! You tell her I might *require* her to bake me a cake with a file in it when they lock me away!" Sighing, she looked about her. "Speaking of cake, what are we supposed to do with all this food? Lollie Pate brought over a whole pound cake we haven't even cut."

"I guess we could freeze it, or, better still, take it to the church. Tomorrow's Sunday and the youth groups will be meeting—they'll gobble it up." Lucy set the cake aside. "Lollie'll never know."

"That was nice of her to help with the serving today, since she doesn't even belong to our church," Ellis said. "Lollie looked tired, don't you think? But she said she wanted to do something to help out, and frankly I don't know what we would've done without her with so many of our circle members out sick."

"Maybe we should join a younger circle," Lucy suggested. "Seems somebody's always ailing . . . let's face it, I reckon we're all getting old!"

"Except Calpernia," Ellis reminded her. "And Shirley/Florence."

Somebody from the faculty had taken Calpernia's sister to the airport soon after dinner, but Poag's family remained. Poag and his sister Myra came into the kitchen to thank them just as Lucy finished wiping off the countertops while Ellis attempted to sweep up the afternoon's assortment of crumbs.

"You two don't know how much this means to me," he said, hugging them in turn. "And I know it would mean a lot to Cal, too." His voice broke when he mentioned her and Myra stepped in.

"Your circle outdid themselves on the food," she said. "Everything was wonderful and we really appreciate your being here." She patted Poag's hand. "And now, little brother, I think you should try to get some rest."

"Good idea," Ellis told her. "There's enough food here for an army, so you might want to freeze some. If you don't mind, though, Lucy Nan suggested taking this pound cake for the young people at the church. Lollie brought it over from Do-Lollie's, so I'm sure it's good, but we really didn't need it."

"That's fine, that's fine," Poag said, turning away, but he didn't look fine at all. His face was gray and drawn and he walked with such a faltering step, Myra steered him into the nearest chair. "I think you need to see a doctor," she said, turning to Lucy, who agreed.

But Poag Hemphill shook his head and after a minute he stood. "A doctor can't help what's wrong with me," he told them. "Only time can do that."

"I meant to ask somebody what happened to Boyd Henry today," Ellis said later as they pulled into her driveway. "Doesn't he usually play with The Fiddlesticks?"

"I heard somebody say they were waiting for him and that's why the service was late getting started," Lucy said. "You'd think he would've called if he couldn't come. I hope he's not sick."

Since Bennett wouldn't be home until the next day, Lucy offered to go inside with Ellis just be to sure everything was okay.

"That's silly," Ellis told her. "I'm used to being here alone with Bennett out of town so much. Besides, you have to go home to an empty house all the time."

"Not anymore. Augusta's there, remember?" Lucy had never become accustomed to coming home with no one there. "I'd feel better about it, really—especially after all that's been going on lately. Humor me, okay? At least let me go with you until you turn on a light. It's as dark as a coal cellar out here."

Ellis shrugged. "Suit yourself. We'll go in the back way and if you beg me, I'll let you give me a hand with those casserole dishes that have to be returned." She snorted as she led the way through the back gate. "I'll swear, it looks like people would learn to use the disposable foil kind!"

They had divided up the dishes earlier: Ellis would return those to circle members who lived near her, and Lucy would do the same with hers. She was struggling with a cardboard box filled with breakable containers and assorted trays when she heard Ellis scream.

CHAPTER THIRTEEN

*L*ucy set down the box in the driveway where she stood and ran through the open gate to the backyard. Ellis had switched on the lights that illuminated the rear of the house as well as the patio and pool area and now knelt at the deep end of the pool clutching a long pole with a net on one end used for scooping out debris. A dark shape bobbed on the shadows a few feet away. A human shape. "Oh, dear God," Lucy mumbled. "Who is it?"

"I don't know! Call nine-one-one, get an ambulance—hurry!" Ellis shouted, and casting the net aside, kicked off her shoes and jumped into the water.

Lucy was torn between helping her friend rescue whomever was in the pool and summoning help, but Ellis seemed to be doing all right without her so she dashed for the house, her heart beating so hard it hurt. Ellis's keys were still in the back door, which was unlocked. Ellis's handbag and a tray of empty dishes sat just inside the door and a faint light from above the stove cast the kitchen in shadow. Lucy flicked on the light over the breakfast bar and reached for the wall phone, stubbing her toe on a stool in the process. Remembering what she had seen on television about emergency calls, she took the receiver with her in case they needed instruction in CPR.

They didn't. Ellis had somehow managed to pull her dripping burden halfway up the side so the head and torso lay facedown on the edge of the pool while the lower half of the body remained in the water. "I think we've found Boyd Henry," she said, shivering in the eerie light that made everything look pasty. "Looks like his foot got caught in the ladder."

"The rescue team is on the way," Lucy told her as the two of them struggled to roll the dead weight that had been Boyd Henry Goodwin onto the side of the pool.

"I'm afraid it's too late," Ellis said. She checked for a pulse and shook her head. "No telling how long he's been in there."

The man's eyes were cloudy and his skin a greenish red, still Ellis began compressions on his chest. The green suede-cloth dress she had worn to the funeral sloshed with every move.

"Ellis, it's no use! Get inside and put on dry clothes. You're freezing." Lucy shoved her friend aside and shuddered as she touched Boyd Henry's cold, clammy skin. His jaw was slack and she noticed what seemed to be abrasions on his cheek and forehead. She had learned CPR years ago as a Girl Scout leader, but it was too late to help her neighbor now. When the rescue squad arrived about five minutes later, Lucy was still crouching over his sodden form, and when someone with warm firm hands pulled her away, she began to cry.

Lucy stood back to watch one of the men examine Boyd Henry while two others waited to lift him onto a stretcher. She recognized the person kneeling beside Boyd Henry as the man who worked in the produce department of the Winn Dixie where she traded. She didn't know his last name, but Lucy had heard some of his co-workers call him Red. Now Red looked up and shook his head at the others. "We won't be needing that yet," he said grimly. "I'm afraid it's too late for this one." Lucy trailed behind him as he went to radio in from the waiting ambulance. "Where will you take him?" she asked.

"We'll have to wait for the coroner now," he said, shaking his head. "That's Mr. Goodwin, isn't it? I used to see him now and then when I was taking some courses at the college. Do you have any idea how this might've happened?"

Lucy told him how they had found Boyd Henry in the deep end of the pool. "No one was here last night and for most of the day," she said. "He must have fallen in somehow."

"Been in there for a while, by the looks of him," Red said. "He might have had a heart attack or a stroke. Of course all that will come out in the pathologist's report."

"You mean they'll perform an autopsy?" Lucy closed her eyes, remembering the *thing* that lay beside the pool, the thing that had been her neighbor.

"Have to when there's a suspicious death," he said.

Ellis, who had changed into a faded exercise suit and purple quilted bedroom shoes, hurried from the house, hair dripping. "Poor Boyd Henry! How do you suppose this happened?" she asked, shivering.

"That's for the police to find out," one of the would-be rescuers said as he carried lifesaving equipment back to their vehicle.

"The police?" For a moment Ellis seemed stunned, then she took a deep breath, averting her eyes from the form that lay only a few feet away. "Well, of course they would be the right people to call in a situation like this! God only knows how long he's been in the water," Ellis said. "And what on earth was he doing in there? You don't suppose he *meant* to drown himself, do you? Come to think of it, he did seem kind of despondent when I spoke with him yesterday." Her hands trembled as she clamped them over her face.

"We can't do anything more for Boyd Henry. I'm more concerned about you right now," Lucy said as she ushered Ellis inside. "Let's get something hot in you before you come down with something."

"You sound just like my mother. You know good and well you don't catch cold from getting chilled," Ellis said, but she didn't object to being hurried inside. There she turned on the oven and pulled up a chair to huddle by the open oven door. "I wonder when the police will get here."

Lucy, filling a kettle at the sink, noticed two uniformed figures approaching from the rear gate. "My guess is right now," she said, and moved to the door to greet them.

"Ed Tillman! No offense, but we seem to be seeing entirely too much of each other lately . . . Watch that puddle there, Sheila. Ellis dripped water all over the steps after she fished Boyd Henry from the pool."

Behind her, Ellis groaned an obscenity.

Two hours later, after taking measurements, photographs, and dusting for prints—or trying to, the investigators roped off the pool area and left, taking the body with them.

Ellis propped her face in her hands and looked at Lucy across the kitchen table. "Now, to add to my other heinous crimes, they think I drowned Boyd Henry," she said. In addition to Ed and his partner, the two of them had also been interviewed by Stone's Throw's police chief, Elmer Harris, and a stiff-faced detective Lucy didn't know who never sat down. Ellis said she thought he suffered from hemorrhoids.

"Then they really aren't operating on all cylinders," Lucy told her. "We won't know for sure until they do an autopsy, but Ed told me the coroner said it looked like he'd been in the water at least twenty-four hours. You've been with me almost the whole time. Just when were you supposed to have done it?"

Ellis sighed. "You wouldn't make much of a detective. He was here with me in this kitchen yesterday until dark. I could've pushed him in before I left for your house."

She drew in her breath and covered her face with her hands. "Dear God, Lucy Nan! Boyd Henry was probably doing the dead man's float this afternoon when I came home long enough to change clothes and heat up my casserole before we went to Calpernia's funeral. I never even thought to glance out back."

"It's just as well you didn't. What good would it have done?"

"None, I guess . . . but *somebody* must've shoved him in there. You know what a private person Boyd Henry was. If he planned to kill himself, I can't believe he'd do it on somebody else's property." She stood at the kitchen window looking out at the pool where their neighbor had died. "I know this sounds silly, but Boyd Henry Goodwin was too polite to deliberately cause such a ruckus."

"I agree. It wasn't like him at all." Lucy made a face. "Most improper—and I read somewhere that, senseless as it may be, most suicides remove their shoes before going in the water. Boyd Henry was fully clothed—shoes and all. Maybe he had a heart attack or something. He always seemed so soft-spoken, so . . . well . . . benign. I can't imagine why anybody would to do this to him."

"Did you notice if he had been hit over the head or anything? I didn't think to look. I wonder if he knew how to swim."

Lucy shrugged. "I don't know about that, but I'm beginning to think he might've known something else."

Ellis switched on another light and double-locked the back door. "What do you mean?"

"He must have known something somebody didn't want him to tell," Lucy said.

Her own kitchen smelled of something wonderful that simmered on the stove. Lucy inhaled the aroma of bay leaves and oregano in a rich tomato sauce as soon as she stepped in the doorway. She tossed her coat on a chair and missed, wishing she hadn't lost her appetite.

Augusta stood on tiptoe to reach the cabinet where Charlie had kept what Mimmer had called his "spirits," and produced a bottle of red wine. "You look like you could use a glass," she said, pouring one for herself as well. "Is anything wrong?"

"I'll say!" Lucy accepted the glass gratefully, stepping out of her shoes on her way to the small family room where her comfortable chair awaited. "Oh, good! I see you've already built a fire. Let's sit in here where we can stretch out and relax and I'll tell you all about it."

She thought it was a pillow until it moved. A shaggy round form of black and white with a splash of brown uncurled itself from the seat of her favorite chair and looked up at her as if to say, "How dare you interrupt my nap!"

"I'm afraid she's quite taken with your chair," Augusta said. "Seems to prefer it to any other."

Lucy had forgotten about Clementine. Now she scooped up the soft warm mound of yawning puppy and deposited her on the floor. "Well, she's going to have to share it," she said, stretching her feet toward the fire. The dog wagged its tail, gave her a quizzical look and promptly jumped up into Lucy's lap.

Augusta laughed. "It seems to me that *you* are."

Lucy nuzzled the animal's soft ears. She had to admit the puppy was cute. Earlier that day she had taken liberties with the truth when she telephoned Patsy Sellers at Bellawood to tell her the little dog had somehow followed the children home on the bus.

Of course Patsy was delighted to give her permission to keep it.

Now Lucy cradled the wineglass in her hand as she told Augusta how she and Ellis had found Boyd Henry's body in the Saxons' swimming pool.

Augusta stared into the fire and sipped her wine. "Do you think he might have taken his own life?" she asked. "Ellis said he seemed a bit distressed when she spoke with him yesterday."

"You mean because of the guilt he felt about the day little Florence was taken?" Lucy frowned. "*After all these years?* His conscience must've taken a long vacation!"

"He could have said something—possibly led police to the couple who took her—yet he didn't," Augusta said. "That's a terrible burden to carry, and then, of course, the poor woman met an unfortunate end right across the street from . . . " Augusta set down her glass so hard Clementine sat up abruptly, ears at attention.

Lucy stroked the dog's head, calming her. "What is it?" she said.

"Florence died on the back steps of the Methodist Church, which is directly across from where Boyd Henry lived. You said he sometimes worked in his yard at odd hours. What if he saw something—someone—that night? It might have seemed perfectly innocent until he learned what had happened there."

Lucy nodded. She and Ellis had already danced around the fact that Boyd Henry Goodwin might have been murdered because of that. "But why Ellis's pool? Now the police will think she had something to do with it."

"That's probably the reason. Ellis had already been questioned in regard to Florence's death. What could be more convenient than to do away with Boyd Henry in her family's pool? I wouldn't be surprised if the poor man wasn't killed soon after Ellis left to come here last night. She said he was there until well after dark." Augusta stood so suddenly, her long necklace swirled. "The stew! I almost forgot about the stew!

"Not a moment too soon!" she called, snatching the lid from the pot and giving its contents a stir. It smelled wonderful, and although she hadn't thought she could eat a bite, Lucy's stomach rumbled as she put together a green salad while Augusta took bread from the oven and brushed the golden-brown top with salted butter.

"And how is Ellis?" Augusta asked as she sliced the yeasty-smelling loaf. "I'm surprised she didn't come home with you."

"She's not taking this too well—and who could blame her? Pulling Boyd Henry from that pool was a chilling experience in more ways than one. We'll probably both have nightmares about it, and I did ask her to stay with us, but her daughter's on the way." Lucy glanced at the kitchen clock, which looked like the face of a cow rolling its eyes. It usually made her smile, but not tonight. "Ellis's husband Bennett will be home tomorrow and Susan plans to stay with her until then. She lives less than an hour away and should be there by now, but I'd better phone to make sure."

Rich brown stew steamed in her bowl when Lucy returned to the table. Susan had answered the telephone and assured her her mother was fine. "Everything's double-locked and the police have promised to keep an eye on the house," she told Lucy, adding that Ellis was convinced they were really keeping an eye on *her.*

Lucy dribbled oil and vinegar on her salad. "If Ellis really wanted to do away with Boyd Henry, she certainly wouldn't have drowned him in her own pool. The real killer's out wandering the streets while the police are bullying Ellis." She snorted. "Doesn't make me feel too secure—especially after what happened while we were at Bellawood yesterday."

Lucy wished she had thought to ask Ed and Sheila if they had any leads on her break-in, but in the trauma of the moment she hadn't thought to mention it.

Augusta glanced at Clementine, who had gulped her supper

and was now earnestly seeking theirs. "But now you have this fe-rocious guard dog to frighten intruders away."

"Oh, yeah, right—if she stepped on their feet!" Lucy laughed.

"I hope Ellis won't take it too personally about the police in-vestigation," Augusta said. "It's only natural they should question her. After all, what would've been Florence's inheritance came to Ellis, and she *was* in the vicinity when Florence was killed."

"So was I. So was Nettie next door. In fact, Nettie probably knew Florence better than anyone. She's never admitted that woman actually *was* Florence Calhoun." Lucy buttered another slice of bread and wondered which part of her already well-padded anatomy would receive the extra fat. "Anybody who knows Ellis would agree it's just plain ridiculous."

"Will her daughter be here long?" Augusta asked.

"Just until Bennett gets home, but she said she'd stay longer if needed. Susan's two girls are six and nine and her husband works out of the home—plus she has great neighbors." Lucy lifted her fork and put it down. "Ellis and her daughter have always been close."

Augusta eyed her across the table. "You don't think your daughter would come if you needed her?"

"You don't see her here, do you?" Lucy forked a fat mushroom from the beefy broth and savored it.

"Does she know what's been going on?" The angel lifted an el-egant eyebrow.

"It's a little difficult to carry on a conversation with someone who won't return your calls," Lucy said.

"Speaking of calls, you might want to check your messages," Augusta said. "I believe you have several on the machine."

"From Julie?" Lucy shoved back her chair.

Augusta touched her necklace, which glowed amber under her fingers. "Your son Roger phoned. He heard about the break-in yes-terday and sounded worried—wants you to call him back . . . and a woman telephoned about decorating for some kind of harvest festival at your church. Ruby, I think her name was. Or maybe it was Pearl."

"Opal. Opal Henshaw." Lucy groaned. "I'd almost forgotten I was on that blasted committee—and with Opal of all people as chairman!" She tossed her napkin aside. "I might as well call her now. She'll drive me crazy until I get back to her."

Augusta stirred cream into her coffee. "Oh, and a gentleman phoned as well."

"A gentleman? Who could that be?"

"I believe his name was Ben. He said you spoke at Bellawood."

"Ben Maxwell? The man who ran us out of his woodworking shop? What on earth could he want?"

Augusta sipped her coffee and smiled. "Why don't you listen to your messages and find out? It sounded to me as if he wants to take you to dinner."

"I don't have time for this," Lucy said, returning from the telephone.

"Time for what?" Augusta was enjoying her second cup of coffee along with a slice of bread oozing strawberry jam.

"Men. Ben Maxwell asked me out—some kind of concert at the college—and dinner as well, he said." Lucy poured a cup of coffee for herself. Augusta never made decaf and she knew it would keep her awake, but she'd probably have trouble in that area anyway, especially after today. "I don't have time for romance. There's too much on my slate already."

"I wouldn't call dinner and a concert romance—although it could lead to that, I suppose. You declined, of course?"

"Certainly not! Do you know how long it's been since anyone asked me on a *date?* Just wait until I tell Ellis."

And then she remembered that Ellis Saxon had more important things on her mind, as did she. Florence Calhoun was dead; Calpernia Hemphill had been killed under suspicious circumstances; and now Boyd Henry had drowned. Who would be next?

CHAPTER FOURTEEN

"What's this I hear about you and Ellis pulling Boyd Henry outa the swimming pool last night?" Nettie McGinnis wanted to know. Lucy was poking about in her backyard to see if she had enough chrysanthemums to make a presentable table arrangement for the harvest festival when her neighbor made her customary entrance through a gap in the hedge. "Dead as a door-nail, too! Do-law, Lucy Nan, that would tend to turn a person's innards plumb to jelly!"

"Mine are still quivering," Lucy admitted, untangling a greedy jasmine vine from her pink daisy mums. She hadn't spoken with Ellis that morning, but she was sure her friend felt the same. She gave the vine a tug. "It was horrible, Nettie. I wish I could just forget about it."

"Don't I reckon? You know that little bottle-blond cashier at the drugstore? Well, she said her boyfriend's cousin has a night job cleaning over at the morgue and Boyd Henry was already colder than a well digger's ass when they brought him in last night."

"Um." Lucy moved on to the purplish blue Michaelmas daisies, the color so vibrant it almost hurt her eyes. "These should last another week or so, don't you think?"

Nettie picked up a stray pecan and put it in her pocket while searching the ground for another. "You know, I wondered about Boyd Henry when I ran into him the other day. Seemed not himself—sort of queer-like. Fretful as an old lady!"

"Boyd Henry's always been kind of different, Nettie."

"Don't I know it! Lived across the street from him all my life. But I think this thing with Florence—if it *was* Florence—really got to him. He asked me if I remembered the day she disappeared—as if I could forget!"

"When was this?"

"Couple of days ago . . . no, before that. Must've been the day after that Shirley woman's funeral. I was in Do-Lollie's—had a notion for some of her lemon chess tarts—when Boyd Henry came in looking like it was ten minutes till doomsday."

Nettie found another pecan and cracked the two together, nibbling the nut meats as she walked. "Then here came Zee wantin' croissants for some kind of sandwiches she was going to make—for that young director fellow, I reckon."

"Was he with her?"

"Waitin' in the car. I saw it parked out front."

"What else did he say?" Lucy asked. Maybe Augusta was right about Boyd Henry seeing something the night Florence was killed.

"I didn't wait around to find out." Nettie made a face. "That Lollie sold the last one of those tarts just before I got there."

Lucy made appropriate consoling noises. "You were right about Boyd Henry being fretful. He told Ellis he actually *saw* the people he believes took little Florence. All this time the guilt must've been gnawing away at him, poor man."

She expected her neighbor to be surprised at this news, but Nettie only nodded. "Uh-huh," she grunted.

"Is that all you can say? Uh-huh? Or did you know about this, too?" Lucy sat on the steps of the summerhouse, knowing full well her pants would be soiled by a season's dust and grime.

Nettie groaned as she joined her. "Let's just say it doesn't surprise me. Boyd Henry was a good bit older than Florence and me and we kinda looked up to him the way small children do. I do remember him selling snow cones that day, only neither one of us had a nickel to buy one. People didn't throw around money like they do today, you know." She tossed pecan shells into the bushes and brushed her hands together. "Of course I didn't know about him seeing the people who took her. Florence was playing in her front yard when Mama called me in to dinner.

"You don't reckon he took his own life?" she added.

Lucy shook her head. "Not like that."

"It doesn't suit, does it?" Nettie said. "Maybe his foot slipped or something. As far as I know, Boyd Henry couldn't swim a stroke. It could've been an accident."

"Let's hope so," Lucy said, but she didn't believe it.

Apparently, neither did Nettie. "I don't know what's happening in our little town, Lucy Nan. Why, I don't remember the police being called on this street since Hortense Pendergrass whacked that door-to-door corset saleswoman in the noggin with a soup ladle for telling her she needed a larger size."

"If you'll tell me what you're looking for, maybe I can help," Augusta said later that morning as Lucy rummaged through boxes in the attic.

"Decorations for the festival. I know I have some ceramic pumpkins up here somewhere. Opal Henshaw's getting some real ones from the farmer's market, but I thought we could fill in with these . . . Ahh! Here you are!" Lucy leaned back on her knees and brought out a grinning jack-o'-lantern. "I made this in my one venture into ceramics when the children were small. It's about as artistic as I ever got."

Augusta examined it solemnly. "It looks like a fine *jack-a-light* to me—and what's this?" She reached into the box for a large tissue-wrapped package with yellow yarn escaping from the bundle.

Lucy smiled as she unwrapped the stuffed scarecrow. "That's Patches! I'd forgotten all about him. My mother made him for Julie when she was about six and he sat on our hearth every fall for years."

Augusta fingered the patchwork jacket. "He still seems to be in good shape—for a scarebird, that is."

Lucy couldn't hide her smile. *Jack-a-light* she could ignore, but *scarebird* was just too much.

"What's wrong? Is it something I said?" Augusta's voice sounded as if it had been wound with a key. Her tenant's reaction to criticism was sometimes far from angelic, Lucy observed.

"It's *scarecrow*," Lucy told her, laughing.

"Oh." Flushing, Augusta smoothed Patches's rumpled coat. "I wonder if Julie remembers this," she said.

"Probably. She always looked forward to putting it out."

"Then why not send it to her?" Augusta smiled, her error apparently forgotten.

Lucy adjusted the scarecrow's straw hat, remembering how much fun they used to have decorating for holidays. "I'll go to the post office tomorrow," she said, rescuing a box of Halloween candleholders from Clementine's inquisitive nose. "But now I'm going to give Ellis a call to see if she's heard any more from the police."

"Nary a mumblin' word," Ellis said. "At least nothing we didn't already know. A couple of uniformed men came by with the same questions we answered last night and I told them the story all over again. I did ask them if Boyd Henry had been hit over the head or something but they said the autopsy wasn't completed." She sighed. "Susan's going home tomorrow. Thank goodness Bennett's here!

"I don't suppose you've heard anything?"

Lucy told her what Nettie had said about Boyd Henry's gloomy visit to Do-Lollie's.

"No telling how many people's he's talked to," Ellis said. "One of them might just be the person who sent him for a swim. You don't suppose he'd be nervy enough to confront whoever he suspected, do you?"

"Not nervy. Naive. It would be like Boyd Henry to want to put things right."

"So I guess we're expected to wait around looking over our shoulders until this psycho decides it's our time to go," Ellis said.

"Unless you're on the decorating committee for the harvest festival with Opal Henshaw cracking the whip. I don't have time to wait around. Don't you want to help round up cornstalks with Augusta and me?"

"*Opal Henshaw?* Thanks, I'll take my chances with the local exterminator. Opal wants you to gather cornstalks? I didn't know she decorated with anything that wasn't plastic!"

"Meow! Meow!" Lucy giggled. "We're going all out this time, but actually it was Augusta's idea. Know where we can find any?"

"There's plenty out at the Folly. Or there used to be. I remember when Susan was on the decorating committee for a class dance back in high school and Poag told them to just go out and help themselves. He rents out a few acres to a local farmer and I'm sure he won't mind if you get some. After all, what are they going to do with dead cornstalks?"

"The Folly? Not on my favorite list of places right now, and I hate to mention it to Poag. It's kind of a sensitive subject after what happened to Calpernia out there," Lucy said.

"Then why mention it, for heaven's sake? Just go out there and chop off a few stalks. They'll be glad to get rid of them." Ellis's voice had an edge to it, which was unusual for her.

"Ellis, are you okay? The police haven't been breathing down your neck, have they? I mean, they can't be serious about your being involved in what happened to Boyd Henry."

"Who knows what they think, but Bennett's talked to a lawyer friend of his who specializes in this kind of thing." She sighed. "I'm letting him handle it."

"Good." Lucy waited. "Ellis, is there something you're not telling me?"

"Damn it, Lucy Nan, I can't keep a thing from you! I wasn't going to tell you this, but that Leonard Fenwick's filed a suit."

"Florence's husband? What kind of suit?"

"Over the inheritance. He wants his share of the property I inherited that would've come to Florence."

"Can he do that?" Lucy asked. "Isn't there a statute of limitations on that kind of thing?"

"I don't think so. He can try—and, Lucy Nan, if Florence were alive, or even if she had children, I would see that they got a fair share, but not Leonard Fenwick! I don't owe him a thing!

"You will take Augusta along when you go for the cornstalks," she added as the conversation came to a close.

"Of course. Wouldn't go without her," Lucy said.

"Better take that big puppy, too—just for good measure." Ellis laughed when she said it, but Lucy suspected she wasn't joking.

"I feel kind of strange about this," Lucy said as they bumped along over the narrow red dirt road that wound through the rolling acres of Bertram's Folly. Clementine, her nose pressed to the window, panted with delight at the outing.

"It shouldn't take long," Augusta said. "And poor Clementine really does need to run about a bit. She's a growing dog, you know."

"Tell me about it! We're about out of dog food already. I'm going to have to start buying the large economy size." Lucy stopped the car in a grassy area on the side of the road and opened the door for Clementine, who immediately took off running.

"Okay, get it out of your system, but you'd better come when I call or you'll have to walk home, you imp!" Lucy yelled as the dog's white-tipped black tail disappeared around a bend in the road.

On the other side of a shallow ditch a field of dry brown cornstalks rustled in a slight wind. "They sound like they're whispering, don't they?" Augusta hopped gracefully over the ditch and looked about. "Well, it looks as if we'll have our choice." She shaded her eyes with one hand. "Just where is this folly you were talking about?"

"About a half mile down the road. It's not far," Lucy said. "I'll show it to you when we're through if you like. It gives me the creeps, though."

Augusta broke off several cornstalks and tossed them into a pile. "Who lives in the little cottage over there?"

Lucy glanced over her shoulder at the rustic house nestled in the trees behind them. In the October woods the cabin was partially camouflaged against the browning oak trees around it. "No one," she said. "Poag and Calpernia used to come here weekends. Calpernia wanted to establish a theater camp here, and I hope Poag will carry out her plans. It seems something positive should come of this place."

Augusta looked about. "It is lovely, but . . . "

"But what?" Lucy asked.

Augusta didn't answer. She didn't have to. Lucy could guess what the angel was thinking. The whole time they had been there she'd felt uncomfortable.

"Let's hurry and get these in the trunk," Lucy said as the pile of stalks grew substantial. "It's getting late and I don't want to be here after dark."

Augusta called to Clementine, who zigzagged ecstatically through brittle stalks of corn and skidded to a stop at the angel's feet. "Do you mind if we walk a little farther?" she asked, swirling her voluminous green cape about her. "I'd like to have a look at that folly."

"As long as you don't expect me to climb it," Lucy said, walking along beside her. Augusta walked fast, and she had to make an effort to keep up, but the weather was crisp and cool and sunlight still streaked the road ahead. Lucy took a deep breath and picked up her pace. She hadn't realized how much she had missed walking. "We should do this more often," she said.

"Is that the folly over there?" Augusta pointed to something up ahead.

"Where?" Lucy couldn't see anything.

"There where the road curves. Surely you see it." The angel shaded her eyes.

"Augusta, that's just a dead tree. How could you mistake it for a tower?" Lucy said. Was something wrong with Augusta's eyes?

"Of course! Now that we're closer, I can see," Augusta said with a slight laugh.

At that point, Clementine, who had been trotting along beside them, growled low in her throat and dashed off in the direction of the cottage, ignoring their commands to return.

"Come back here, you rotten dog!" Lucy yelled, starting after her. The puppy was probably chasing a raccoon or a squirrel, she thought, but Clementine was already lost to her in the woods surrounding the cabin.

"Wait." Augusta spoke softly beside her. "We don't know what—or who—could be up there. It's best to hold back a bit."

Lucy agreed. After all, Augusta *was* her guardian angel, and she was content to walk slowly alongside her until they came to the small house set back from the road where Clementine raced back and forth barking in the clearing.

"She senses something," Augusta said, clapping her hands. "Enough, Clementine! Come here!"

Lucy sensed it, too. Someone was watching them; she knew it. Suddenly she wanted to run, to hide. When the puppy raced toward them, responding to Augusta's call, Lucy felt as if an iceberg melted in her stomach. Grabbing up the squirming dog, she held her close as they hurried to the car, but Augusta paused to bend down and scoop up a glob of mud, cradling it in her hand.

"Are you crazy? What are you doing?" Lucy turned back to wait for her.

Augusta stared at the clay in her hand. "Nancy Estridge," she said.

"Nancy-schmancy! We don't have time to make mud pies. Come on, Augusta! Hurry! Something's not right here." Lucy must have blinked because the next time she looked, the angel was waiting at the car holding the door open for Clementine.

"How did you do that?" Lucy slid behind the wheel and locked the doors before turning the key in the ignition.

"You *said* you were in a hurry." Augusta didn't smile, but she looked as if she wanted to.

Lucy watched her deposit the blob of clay on a scrap of paper. "What's that for?" she asked.

Augusta wiped her dainty fingers on a tissue and glanced back at the cottage as they drove away. "Something is most definitely wrong here," she said. "If I'm not mistaken, this is the same type of clay we saw on that woman's shoes—the woman claiming to be Florence Calhoun."

Lucy had forgotten all about the shoes, which she supposed were still on a shelf in her hall closet where she had left them earlier. Tomorrow, she thought. Tomorrow I'll take them to the police. "And what does Nancy Estridge—whoever she is—have to do with it?" Lucy asked.

"Nancy Estridge was one of my earlier charges. Goodness, it doesn't seem so long ago, but she lived in a log building much like that one and carried her water from a spring. When darkness came, she had only a lantern for light." Augusta reached behind her to trail her fingers along the puppy's nose and smiled when Clementine licked her hand. "I have a problem remembering time, but it must have been many years ago."

"Before the invention of the electric light, I imagine," Lucy said, wondering where this was going.

Augusta nodded. "Nancy lived with her two children—no more than babies, really—and she had to take care of her family as her husband had been killed in a war. She did it by making pottery—rather crude vessels at first, and then she became quite adept at what she did. Some of her pieces were lovely, and the clay was much like what we saw here—grayish-white with an occasional streak of blue. It came from the bank of a creek near her cottage, and from what I learned, is not all that common."

"Kaolin. I've read somewhere that some kinds of clay contain kaolin. Porcelain is made from the pure white kind." Lucy frowned. "Do you think the smudges we saw on Florence's shoes are the same as what you found here?"

"I wouldn't want to spring to conclusions," Augusta said, "but it's certainly a possibility."

Lucy turned onto the main road, glad for once to merge into traffic. If the clay on Florence's shoes turned out to match the other, she must have been at the Folly before she was killed.

CHAPTER FIFTEEN

That silly puppy was probably barking at Poag," Ellis said when Lucy telephoned her later that night. "I mean it *is* his cabin and I expect the poor man came out there for some peace and quiet after all this mess. Could've been out in the yard for some reason or other when the dog got his scent."

"Maybe, but I didn't see his car and he usually parks on that graveled area out front. Besides, Poag would've come out and spoken to us. You know how he is."

"Are you sure this person was actually *in* the cottage?" Ellis asked.

Lucy thought for a minute. "No, could've been behind it or in the woods somewhere, but I'm sure we were being watched."

"*You* were being watched," Ellis said. "Remember, most people don't see Augusta. Do you think somebody deliberately followed you there?"

"Nobody knew I was going except you . . . and Opal."

"Oh, well! You might as well holler it from the street corners," Ellis said. "She's told everybody in town by now."

"And come to think of it, I did mention it to Nettie. She knew I was scrounging up decorations for the festival this week."

Ellis groaned. "Say no more. It'll probably be on the evening news tonight."

"Speaking of news, I have a tidbit to share," Lucy said, and told her about her upcoming evening out with Ben.

"Ben Maxwell? Really? I've always thought he was good-looking in a rugged sort of way, but can he *talk?* The man scarcely said two words to us when he was working on our hutch."

"Does it matter? He's taking me to dinner and a concert and his eyes are the color of my Michaelmas daisies."

"Hmm . . . what kind of concert?" Ellis wanted to know. But Lucy hadn't thought to ask.

"You're going out with *who?*" Roger asked when he came by the house the next day.

"Benjamin Maxwell. I'm sure you've heard of him, Roger. He made that beautiful walnut desk in the dean's office at Sarah Bedford."

"Oh, that Ben Maxwell! Do you think you might get a special price on a drop leaf table? Jessica's been asking for one for years."

Lucy laughed. "Don't get your hopes up. It's only dinner and a concert." With soothing words and a generous slice of Augusta's apple pie, Lucy had managed to convince her son that the body in the swimming pool and her recent break-in had absolutely no connection and that she wasn't in danger of being abducted by villains with evil intent.

He did give her strict orders upon leaving, however. "I want you to promise you'll call me immediately if you have even the faintest suspicion of anything wrong!" Roger kissed her cheek. "You know you're welcome at our house anytime, Mom!"

"I know," she said, and resting her cheek on his shoulder, Lucy held her son a little tighter than usual. At least one of her children cared.

"You aren't wearing the green frock?" Augusta wanted to know when Lucy came downstairs the next evening."

"A little too fussy, don't you think?" She had tried on the green dress the night before and decided in favor of her plum-colored pantsuit with an ivory silk overblouse. Lucy had become fond of anything you didn't have to tuck in.

"Ah, but it brings out the color in your eyes and your silver shoes would look elegant with it." Augusta glanced at her own shimmery gold slippers and did a quick pirouette.

"Augusta, I'm just going to a concert at Sarah Bedford—not Carnegie Hall." Lucy sighed. "I think this looks all right."

"You're right, it does. It looks *all right,*" Augusta said.

Lucy looked at the clock. She just had time enough to change. "What if he shows up in khakis and a sport shirt?"

"He won't," Augusta assured her.

And he didn't. In fact, Lucy thought, Ben Maxwell cleaned up real well.

"Would you like to come in for a few minutes?" she asked, shoving Clementine away with her foot.

"I'd like to," he said, glancing at his watch, "but I made dinner reservations for six-thirty." He hesitated at the door, wearing a nubby tweed sport coat with a burgundy tie and gray pants. The tie, she noticed, had tiny horses on it. "Do you ride?" she asked.

He laughed. "No, but my sister does. She gave this to me last Christmas. In fact, she's given me all four of my ties, I think."

Clementine by this time was slobbering all over his shoe. "Then I guess we'd better be off," Lucy said, only pausing long enough for him to help her with her coat. She thought he could've at least told her how beautiful she looked and how the dress brought out the green in her eyes, especially after she'd burned her forehead with the curling iron and gone to the trouble to change. As they left, she glanced back to see Augusta, sitting on the stairs, raise her hand in a three-fingered wave.

At the restaurant, Ben made a joke out of straining to read in the dark as he studied the menu by candlelight. "Everything on here looks good to me," he told Lucy. "I passed through Greenville on my way back from a visit with my son in Atlanta today and stopped to hike that trail to Caesar's Head. Sure worked up an appetite! I'd forgotten how steep it was—but what a view!"

"My husband and I hiked that when the children were younger," Lucy said. "Charlie had to carry Julie most of the way and I remember wishing I had somebody to carry me—but you're right. Those falls are worth the climb."

She gave her order of shrimp and grits and turned back to him. "Is hiking a habit or was that a spur-of-the-moment decision?"

Ben gave the waitress his menu, deciding on the pork tenderloin with sweet potatoes. "A little of both, I guess. There's something of the vagabond in me—must've been a gypsy in my other life. Whenever I see a trail, I want to know where it leads, and that one's right in our area yet I'd never had a chance to explore it." He sipped his Scotch and water and turned the glass in his hand. "Do you still enjoy hiking?"

Lucy laughed. "I haven't done much since Charlie died, but I think the trails are calling to me."

"Let me know when you're ready to answer," Ben said, lifting his glass to hers. Their fingers touched as they toasted and neither seemed in a hurry to move away.

"Frankly, I guess you could say I've been at loose ends lately," Lucy admitted. She told him of Bud Fincher's retirement and the subsequent loss of her job. "I didn't make much money but it gave me a purpose, especially after Charlie died," she said. "And soon after that, the student I tutored in the adult literacy program got her certificate and is now studying for her GED."

"That's wonderful! I've thought seriously of doing that myself but somehow just never got around to signing up for the course," he said. "Tell me about it. It must be very rewarding."

Lucy smiled. "It's never too late, you know. My student and I came to be good friends."

Ben Maxwell waited until they had ordered dessert to mention Boyd Henry's death. "I'm sure this must be a sensitive subject, but I did want you to know how sorry I am that you and your friend were subjected to such a terrible experience," he said.

"It was a lot more terrible for Boyd Henry than it was for us." *Now why did I say that?* Lucy thought, and in her confusion spooned entirely too much sugar into her coffee. "I just hope they won't waste time finding who did it."

He met her eyes with a steady gaze. "Do you think the police are wasting their time?"

She sipped her coffee. "I'm afraid I do, yes."

"Why?"

Lucy told him of her concerns for Ellis. "It seems as if somebody wanted to throw suspicion on her by drowning Boyd Henry in her pool. Meanwhile, whoever did it is going free." Lucy spoke softly. Although the restaurant was in a neighboring town, people from Stone's Throw came there often and the seating was fairly close. Tonight, however, she didn't recognize anyone she knew at the candlelit tables around them.

Dessert came: chocolate mousse for her and a brownie topped with ice cream for him. "I'm a fool about ice cream," he admitted, and Lucy, who shared that same passion, almost forgave him for not complimenting her on her dress.

"Have they considered that Boyd Henry's death might have been accidental?" he asked as they waited for the bill.

"I think they're waiting for the autopsy," Lucy said. "I wish it would be that simple."

"Well, they'll sure miss him out at Bellawood. That fellow practically ran the place." Ben smiled. "Peculiar old gent, but I liked him."

"Did you notice any difference in Boyd Henry's behavior during the last week or so?" Lucy asked. "I don't suppose you saw him talking with anybody for an unusual length of time."

Ben shook his head. "I really wasn't around him that much, but from what I could tell, Boyd Henry Goodwin didn't get involved in long conversations."

The auditorium at Sarah Bedford was crowded, as many of the students attended tonight's performance, a rhythm-and-blues concert by a popular group. Ben and Lucy found that their seats were directly in front of Lollie Pate, who kept up a one-sided conversation until the house lights dimmed:

I declare, my feet are killing me! I'll bet I didn't get to sit down five minutes all day . . . and how is Ellis? Poor girl, what a dreadful thing to discover! And I hear you were there, too, Lucy . . . I wonder if they've made any progress in finding out who's responsible . . . seems all we've done lately is go to funerals . . .

Lucy, noticing Poag Hemphill across the aisle, put a finger to her lips hoping to shut the woman up, but it did no good.

Didya know they're dedicating this concert tonight in memory of Calpernia? Everybody seems to think it was an accident . . . sure makes sense to me . . . Now, aren't you going to introduce me to this handsome fellow you're with?

Lollie looked lovely, Lucy had to admit, in a simple black dress and pearls that set off her fair hair, worn tonight in an elegant chignon, and Ben managed a private wink in Lucy's direction while enduring her flow of chatter. When a member of the faculty came out on the stage to introduce the musicians, Lucy had more than one reason to applaud.

Later, during intermission, Lucy sighted Zee and Jay Warren-Winslow at the rear of the auditorium as they weaved their way through the mesh of bodies to what her husband Charlie had referred to as the "yack and yawn" area. This was where people congregated to stretch their legs, sip wine and hug acquaintances they only saw once or twice a year. The line to concessions was so long Ben and Lucy gave up on the drinks, but Lucy was glad to stand for a while as long as she could avoid Lollie.

Zee, standing with her young tenant by the water cooler, seemed relieved when Lucy and Ben approached them. "How are you, sugar?" she asked, enfolding Lucy in bony arms. "I tried to call you yesterday but you were out and I didn't want to leave a message—hate those blasted machines! Anyway, I'm relieved to see you're okay. God, will this shit never end?" She kissed her cheek, whispering, "Who's the hunk? Have you been keeping something from me?

"Oh, you're the one who made that beautiful hutch for Ellis! What a fine piece of furniture!" she said when Lucy introduced Ben to the two of them. Lucy was searching for something acceptable to say about Jay when she noticed Poag Hemphill approaching.

"Oh, crap!" the young director uttered under his breath.

But Poag, although he wasn't smiling, seemed genial enough, and after dutifully kissing both women and speaking to Ben, whom he knew through some work Ben had done for the college, turned and offered his hand to Jay. "I must apologize for the way Calpernia's sister spoke to you at the service the other day. I don't believe you had anything to do with what happened to Calpernia, Jay, and I feel I had to let you know. I can't imagine what she was doing in that tower unless it was to get a better view of the surrounding area, but whatever her decision concerning you and the facility she planned out there, it had *nothing* to do with the way she died. I'm convinced of that, and I believe the police are coming around to that theory as well."

For a few seconds Jay seemed too stunned to respond, and then, with trembling lips, he managed to stammer his thanks.

Lucy thought he was going to cry, and although she didn't especially care for the man, she had a compelling desire to gather him into her arms. Instead she reached for his hand, patted it, and told him she was glad for him. If Poag thought Jay was innocent, it was good enough for her. "By the way," she said, turning to Poag, "I hope you don't mind, but I helped myself to some cornstalks out at the Folly yesterday. You weren't at the cottage by any chance, were you? I thought I saw someone there."

He shook his head, frowning. "I haven't been out there lately, but it could've been Ted Driscoll, the fellow who farms that plot—and I'm sure he wouldn't mind sharing some of his cornstalks."

Lucy had never met Ted Driscoll, but she couldn't help wondering why he didn't make an appearance. Surely he must have seen her.

Ben took advantage of a lull in the conversation to tease Lucy about dognapping a puppy from Bellawood. "She *says* the dog was a stowaway on the bus, but I think she plotted the whole thing!"

Everyone laughed, and Lucy spent the next few minutes telling them about Clementine until the lights blinked to summon them back to the performance. As they started inside, she noticed that Poag didn't follow them but instead slipped out a side door. He and Calpernia usually attended these events together, and Lucy imagined how difficult if must be for him, especially since tonight's performance was in memory of his wife.

Throughout the course of the evening, Lucy saw and spoke to numerous friends and acquaintances, and for the most part, she thought, they seemed pleased to see her with an escort. After the concert was over, she smiled as Ben took her arm, guiding her through the crowd. She hadn't let herself acknowledge how much she had missed the attentions of a man, and after three long years it was a welcome adjustment—no matter how temporary it might be.

In fact, as Ben walked her to her door, Lucy Nan Pilgrim made up her mind she would invite him in for coffee. Earlier, Ben had mentioned the possibility of a picnic and hike at King's Mountain and Lucy hoped they could pursue the idea before colder weather set in. While she stood searching for her key, however, Lucy couldn't miss the figure in the shadows at the top of the stairs. Augusta had tried to make herself inconspicuous, but the gleam of her necklace and soft iridescence of her rose-colored shawl gave her presence away.

Clementine banished what could have been an awkward moment by greeting them at the door, and Ben laughed, then kissed Lucy on the forehead and told her good night.

"Tea or coffee?" Augusta asked a few minutes later as Lucy shed her shoes in the kitchen.

"I don't care, as long as it's hot." Lucy practically melted onto a chair. It had been a long day.

"Then I believe I'll join you." Augusta smiled as she poured steaming cider into ceramic mugs. The brew smelled of apples and cinnamon. "How was your evening?"

"Nice." Lucy told her about dinner in the small but elegant restaurant and how they had ended up sitting in front of Lollie Pate during the concert. "She was quiet for the second part of the performance, thank goodness! Seemed kind of put out about something. I hope it wasn't because we didn't talk with her, but my gosh, she didn't give us a chance to get a word in edgewise! I was afraid the woman was going to run out of breath."

Augusta seemed indifferent to that. "What about your friend Benjamin? Did you enjoy his company?"

"Yes, I did. He's very nice."

The angel lifted an eyebrow. "Nice."

"Yes, nice. His wife died several years ago and he has a son who's a doctor in Atlanta. Actually, we have a lot in common." Lucy told her about the proposed hike and Ben's interest in the adult literacy program. "And in spite of what Ellis says, he *can* talk after all! We found we even enjoy some of the same books and music, although I don't think he's much for dancing."

"He's nice-looking, too." Augusta glanced away.

"Why, Augusta Goodnight, I do believe you have a crush on Ben Maxwell!" Lucy grinned. "And I think he's a bit of a history buff, too. That should be right up your alley."

"Lucy Nan Pilgrim, don't talk such foolishness!" Augusta leaned over to scratch Clementine's ears, but Lucy thought the angel didn't protest too much.

"My friend Zee was at the concert tonight with that director who rents her apartment." She told Augusta what Poag Hemphill had said during intermission. "I thought it was awfully kind of him, and I could see the relief on Jay's face."

Augusta nodded solemnly. "I suppose we'll have to wait and see if the local police agree." She leaned closer. "And speaking of face, what have you done to your forehead, just below the hairline there?"

"Must be the place I burned with the curling iron tonight." Lucy touched the tender spot. "Ouch! Still hurts. You're lucky, Augusta. Your hair is naturally glorious."

But Augusta, usually receptive to compliments, didn't acknowledge the praise. "Curling iron, of course!" she said. "Years ago, people used to heat them in the fire. Didn't you tell me the woman who came here had something like a burn mark on her forehead?"

"Yes, that could've been what it was," Lucy said. "I didn't look at it closely, though."

"And she wore an entirely different lipstick from the tube found in her handbag?"

Lucy nodded. "Nettie said it didn't suit her."

Augusta let her necklace slip through her fingers while she thought. "It seems to me that your guest—whoever she was—had recently undergone some kind of cosmetic makeover."

CHAPTER SIXTEEN

Lucy Nan, if you're going to the grocery store, would you please pick up a few things for me?" Ellis asked when she phoned the next day.

"Of course. You know I practically live there. They're thinking of charging me rent. You aren't sick, are you?"

Ellis's response was more like a gag than a groan. "Just sick of being suspected of murder! I can just feel people looking at me wherever I go, and I know what they must be thinking."

"Ellis Saxon, you know that's not true! Everybody in Stone's Throw knows you better than that."

"No, they don't." Ellis's voice was choked.

"Who? Name one," Lucy demanded.

'That woman who works at the video rental place. Susan and I ran in there yesterday to grab something to watch last night. Thought it would keep our minds off the current dilemma—for a little while, at least."

"The woman with the big hair? Wears enough jewelry to sink a ship?"

"That's the one. When I paid her she acted like my money was contaminated, and I saw her whisper something to that man she works with as we left."

"Maybe your slip was showing." Lucy tried to make light of the situation, as she could tell her friend was on the verge of tears.

"Slip, my foot! I know what she was talking about, and I'll never go in there again!" Ellis sniffed. "I feel like moving into the closet and never coming out!"

"Ellis, that silly woman has beans for brains. I can't believe you'd let her get to you this way. What does Bennett say?"

"He thinks I'm overreacting . . . pats me on the back."

"And Susan? Where's she?"

"Left early this morning. Her girls are both down with a virus."

"I'll be there in a minute," Lucy said. "I have to run these shoes Shirley/Florence left here by the police station."

"Do give them my regards—what shoes?"

"The ones she left in Julie's closet when she took my boots and coat. I'd forgotten all about them until Augusta noticed the mud the other day." Lucy could have kicked herself for not getting the shoes to the police earlier. It seemed something else was always getting in the way.

"What mud?" Ellis asked.

"From the Folly—but I'll tell you when I see you. Be making out your grocery list," Lucy told her. But she had no intention of doing Ellis's shopping.

"Keep your old list. You're coming with me," she said a few minutes later when Ellis met her at the door, list and money in hand. "And grab that rented video while you're at it. We'll pay a visit to little Miss Puffyhead."

"What kind of friend are you?" Ellis whined. "Very well, I'll just ask Idonia to go."

"No, you won't! Do you want people to believe this crap? Straighten your shoulders and hold your head high. Where's your mettle?"

"I don't even know what mettle is. It sounds painful," Ellis said, but she reluctantly allowed Lucy to help her into her coat and out the door.

"That's *nettle*, and it can't be more painful than what you're going through," Lucy told her.

"What's all this about Florence's shoes?" Ellis asked as they waited at the traffic light.

"I dropped them off at the police station on my way over," Lucy said, and told her what Augusta had discovered. "If it turns out to be the same kind of clay—"

"—it would mean that Florence had been out to the Folly. But what would she be doing out there?" Ellis gasped. "Lucy Nan, you don't think she had anything to do with what happened to Calpernia, do you?"

"I don't know if she ever met Calpernia. It sure beats me," Lucy said, "but I intend to find out!"

"Please don't make me do this, Lucy Nan!" Ellis pleaded as they parked in front of the video store a few minutes later.

"Oh, come on, you'll love it! It'll be fun. Can you imagine what she'll *think*? Besides, what do we have to lose?"

Ellis smiled and began to look almost like her old self again. "Well . . . if you promise not to run off and leave me like you did that time back in high school."

"Ellis Calhoun, is there an animal in here?" Lucy mimicked Miss Winfield, their high school librarian, who was convinced a cat was hiding in the stacks. What a joke that had been! The

straitlaced woman never knew the two of them had been responsible for all the meowing.

"And don't you dare make me laugh!" Ellis added.

The woman barely nodded in greeting when they came in, but
Lucy saw her stiffen noticeably when she recognized Ellis. They
returned the rented video and disappeared behind the shelves
pretending to inspect the movies offered there.

"I just hate violent films, don't you?" Lucy said in a loud voice.

"Oh, no. The bloodier, the better," Ellis answered. "And I find
the methods most interesting. In fact, I'm doing a little research
of my own."

"Really? Have you considered poison? And of course there's
great-granddaddy's sword just killing time in the attic—if you'll
pardon my pun."

Ellis covered her mouth to keep from laughing. "So many vic-
tims, so little time," she said. "I wonder who'll be next."

A couple of minutes later, when the two left empty-handed,
the woman with the big hair stood as far away as she could, with
a roomful of shelves between them. "Bye, now!" Ellis called to
her, waving as they walked out the door.

"Damn, that was fun!" she said, grinning, and Lucy knew the
old Ellis was back. But for how long? she wondered.

Augusta laughed when she told her about it later. "I'm pleased
you were able to make your friend laugh, but I'm afraid she's going to need more earnest support." It was a mild day and they sat
on the back steps drinking coffee while Clementine played at

their feet. Now Augusta lifted the puppy onto her lap and stroked her tummy. "Lucy Nan, do you honestly think anyone you know had a hand in any of this?" she asked, turning to Lucy with her clear-eyed gaze.

"I can't imagine who it might be," Lucy said. "Nothing like this has ever happened in Stone's Throw before." She didn't even like to think about it.

"Then it seems to me it might be time to enlist some help. Why not call on some of your friends? One person might have information another doesn't. You never know what might come of it until you put the pieces together," Augusta said.

"The Thursdays aren't supposed to meet for another couple of weeks, but I don't see any reason why we couldn't get together sooner."

Augusta nodded. "The sooner the better," she said.

"Zee says Jo Nell and Idonia aren't speaking to her because she came to Calpernia's funeral with Jay. That might present a problem," Lucy said, watching the puppy wobble down the steps. It looked so cute she scooped it onto her knees, where it proceeded to puddle on her lap.

Clementine! Setting the dog on the steps, Lucy jumped to her feet, a damp spot spreading across the front of her pants. "Oh, sure, go ahead and laugh!" she said, noticing that Augusta didn't even try to hide her amusement. "She didn't wet on *you*." But she found herself laughing as well and shrugged. "Oh, well, at least they're washable."

The next afternoon The Thursdays, with the exception of Ellis, gathered in Lucy's living room. Augusta had agreed with her that Ellis should be excluded since they were meeting to share information that might clear her name. "She would either want to be in on it or she'd put on a big act about not needing any help," Lucy had explained to the others.

"You might want me to sit in another room since there are *some people* here who might not want to share the same air with me," Zee said, shedding her jaunty red jacket on the back of a chair.

"That's not true, Zee Saint Clair, and you know it," Idonia said, taking the seat beside her. "Jo Nell and I were upset—and rightly so—since you chose to accompany *that man* to Calpernia's funeral. To be honest, I was afraid if I spoke, I'd say something I might regret."

"Since when has that stopped you?" Zee said.

"Well, it's all behind us now, so let's just forget it," Jo Nell said. She leaned over to kiss Zee's cheek. "We've been through too much together to let this silliness come between us. Besides, Ellis needs our help."

"Do you think the police are seriously considering Ellis as a suspect?" Claudia asked Lucy.

"She seems to think so, and they did ask her not to leave town," Lucy answered. "I thought if we pooled our information, we might come up with something to shed some light on the subject."

"I'm afraid I don't have any information," Idonia said, "but it all seems to begin with Florence's coming to Stone's Throw."

"She took a bus from Chicago," Lucy reminded them, "but nobody here remembers seeing her get off the bus." She frowned. "I meant to get back to that man who clerks at the station here. There was a substitute driver that day and he said he'd try to find out who it was. It's a long shot, I know, but if we can track him down, maybe the driver will remember where Florence got off."

"Or if somebody got off with her," Claudia added. "I can do that right now. I'll use the phone in the kitchen and see what I can find out."

"Good. Thanks!" Lucy turned to her neighbor. "Remember,

Nettie, you commented on the lipstick she wore. Said it didn't match her complexion."

"Or her dress," Nettie said. "And didn't you tell me you found a different color tube in the lining of her purse?"

"What's so strange about that?" Zee asked. "I couldn't begin to count all the lipsticks I own."

"But that wasn't the color she was *wearing*," Nettie reminded her. "What happened to that?" She clicked her teeth absently, thinking. "And her hair smelled of shampoo—remember, Lucy Nan? Like it had just been washed."

Lucy thought of the woman's sleeping face. Her rouge had been carefully applied and she still wore a dusting of eye shadow. She doubted if a woman in Florence's state would have been able to do such a professional job.

"She had obviously paid a recent visit to a beauty salon," she said. "But where? And when?"

"Maybe she went before she left Chicago," Idonia said. "Assisted living facilities—even nursing homes—offer services like that now." She made a face. "Dear God, I'll probably have to take advantage of them soon enough!"

"Relax. I doubt if your room's ready yet," Lucy told her. "And Florence's makeup looked fresher than that. Her hair still smelled like apricots, and according to the bus schedule, she should've arrived in Stone's Throw a couple of days before she came to me. So where was she all that time?"

Across the room, Augusta waved to get her attention and pointed to her shoes.

"I'm coming to that," Lucy said aloud.

"Coming to what?" Idonia wanted to know. "And by the way, didn't you tell me Florence said something about California? Wonder what she meant by that."

"That's right, she did!" It was getting darker and Lucy rose to turn on a lamp by the window. "We were sitting in the kitchen and she'd been asking about her mother. That's when she told me her mother was a Thursday. Said something about her not being here because she was at a meeting of The Thursdays . . . And then she said, *I knew she wasn't in California!*"

"Poor little thing! That just breaks my heart!" Jo Nell searched in her bag for a tissue until Zee put one in her hand. "Somebody must have told her her mama was in California." She frowned. "Now, why would they do that?"

"I reckon it's the first place that came to mind," Idonia said. "Would you want to tell a seventy-year-old woman who thinks she's five that her mama has been dead forty years?"

Claudia appeared in the doorway just then to tell them she'd finally gotten through to the bus station. "Number was busy, so I had to redial a bunch of times, and a lot of good it did. The man I spoke with—Horace, I think he said his name was—said he tried but he never could track down that fellow who was driving the bus that day. Said he hasn't seen him since, but if he does, he'll give you a call. I gave him your number."

"So, other than *some* beauty parlor *somewhere*, we don't have any idea where Florence went before she came here," Zee said.

Lucy glanced at Augusta. "As a matter of fact, we do," she said and told them about the shoes.

CHAPTER SEVENTEEN

Jo Nell leaned forward so quickly she almost fell out of her chair. "Good heavens! You don't suppose Florence pushed Calpernia from the Folly, do you?"

"Good old Florence! I'm beginning to like her more and more," Zee said with a smile.

"Oh, hush!" Idonia told her, but Lucy noticed she laughed when she said it. "If the mud came from the Folly, what was she doing there? And what's the connection between Florence and Calpernia?"

"Well . . . they're both dead," Claudia said, and everyone turned to look at her before they laughed. Small, blond and serious, Claudia Pharr rarely cracked jokes—not intentionally, anyway. At forty-five, she was the youngest of the group, invited to join only because her mother had been a member, and her grandmother before her. Lucy found her rather colorless, but she had to admit Claudia did make a mean pound cake and was eager to take on jobs nobody else wanted.

Now a shy smile broke out on Claudia's girlish face and she shrugged. "Well, they *are*, aren't they? And they surely didn't kill each other—so who did?"

"Good point," Nettie said. "What did you do with the shoes, Lucy Nan?"

"Took them to the police. I hope they'll be interested enough to do some investigating on their own. I understand they have ways to analyze things like that."

Idonia stood and warmed herself by the fire. "When did you take them?" she asked.

"Yesterday."

"I'd call them tomorrow and find out if they pursued it. Those clowns will drag their feet from now till doomsday if we don't stay on their case." Idonia turned to warm her other side. "Sounds to me like Florence might've stayed out there during those two missing nights."

"At the Folly? Why?" Jo Nell asked.

"Probably stayed in the cottage," Idonia said. "How else would she get that clay on her shoes? Assuming it came from there."

Lucy, who had started to the kitchen for refreshments, stopped in mid-stride. "I just thought of something," she said. "I didn't think anything about it then, but Florence mentioned something about having breakfast twice, and the day Calpernia was killed, the police found breakfast dishes in the sink out at the cottage. Naturally they assumed Calpernia had spent the night there alone, but maybe she had company."

"But twice?" Nettie frowned. "Why did she say she'd had breakfast twice? And what would those two be doing together?"

"I haven't the faintest." Lucy turned to Zee. "Do you think Jay might have seen her? He was out at the Folly that day. After all, he was the one who discovered Calpernia's body."

Zee groaned. "Don't I know it! I'm sure he would've mentioned it, but I'll ask." She started to rise. "How 'bout if I give you a hand in the kitchen?" she said to Lucy.

"Doesn't it make you nervous with that man living right there in your guest house, Zee?" Jo Nell asked. "It gives me the shivers just thinking about it."

Oh, dear, Lucy thought. Here we go again! But she was surprised when Zee began to laugh. "Jo Nell Touchstone! A four-year-old in a Batman cape would give you the shivers. For your information, even Poag Hemphill admits he doesn't suspect Jay of having anything to do with Calpernia's death." She stood and looked about her. "And since we're sharing, I'll share this: Jay tells me he wasn't even aware that Calpernia had changed her mind about hiring him to head up her project—and what's more, I believe him."

Lucy thought she was going to choke on the silence until Claudia spoke up. "So where is Jay this afternoon? I expect he finds the possibilities for entertainment rather limited here in Stone's Throw."

"Oh, he manages to keep occupied," Zee said. "Today he's sitting in on an art class at the college—some of that modern stuff."

"You sound less than enthusiastic," Nettie said. "Don't tell me the bloom's wearing off the rose."

Zee shrugged. "I found we have different interests—which shouldn't surprise me, only for some reason it did. Can you believe the man has never read *To Kill a Mockingbird* or *Huckleberry Finn?* And the other day was the last straw!"

"What do you mean?" Jo Nell gripped the arms of her chair.

"I said I wanted to get a Perry Como Christmas CD when we were in the mall last week, and he said, 'Perry *who?*'"

This brought a howl from everyone, and Zee laughed along with the others. "Of course he'll continue to live in the guest house as long as necessary," she said. "Did you know he's a gourmet cook? I'll have to throw a dinner party before he gets away from us. Good food knows no generation gap."

"I've been wondering how that woman found her way to your house," Nettie said over the spiced tea and scones. "Somebody must have brought her. Didn't you notice a car or anything?"

Lucy shook her head. "Just the one at the stop sign on the corner."

"Do you remember what it looked like?" Nettie washed down the last of her scone with a gulp of tea and set her cup aside. "Maybe they dropped her off."

"Gray or blue, I think, and I have no idea of the make. I wasn't paying much attention."

"I think we need to check with the local beauty parlors," Idonia suggested. "Maybe somebody will remember Florence."

"That shouldn't take long," Nettie told her. "There can't be more than five. I'll ask Addie at the Total Perfection when I go for my shampoo and set tomorrow. And Claudia, why don't you check with that artsy place you go to downtown—the one that takes men and women?"

Lucy smiled. Most beauty salons now welcomed both male and female clients, but any man who dared to enter the sacred portals of the Total Perfection would be reduced to a spineless wimp in seconds by the Blue-Haired Freeze.

"I'll be glad to," Claudia said, "and while I'm at it, I'll drop by Cleo's Clips down the street, but there are a lot of people who do this kind of thing out of the home. How do we find them?"

"You're right," Nettie said. "They have their own small group of customers and they don't advertise. I know Emma Joiner over on Forsythia Street does practically everybody from my Sunday school class. You did it for a while, didn't you, Zee?"

"Lord, that was ages ago, before Melanie was born! Didn't last long. What a catastrophe!" Zee made a face over her cup. "Opal Henshaw never has forgiven me for that permanent I gave her. Said it made her look like the Cowardly Lion . . . Lucy Nan, have you been taking a cooking class? You've always been a good cook, but these scones just melt in your mouth. Are those cranberries in there?"

"New recipe," Lucy said, nodding in Augusta's direction.

"I'd sure like to have it," Jo Nell said. "This is scrumptious." She dabbed her lips with one of the last of Lucy's scarecrow napkins. "By the way, did Florence's rings ever turn up? You said she was wearing some rather large stones, didn't you, Lucy Nan?"

"I'm sure we would've heard about it if they had, and I could be wrong, but they didn't look worth stealing to me," Lucy said.

Idonia snorted. "The scum who took them wouldn't know that. Imagine being so cruel to that poor soul. How could they live with themselves?"

"How do you know somebody took them? For all we know, Florence might have left them here." Zee held out her cup for more tea. "Whoever broke into this house was looking for something. Those rings might be worth more than you think, Lucy Nan."

"If they were after money, they came to the wrong place," Lucy said. "Besides, where could she have left them? We've looked under the bed—everywhere, And she had a habit of slipping them off and on, so she could've lost them somewhere between here and the Methodist Church."

"Did you tell that to Ed and Sheila?" Claudia asked.

"Didn't think about it, but I will," Lucy said. "They're welcome to come and look for them, but I'm sure I would've noticed if she dropped anything that gaudy in our yard." She pulled her chair closer into the circle. "Maybe you'll find a ruby among your chrysanthemums, Nettie! She had to cut through our backyards to get there or we would've seen her when we were out front picking up all that mess from the garbage cans."

Jo Nell reached across to pat Lucy's arm. "I just hope these hoodlums don't come back. If I were you, I'd get my locks changed, Lucy Nan. With all this meanness going on, I'm almost afraid to go out in broad open daylight, and now look what's happened to poor Boyd Henry! Why, Bernice Okey told me she heard he had a bruise in the middle of his back like somebody'd poked him with a stick or something."

"How does Bernice know that?" Lucy asked. Jo Nell's next-door neighbor always seemed to know everything even before it happened, but Lucy thought surely the police would have notified Ellis about it first. Or not. She frowned. Now they were certain to think Ellis had something to do with it.

"Said everybody was talking about it at the doctor's office this morning," Jo Nell said. "You know how poor Bernice suffers from bronchitis."

"This doesn't look good for Ellis," Nettie said, slipping out of her shoes. "Ahh!" she said. "That's better! Blasted callus is killing me . . . "

After a brief moment of shoeless bliss, Nettie McGinnis looked about. "Girls, we have a murderer in our midst! Sure as I'm sittin' here, somebody drowned Boyd Henry Goodwin because of something he knew—or saw."

"What do you mean, *in our midst?*" Claudia asked. "Surely you don't think one of The Thursdays—"

"Of course not!" Nettie told her. "I meant here in Stone's Throw, and I'm gettin' sick and tired of it. I'm almost sure I remember seeing Boyd Henry out there working in his tulip bed when I left you that night, Lucy Nan."

"What do you mean, *almost* sure?" Idonia asked.

"Well, it was dark, for one thing, and I was about to freeze. Lucy Nan and I had been out there cleaning up all that garbage some fool knocked over and I was ready to get home, but I seem to remember seeing Boyd Henry out there planting bulbs. At least I reckon it was Boyd Henry. I wondered at the time how he could see what he was doing, with it being so dark and all."

Lucy moved about with a tray collecting cups and plates. "If we can find out what happened to Florence, I think the rest will fall into place. If she didn't get off the bus in Stone's Throw, then where *did* she get off?"

"Let's start here. Claudia, I'll help you cover the beauty salons tomorrow," Zee offered. "And Nettie's going to check with Addie at the Total Perfection—right? But what then? How are we going to trace her back all the way to Chicago?"

"Let's all sleep on it," Idonia said. "Maybe we'll come up with something." She looked at her watch. "I didn't realize it was this late and I still have to get to the grocery store. Promised I'd bake cookies for the harvest festival, and here it is only two days away."

Jo Nell said she was making popcorn balls and Claudia, chocolate cupcakes, and for a few minutes, hearing them chatter as they prepared to leave, Lucy was reminded of happier autumns. She wondered if Julie had received the Patches doll she sent.

The house seemed quiet after everyone left and Lucy finished gathering cups and napkins and took them into the kitchen. Augusta sat reading the newspaper in the rocking chair by the window, with Clementine on the rug at her feet. "Doesn't seem to be anything but bad news in here," she said, laying the paper aside. "Oh, and there were several leaflets in your paper box. I put them on the table."

"Just junk, usually," Lucy said, shuffling through them before throwing them in the trash. "People advertising maid service and pizza, trying to sell memberships at a spa."

"But you read them first," Augusta said, "so it must be worth the effort."

"I guess it pays off or people wouldn't keep doing it," Lucy said. "And it is a cheap way to advertise."

Augusta pulled the puppy into her lap and nuzzled her ears.

"Suppose you wanted to advertise in another town?" she asked. "How would you go about it?"

"You'd have to distribute them somehow. Go there yourself or have someone else do it. Why?"

Augusta Goodnight didn't answer. She only smiled.

"Augusta, have I ever told you you're an angel?" Lucy asked.

"You might have mentioned it once or twice."

"This is exactly how we need to go about trying to find somebody who might have ridden the bus with Florence! The man at the bus station here gave me the schedule from Chicago . . . hold on a minute, let me get it."

"Okay, once it got past Kentucky," she continued, "the bus stopped in Knoxville, Tennessee, then Asheville, North Carolina," she said. "I suppose she could have gotten off in one of those places, but that's a long way from here."

"Then what?" Augusta stroked the puppy's soft neck.

"It stops in Hendersonville, North Carolina, before crossing into South Carolina for passengers in Greenville, then Greenwood. That's the last stop before this one. Those last two cities aren't very far from here. We could make a day trip out of it—post flyers in and around the bus station."

"What about those other places, the ones between Knoxville and Chicago? You can't possibly travel everywhere," Augusta said.

Lucy stooped to rattle dog food into Clementine's bowl and the puppy immediately abandoned Augusta's lap to begin gulping it down. "Darn it, Augusta!" she said. "Aren't you supposed to be able to fly?"

Augusta shivered. "It's October! You know how cold-natured I am." She brightened. "But couldn't you use that new beeping machine?"

"Beeping machine?" Lucy frowned.

"The one that buzzes and spits out paper—makes all kinds of noise."

Lucy grinned. "A fax! Of course we could if they have a machine. But we'd have to depend on somebody else to post the notices for us. My old college roommate lives in Asheville. I'll bet she would put up a few, and Nettie's niece teaches in Knoxville. We'll get them out one way or another."

"I'll call her tonight," Nettie said when Lucy phoned her a few minutes later. "I'm sure she'll be glad to help, but aren't you forgetting something?"

"What?"

"We'll need a picture of Shirley/Florence," Nettie said. "Wasn't there one at the funeral? Seems I remember seeing a photograph of her next to a vase of roses in the narthex. Leonard brought it, I reckon, but he probably took it back home."

"There's only one way to find out," Lucy told her, and punched in Ellis's familiar number.

"It's right here," Ellis said. "Why do you want a picture of Florence?"

Lucy told her of her plan to circulate the woman's photograph. "Maybe *somebody* who remembers her from the bus will get back to us," she said. "I can't tell you how relieved I am that you still have the picture. Nettie and I were afraid Len had taken it home."

"Luther found it in the narthex the day after the funeral," Ellis said, speaking of the sexton. "I forgot all about it with everything else going on, and Leonard never mentioned wanting it back. He never would've brought it in the first place if I hadn't asked him to."

Lucy hesitated to ask the question foremost on her mind, then decided to plunge in anyway. "Is it true that Boyd Henry had a bruise on his back?" she said.

"Several, in fact, and that detective couldn't wait to tell me they might've been made with the handle of our pool net."

"What detective?" Lucy asked.

"The one with the hemorrhoids. Remember? The one who wouldn't sit down. But Lucy Nan, anybody could've used that net scoop. We keep it hanging beside the pool. And he said the abrasions we noticed were probably made when his face scraped the side of the pool."

"Oh, Lord, Ellis! Poor Boyd Henry!" Lucy heard the clatter of dishes on the other end of the line. "I'm not interrupting your supper, am I?"

"Nope, Bennett and I had waffles tonight and I'm stacking the dishwasher," Ellis said. "He offered to take me out, but I'm leery of the paparazzi."

"You're a nut!" Lucy told her. "I'll be by to collect Florence's photo tomorrow."

"What if somebody does recognize her?" Ellis asked. "What then?"

"Then I'm hoping they can tell us where she got off the bus."

Lucy remembered Mimmer's batter-spattered recipe for waffles pressed between the pages of her grandmother's cookbook and rummaged in the cabinets until she found it, then hauled out her old waffle iron. "Tonight I'll stir up something heavenly for you," she told Augusta, assembling the ingredients.

The two of them had just sat down to eat when the telephone rang. "Drat!" Lucy put down her fork. "It never fails! Bet that's

Opal Henshaw bugging me about those decorations for the harvest festival. Well, if she wants any more cornstalks, she can get them herself!"

Reluctantly she pushed back her chair and went to answer the phone.

"Mom?" Julie said. "Guess what came in the mail today!"

CHAPTER EIGHTEEN

$\mathcal{I}$ ran across Patches in the attic the other day and thought you'd like to have him," Lucy said. "After all, your grandmother made him for you."

"Thanks, Mom. Remember how I used to sleep with him? He's propped up on our bed right now, and I don't think he's aged a bit."

Our bed. Lucy managed to suppress a shudder. "And how is Buddy B—uh . . . is everything all right?" *Please tell me he's volunteered for a year-long experiment on the moon!* If so, it would be the longest stretch he'd ever worked at a time, she thought. Her daughter's boyfriend drifted from one job to another with less sticking power than a stale wad of gum.

"Fine, Mom, and guess what? I'm finally getting a chance to write features! Did one this week on this man who makes jewelry out of chicken poop. Encases it in acrylic. I'll send you a copy."

Lucy laughed. "Just don't send me any of the jewelry!" she said. Julie had been writing for a newspaper in a small Georgia city since graduation from college and Lucy was grateful she had at least one stable thing in her life. "So, things are going well at work?"

"Great! I'm learning a lot." Did her daughter's voice have a forced brightness, or was she just imagining it?

"I'm glad, honey. And are things about the same with you and Bu—"

"Hey! What's all this about the mystery woman who turned up on your doorstep?" Julie said. "Even the Associated Press picked it up. Did she really get mugged behind the Methodist Church? What's going on over there in Stone's Throw?"

Lucy told her daughter what she wanted her to know. "We're planning to circulate some leaflets with Florence's photo to see if we can locate anyone who might have seen her on the bus," she said.

"Who's 'we'?"

"Oh, just some of The Thursdays," Lucy said.

"Want me to post some around here?"

"The bus doesn't come through Georgia on that route, but I don't suppose it would hurt. Thanks, I'll put some in the mail this week . . . And, Julie, you will try to get home for Thanksgiving, won't you?"

"I don't know if I can get off, Mom. We'll see."

Lucy met Augusta's calm eyes from across the room as she replaced the receiver. "She said we'll *see*," she told her. "It sounds like Julie may be here for Thanksgiving after all!"

Augusta shook out the cloudlike shawl she had been knitting and laid it neatly aside. "I hope you're right, Lucy Nan, but it's wise not to count your eggs before they're laid."

"Oh, good! You've made copies of Florence's picture," Zee said when Lucy dropped by the next morning. "Claudia's supposed to come for me in a few minutes and this will save us from trying to describe what the woman looked like—especially since neither of us ever saw her."

Lucy had made a few copies before leaving the original with the printer who was to make up the fliers. "The printer said somebody had just canceled a big order, so he'll be able to get these ready by tomorrow morning," she said.

"Good!" Zee examined the photo at arm's length. She had yet to admit she needed reading glasses. "Does Ellis know we're doing this?"

"Had to tell her. How else could I get the photograph?" Lucy told Zee how Leonard had left it behind.

"I'm not so sure about that one," Zee said, frowning. "Do you suppose he *knew* what Florence was planning?"

"About coming here, you mean?"

Zee ran long fingers through her short dark curls: *Arabian Starlight # 5, available at your local drugstore*. "*And* that she might come into money," she said.

"I wouldn't put it past him. He's suing, you know."

"So I heard . . . oh, and before I forget—I asked Jay if he happened to notice anyone else at the Folly that morning, and he said the only living creatures he saw were Calpernia's two dogs."

"That must have been an awful experience, finding Calpernia like that," Lucy said.

Zee nodded. "Pretty bad. He doesn't like to talk about it." She frowned at her reflection in the hall mirror and pinched her cheeks for color. "I don't guess you've heard anything yet about the clay on Florence's shoes?"

"You guess right. I went by the police department on my way here and they told me they hadn't heard anything yet. To tell you the truth, I'm not even sure they did anything about it—although they swear up and down they did. I get the impression they think I'm poking my nose in where it doesn't belong."

"Who cares what they think?" Zee said, walking with Lucy to the door. "I'll call you as soon as we talk with these hairdressers. Maybe somebody will recognize that poor woman. Need any help getting those fliers out?"

"I thought I'd mail some to my old roommate in Asheville and Nettie's niece in Knoxville as soon as I pick them up tomorrow, but we'll need to phone the rest of these bus stations to get their fax numbers *and* hope they'll be willing to put them up."

"I can do that this afternoon," Zee said. "I know you have your hands full decorating for the festival tomorrow. You don't happen to have that bus route with you, do you?"

Standing on the front steps, Lucy dug in her handbag for the folded piece of paper and gave it to Zee; as she did, a car door slammed and Jay Warren-Winslow gunned down the driveway, scattering gravel. He waved as he drove past. On the way home, Lucy wished she had thought to ask Zee not to mention what they were planning to her guest. Poag Hemphill seemed convinced the young director had nothing to do with his wife's death, as did Zee. But Lucy wasn't so sure.

She spent the rest of the morning and most of the afternoon in the church fellowship hall trying to dodge Opal Henshaw's pointed questions while propping up cornstalks and placing pumpkins about for the festival the next day.

"I know Zee's a friend of yours, Lucy, but somebody ought to tell her how improper it looks with the man who probably killed Calpernia living right out there in her guest house!" Opal smoothed the long yellow tablecloth with her long yellow fingers and tucked autumn leaves behind a pumpkin, then stood back to admire her work.

At the other end of the table Lucy heaped dried corn and gourds around mounds of bronze chrysanthemums and tried to ignore her. Fall was one of her favorite seasons and she was hoping to enjoy this brief respite from the troubles that had come tumbling around her.

Now Opal stepped up to Lucy's display and moved a pot of mums a half inch to the left. "All I'm saying is, Zee better watch her step or she may wake up one morning murdered in her own bed."

Lucy laughed as she moved the pot back where it had been. "If she were murdered, I doubt if she'd *wake up*, Opal!"

Across the room, several members of the senior high youth group scooped out pumpkins for jack-o'-lanterns and hung apples on strings for a children's game while a constant parade of women bearing cakes and pies for the cake walk filed through the adjacent church kitchen. Lucy was glad when Opal huffed away to supervise somebody else, allowing her to escape into the kitchen for one of Idonia's molasses cookies. In spite of Opal's grim predictions, the mellow October smells of candle wax and pumpkin, the laughter and flurry around her granted a temporary retreat from a world gone crazy.

It didn't last long. Upon arriving home, Lucy found a patrol car parked behind her house and a young policeman coming down her back steps. Removing his hat, he identified himself as Sergeant Duff Acree. "Lieutenant Tillman said to ask your permission to search your yard for the rings that woman might've been wearing when she was killed the other night. If it's all right, would you mind signing an agreement?" He glanced in the direction of Nettie's backyard. "Your neighbor said it was okay with her."

Lucy nodded, scribbling her name on the slip of paper. She had mentioned the possibility of Florence's losing the jewelry when she had stopped by the police station earlier.

"She did have a habit of slipping them on and off," Lucy told him. "Who knows? Maybe you'll find something." But she didn't think he would.

Inside, she found two telephone messages waiting. The first was from Zee informing her that she and Claudia hadn't had any luck in finding a local cosmetician who remembered Shirley/Florence.

"We're going to have to stop calling that poor woman Shirley/Florence," Lucy said when she returned Zee's call. "It strips her of her identity."

"Her husband was willing enough to let her be buried here in the Calhoun family plot," Zee said. "Guess that's identity enough for him."

"But what if she wasn't Florence Calhoun?" Lucy wondered aloud. "What if the DNA sample doesn't match?"

"Then the whole thing would be a hoax—and Leonard Fenwick wouldn't have any grounds for a suit against Ellis," Zee said.

"That's worse than if it were true—to think anyone would use that sad, bewildered woman in a scheme like that," Lucy said. "If we could just find someone who *saw* her!"

"Maybe we will," Zee told her. "Just about everybody I called on the bus route who has a fax machine has agreed to post a flier on their bulletin board."

"Great! I'll pick up the fliers in the morning and get them out first thing . . . and Zee, I think it would be a good idea to keep this to ourselves." She hoped she wasn't too late with her warning.

Lucy hung up the phone feeling a zing of buoyancy that had been missing in her life, and the second message did nothing to deflate it. The call was from Ben Maxwell.

Lucy walked through the house eager to share her news with Augusta, but the angel was nowhere to be seen. In the kitchen, Clementine looked up from her nap on the rug with a thump of her tail and Lucy stooped to pet her, glad of another warm presence in the room. The house seemed almost hollow without Augusta there, as if she had taken her energy with her, and Lucy glanced through the kitchen window to see if she was on the porch or out in the yard, but all she saw was the young policeman pawing through the underbrush, presumably looking for Florence's rings.

Now Lucy put a match to the fire Augusta had laid in her den and sat on the floor watching the flames grow brighter. In addition to the picnic on Sunday, Ben had asked if she wanted to see a movie the next night, the night she had planned to take Teddy to the church festival, and she was torn in two directions. Augusta would know what to do.

And where was Augusta? A little knot of fear began to grow in her chest and when a voice spoke behind her, Lucy whirled instantly to her feet.

"Oh, good! You've lit the fire!" Augusta ran to warm her hands at the blaze. "Did you know there's a man crawling around in your yard?" she asked.

"He's looking for Florence's rings . . . and where have you been? I was getting worried."

"With Ellis." Augusta sat across from her and regarded her with quiet eyes. "She needed me today. "Things have been rather turbulent for her since this latest incident."

Lucy nodded. "I know." Her conscience gnawed at her for wanting Augusta to herself. "How is she?"

"Worried. And lonely, too, I think." Augusta smiled. "But Bennett's with her now."

"Maybe somebody will recognize Florence's picture from the flier," Lucy said. "I'm sending them out tomorrow. So far, we've had no luck with the beauty operators. None of them remembers seeing her." Tucking her feet under her, Lucy told Augusta about her day, including the message from Ben Maxwell. He's asked me out for a picnic Sunday, and for tomorrow night as well. That's the night of the church festival."

"I don't see the problem," Augusta said. "Why not do both?"

Lucy remembered how Ben had reacted when the children chased through his workroom after escaping puppies. He had overwhelmed the little ones with his deep, booming voice. "I'm not sure that's his cup of tea," she said. "We can go to the movies another time."

"Of course." Augusta let her necklace trickle through her fingers, reflecting the glint of the fire.

"Teddy's been looking forward to the festival. And so have I. I made him a promise, Augusta." Lucy sighed. "Besides, I doubt if Ben would enjoy it."

"You might be surprised." Augusta smiled. "Don't be afraid, Lucy Nan."

"Afraid? What do you mean? Afraid of what?"

"To take a chance. Just think about it." Augusta touched her shoulder on her way to the kitchen. "Does tomato bisque sound good to you?"

It was not until later that night that Lucy finally worked up the courage to return Ben Maxwell's call. He would be delighted to attend the church festival with Lucy and her grandson, he said, and would be at her door at five. Afterward, Lucy sat with the receiver in her lap wondering why she dreaded the assumed intimacy of such an evening with Ben. It was one thing to sit cloistered in a restaurant or a darkened theater, but the thought of being on display at Stone's Throw Presbyterian in front of God and everybody scared her half to death.

When the phone rang again as she was getting ready for bed, Lucy halfway hoped it was Ben calling to tell her he'd changed his mind. Instead she heard the familiar rattle of Nettie's upper plate.

"You reckon that young Acree fellow found anything out there today?"

Lucy yawned. "Didn't look like it; besides, I doubt if they'd tell us if he did."

"I saw him scratching around out there till it was almost too dark to see, but it isn't going to do any good. If that woman really was Florence and she wanted to hide something, it would be somewhere in your house."

"Nettie, somebody's already broken in here and turned the house upside down, and the police have searched this place from top to bottom. If anything was hidden, they would've found it."

"Maybe. Maybe not . . . Nettie paused. "Like most little girls, Florence liked secrets. She had her hiding places."

"*Where?*" Lucy put down her hairbrush and sat on the bed. "Do you remember where?"

"Not right offhand. I'll need to think about it," Nettie said. "But I got to thinking about that time we stole the lemon drops."

"Stole *what?*"

"Lemon drops. Florence's mama had a terrible cold and she kept these lemon drops in a dish by her bed. We weren't supposed to have any, but of course we did—went in there and grabbed as many as we could carry and Florence hid them away in what she called her secret place."

"But you don't know where that might be?" Lucy asked.

"Well, not right now, but I'm hoping it will come to me in time," Nettie said.

Lucy looked at the clock. It was a quarter past ten. "If it doesn't come within the next thirty minutes, put a hold on it, will you? Because I'm going to bed."

When the telephone rang again, Lucy, awakened out of a deep sleep, struggled to sit up and turn on the light. It was almost three in the morning! Her first thought was of her family. Had something happened to Julie or Roger? Had Teddy been taken ill? Her hand shook as she snatched the receiver from its cradle.

"I know where it is!" Nettie McGinnis said. "Turn on the porch light. I'm on my way."

CHAPTER NINETEEN

Lucy stood on the back porch shivering in her robe as Nettie picked her way through the hedge and across the lawn. "For heaven's sake, it's the middle of the night," she said, holding open the door. "Couldn't this wait until morning?"

"By morning I might forget it." Nettie took her time coming up the steps and paused at the top to catch her breath. "Law, I hate to think how long it's been since I've been out this late, Lucy Nan. Old time's catchin' up with me."

Lucy reached for her hand and pulled her neighbor inside, then hurried to lock the door behind them. "Come in here and get warm—and good grief, Nettie! You're still wearing bedroom shoes!"

Nettie looked down at her fuzzy blue slippers which now had leaves sticking to them. "Reckon I forgot . . . oh, well, I'm here now." She sniffed. "Your house smells just like strawberries. I've been noticing that lately. You been doing a lot of baking?"

"Must be the air freshener," Lucy said, helping Nettie off with her coat. "Now, are you going to show me this secret hiding place or not?"

"That's what I came for." Stepping carefully around Clementine, who opened one eye and went back to sleep, they made their way through the kitchen.

"Where now?" Lucy asked, and Nettie pointed upstairs. "Julie's room," she said.

Upstairs, Nettie paused in front of the open closet door and switched on the light that came from a bulb dangling from the ceiling. "We'll need to take out some of these clothes," she said, grabbing an armful of summer wear Lucy *hoped* she'd be able to fit into again next spring. Lucy swept out another bundle and laid it across the bed, hoping Nettie wouldn't notice the cobwebs in the corners of the empty closet. The cubicle smelled musty with a lingering fragrance of the rose sachet she had tucked among the clothing, and the interior was of white-painted wood with an overhanging shelf of the same. Although it was straightened and cleaned on a more or less regular basis, the closet hadn't been painted since they moved into the house over twenty years before.

Now Nettie stood on tiptoe and strained to look over the shelf.

Lucy pulled up a chair and stood on its seat. "Where?" she said. "Tell me where to look."

"It was over here somewhere," Nettie said, pointing to the left corner of the closet. "Up high. We had to stretch to reach it."

"I don't see anything. What's it look like?" Lucy probed behind the shelf.

Nettie frowned, crowding in to look up. "It was just a little opening, no bigger than a deck of cards. Maybe it's been sealed up."

"I don't see anything like that," Lucy said, climbing down from the chair. "Are you sure it was this side?"

Nettie nodded. "Up high."

"But you could reach it if you stretched?"

"Right." Nettie shoved a strand of hair from her face. "Sometimes she put treasures in there, too—little things like marbles and pieces of colored glass. She kept them in a can."

"Nettie, you were children then. You couldn't possibly have

reached as high as that shelf. It must have been lower." Lucy shoved the chair aside and ran her hand underneath until her fingers came across a crevice in the corner. "There's something here . . . " She felt inside, hoping she wouldn't come across what was left of a sixty-year-old lemon drop.

"Does it feel like a ring?" Nettie asked.

"No, it's something with a clasp—ouch! I stuck myself! I wish I had longer fingers; there's a lot of dust and lint in here." Fumbling, Lucy finally drew the trinket from the space beneath the shelf and held it up to the light.

"What on earth is it?" Nettie adjusted her bifocals. "Looks like some kind of costume jewelry. Do-law, you reckon it's been in there all these years?"

"No, I don't," Lucy said, looking closely at the pin, "and I don't think it's costume jewelry, either. This is a beautiful piece of work. It looks handmade." The artist who designed the jewelry had used sapphires and emeralds to create the likeness of an iris rising from green fronds with a tiny diamond dewdrop on one blue petal.

Nettie turned it over in her hand. "It is a pretty thing. Looks like it's set in silver."

"More like platinum, I think," Lucy said. "But where on earth did it come from?"

Nettie made a space for herself on the bed and sat, still holding the pin in her hand. "Florence must've put it there—had to have been Florence. Nobody else knew about this place but me."

"So it really was Florence we buried in the family plot." Lucy felt a mixture of relief and sadness wash over her.

"Seems so. Whoever did her hair must've applied her lipstick, too. It made her mouth look fuller. Didn't look the way I thought." She gave the pin to Lucy. "Here, you take this thing. I don't want to be responsible for it."

Lucy slipped the pin into her pocket and patted it with her

hand. "I don't know what to do with it, either. It must've been somewhere on her clothing when she came, but I didn't see it. It certainly wasn't in her purse. Do you suppose she could've stolen it somewhere?"

"Her husband would know if it were hers, wouldn't he?" Nettie scowled as she clicked her teeth. "But I don't know if I'd trust him—looked shifty-eyed to me."

"We'll have to tell somebody," Lucy said. The pin felt like a hot lead weight in the pocket of her robe.

Nettie patted Lucy's arm and yawned. "Wait till we all get together. The Thursdays will decide what to do. Are you sure there wasn't anything else in there?"

"I'll check again." Lucy reached once more into the crevice but all she found was more dust and debris. "Were you hoping for a lemon drop?" she said.

After Nettie left, Lucy went back upstairs and stood in the door-way of Julie's old room, the room that had belonged to Florence. *If you could only speak,* she thought, looking around at the violet-colored walls, the wide floorboards, the tall double windows over-looking the street. It was a comfortable room; the child Florence had been happy here, and it was to here she had come home. Once more Lucy went to the closet and explored the small space with her fingers, but there was nothing there. The clothing still lay heaped on the bed and weariness fell so heavily upon her, Lucy felt as if she were facing a mountain. Even her arms seemed weighted.

She turned at a touch on her shoulder to find Augusta behind her. "I'm so tired," Lucy said.

Augusta smiled. "Go to sleep." She nodded toward the pile of clothing on the bed. "We'll take care of this in the morning."

Lucy fumbled in her pocket for the pin. "We found this piece of jewelry in the closet. Florence must've put it there, but where did it come from? Augusta, I don't know what to do."

"I know," Augusta said, guiding her downstairs to bed. "We'll think about that tomorrow."

It was almost nine when Lucy woke to the telephone ringing the next morning. "The DNA's a match," Ellis said.

Lucy tossed aside the covers and searched for her slippers. "What? You mean—"

"The little curl of hair that was in Florence's baby book—it matched up with the sample they took from your visitor."

"I know," Lucy said.

"What do you mean, *you know?*"

Lucy told her about Nettie remembering the hiding place in the closet and how they had found the pin. "It had to have been Florence who put it there," she said. "Nobody else would know about it but Nettie."

"And you found this *in the middle of the night?* What does it look like?"

"That sounds familiar. I think I've seen it somewhere," Ellis said after Lucy described the jewelry.

"Come and take a look at it. Have you had breakfast?" Lucy poked her head into the kitchen. "Augusta's whipping up a cheese omelet and it looks like there's enough for three."

"I've already eaten my cereal and skim milk. Don't tempt me," Ellis said.

"Okay, but I could really use some help getting these fliers mailed out this morning . . . and I don't even want to tell you about the blueberry pastries she's taking out of the oven."

"Be there in three shakes!" Ellis said. She got there in two.

"I know I've seen this pin somewhere before," Ellis said as they sat at the table after breakfast. "I just wish I could remember where."

"I suppose we need to find out for sure if it belonged to Florence," Lucy said, "but we'd have to involve Leonard."

"Not necessarily." Augusta leaned back in her chair. She had just finished her second cup of coffee and was eyeing the pot as if she considered having a third. "Why not contact that residence where she stayed? Maybe someone there would remember the pin. They might even be willing to let you communicate with Florence's husband through them, since the lawsuit has strained your relationship somewhat."

"What relationship?" Ellis snorted. "But you're right, Augusta. That's the best route to take. I'll phone them today."

"Well, for Pete's sake, don't describe the pin to Leonard," Lucy warned. "That greedy jerk would claim it whether it's hers or not. Just ask him for a description of her jewelry."

And so it was agreed that Ellis would see what she could find out about ownership of the pin as soon as they collected the fliers. "We're missing a link somewhere," Lucy said as they drove to the printer's together. "I'm hoping somebody somewhere will remember Florence's face."

Ellis stared silently out the window. "Are you absolutely sure Florence put that pin in there?" she asked finally.

Lucy frowned. "Who else could it have been?"

Ellis shrugged. "Have you considered that it might have been Nettie? I mean, it did seem to come to her all of a sudden, and she's had ample opportunity to hide it there."

"But why?" The thought hadn't occurred to Lucy. "It doesn't make any sense."

"I know it doesn't. Of course it doesn't! What's wrong with

me?" Ellis's eyes filled with tears and she turned her head away. "Here I go thinking terrible things of old and dear friends because my own life is under a shadow. Just slap me, Lucy Nan!"

"Can it wait? I'm driving right now." Lucy pulled to a stop in the parking lot behind the printer's. "You are coming to the festival tonight?" she asked.

"Have to. Bennett's helping with the stew. He's gone to pick up the shrimp right now."

"Mmm! We'll be there. Save us a place at the table!" Every year the men of the church served Frogmore stew at the harvest festival and Lucy looked forward to the mouth-watering combination of shrimp, kielbasa sausage, corn and potatoes which they sopped up with fresh loaves of crusty bread. Just about everybody in town came, including students and faculty from the college, so people usually ate in shifts.

"Jessica's circle is in charge of the auction, so she's dropping Teddy by the house this afternoon while they get everything together; then later we'll bring him to the festival with us."

Ellis lifted an eyebrow. " 'Us'?"

While they waited for the clerk to bring them the printed fliers, Lucy told Ellis of her plans with Ben.

Ellis laughed. "Good for you! It's time you had a little romance in your life."

Lucy felt her face grow warm. "I don't know. To tell you the truth, I'm kinda dreading tonight, and it's all Augusta's fault. She practically twisted my arm."

Ellis patted the aforementioned limb. "Yeah, right. It must hurt a lot."

Jessica had hardly stepped through the back door that afternoon before Teddy rushed past her to play with Clementine. "Now,

Teddy, don't get so close! It won't bite, will it, Mama Lucy?" Jessica backed away from the puppy's playful advances and put a paper bag on the table. "A change of clothing—just in case," she said.

"He'll probably need it. I thought we'd take Clementine for a run . . . and don't worry, Jessica. She's really a gentle dog. She's just full of herself at this stage."

Jessica nodded. "She certainly has large feet." She gave her son a kiss. "Well, I'd better get out there and start rounding up the treasures."

"Can't you stay for a cup of coffee—I mean, tea? I have some nice herbal mint." Jessica wouldn't drink anything with caffeine in it.

Jessica smoothed back a straying wisp of ash-blond hair and smiled. "I'd really like to, but I have a lot of things to collect, so I guess I'd better get on with it." She wore slim black pants with a white turtleneck sweater, and a long fringed gray-and-black shawl thrown about her shoulders made her look elegant and tall—which, of course, she was. Lucy just wished her daughter-in-law would wear more color and relax more. She was always in such a hurry.

"I suppose Lydia Tillman's donating one of her dolls with the crocheted dresses?" Lucy said.

Jessica made a face. "Of course. Somebody will bid on it. They always do. And Jo Nell's holding a couple of her oil paintings for us."

"Oh dear!" Lucy laughed. Her cousin turned out dreadful paintings year after year to donate to the annual auction. People usually bid generously as the proceeds went to the local care center, then stored the atrocities in the attic. "Don't we have anything *good*?"

"Oh, sure! A beautiful quilt from the sewing circle, hand-smocked dresses for little girls, and a lot of Christmas ornaments. The town merchants have been generous, too. This year we're adding a raffle, so don't forget to buy some tickets. Lollie Pate's giving us that gorgeous soup tureen that's been in her window, and the Tea Room's donating several gift certificates."

Lucy had been eyeing the tureen as a possible Christmas gift for Julie, but it was a little more than she could afford to pay. Maybe I'll get lucky, she thought as she and Teddy ran with the puppy that afternoon in Rutledge Park. It was a golden kind of day, with the crisp scent of leaves and just enough breeze to send them flying. They paused to watch the fish in the lily pond, tried the drinking fountain that seldom worked and were rewarded with a warm, metallic-tasting splash. Lucy listened to Teddy's laughter as he and Clementine rolled and tumbled in masses of autumn color on the grass and chased each other around the monuments in the park. If only Charlie were there beside her, Lucy thought, then smiled. Somehow she felt he was—and he was smiling, too. Watching them, she knew these moments would make an indelible imprint on her heart. All in all it had been a satisfying day. Earlier she and Ellis had faxed the photo of Florence to the bus stations that had fax machines along the route and mailed out fliers to others—including Lucy's former roommate, Nettie's niece and Julie in Georgia.

Before sealing the envelope to her daughter, Lucy had slipped in the final draft of a note written the night before:

My own Julie, although we might not always agree, your friends have always been, and remain, welcome in our home, and I do hope you and Buddy will be able to join us for Thanksgiving. With much love always, Mom.

Now all she could do was wait.

The church fellowship hall was already crowded when they arrived at a little after five that afternoon. Teddy, who hadn't been too sure about the bearded man with the big voice, had gradually warmed to Ben Maxwell's gentle manner and now walked hand in hand with his new friend to try his luck at the ring toss booth while Lucy left her butterscotch brownies for the circle cake walk. After Teddy had had a turn at all the games, had his face painted like a clown, and won a bag of Halloween candy and a noise-maker, they progressed to the display of donations up for auction. Lucy put in a silent bid on a hand-embroidered baby bonnet for a friend's grandchild and a set of Christmas place mats for Ellis, then paid ten dollars for as many raffle tickets on the soup tureen.

"I know I won't have a chance," she whispered to Ben, "but my daughter would love this!" Julie liked anything purple and the tureen had a hand-painted design of pansies in almost every shade of that color. Even the handle on the lid was fashioned like a flower.

In the area set aside for dining she waved at Ellis, who made room for them at her crowded table. Lucy was glad to see Poag Hemphill there with some of the faculty from the college. He ac-knowledged her greeting with a smile, but his eyes lacked their usual keen sparkle. Calpernia's death weighed heavily on him, she thought, although he tried to hide it.

"What's the matter with you, boy? Don't you know what's good?" Ben teased as Teddy, like most children there, chose tomato soup and a peanut butter sandwich over the Frogmore stew. Lucy was surprised when he even persuaded her grandson to taste one of the shrimp.

"I think they're getting ready to draw for the raffle now," Bennett said later, as he collected their plates. Most people had eaten by now and the clean-up crew was busy in the kitchen when Lucy and Ben, herding a tired little boy along with them, hurried to learn who was the winner. Lucy crossed her fingers as their minister, Pete Whit-taker, reached into the basket to draw out the winning number. It wasn't hers.

"Oh, glory!" Opal Henshaw shrieked from the back of the room. "It's mine! I've got the number right here!" And she scurried to collect it.

Lucy turned to Ben and made a face. "Rats!" she said as Opal, resisting offers to help, carried her prize to her car.

"Never mind, Mama Lucy," Teddy said sleepily. "Maybe you'll win something else."

And she did. The second drawing was for a simple ceramic pitcher in silver and bronze from a local craftsman, and Lucy was delighted to claim it. The colors would be perfect in Jessica's dining room if she could just keep it a secret until Christmas. And although she didn't get the place mats, she did put in the highest bid on the baby bonnet, so the evening had been a success in more ways than one.

After turning Teddy over to his parents, Lucy and Ben offered their assistance to the few who remained in the kitchen. Bennett, scrubbing out the last of the huge pots, threw them a couple of dish towels and gratefully accepted. Lucy was sweeping the floor when she heard angry words just beyond the door.

"I can't believe I paid good money for a ticket on a broken tureen!" Opal Henshaw said, "No wonder you donated it, Lollie Pate! The lid has a great big crack in it!"

"Then you must've dropped it," Lollie said. "It wasn't like that when I gave it to them. Just ask Jessica. She's the one who collected it this afternoon. She'll tell you it wasn't broken."

"Well, it's broken now, and I want a replacement," Opal said. "It should be your business to make good on it."

Lollie's voice was low and dull but it had a final edge to it. "I'm sorry, Opal. I can't do that," she said.

"Then I'm sure you know you'll be getting no more business out of me!" the other woman snipped.

Lucy jumped when she heard the outside door slam and laid the broom aside to find Lollie leaning against the wall, her makeup streaked with tears.

"Lollie, are you all right?" Lucy seated her in a chair and Ellis brought a glass of water from the kitchen. "Here, drink up. That was a nasty thing for Opal to say and I hope you'll just consider the source."

Lollie nodded and tried to smile. "It wasn't broken," she said hoarsely.

"Of course it wasn't," Ellis said. "I saw it myself. That idiot probably dropped it in the parking lot."

"I'm sorry this happened, Lollie," Bennett told her. "You were more than generous to let us have it." He helped her get to her feet. "Would you like us to take you home?"

She shook her head. "No, thank you. I have my car."

"Then we'll walk to the parking lot with you," Ben offered.

"Poor Lollie," Lucy said as the four of them stood watching her drive away. "Somebody should swat Opal Henshaw for making her cry like that!"

"Or just on general principles. I'd like to get in line to kick her butt," Ellis whispered to Lucy as they went inside together. "She certainly didn't help matters any, but I noticed Lollie coming out of the ladies' room earlier tonight and I could almost swear she'd been crying."

CHAPTER TWENTY

"Who's not here?" Idonia asked, looking about. "Seems like somebody's missing."

Zee spoke up, raising her coffee cup. "All present and accounted for."

It was Monday morning and The Thursdays sat around Lucy's kitchen table with an account of their findings of the past few days. Ellis, who had been allowed to come since she knew what was going on anyway, grinned at Lucy across the table. Augusta had left the day before for a visit with her former apprentice, Penelope, and The Thursdays, although not aware of the angel's presence, seemed to sense the void.

"All right then, let's get on with it," Lucy said. "Zee, why don't you and Claudia tell us what you found when you showed Florence's photograph in the beauty shops?"

Nettie waved a hand and half-rose from her seat. "Don't you want to tell them about—"

"Later!" Lucy shushed her. "One thing at a time."

"Tell us about what?" Jo Nell wanted to know.

With a nod from Lucy, Zee ignored her and announced in a loud voice their lack of success with the cosmetologists in the area. "Of course we might have missed some, but we covered as many as we could."

"Lucy and I faxed the flier to several of the bus stations and mailed out the rest," Ellis said. "Let's hope something comes of it." She didn't look too hopeful.

"Some little old policeman who looked about twelve years old was over here looking for those rings the other day," Nettie said, "but I don't think he found anything. Florence must've had'em on her when she died."

"If it was Florence," Jo Nell said, shaking her head.

"It was." Ellis spoke softly. "The DNA was a match."

"I knew it! I just knew it!" Jo Nell said. "Imagine finding her way home after all these years just to wind up dead before we had a chance to welcome her back."

"At least she got to sleep in her old room again," Idonia muttered, shaking her head.

"Which leads us to this," Lucy said when the chatter died down. She took the pin she had been guarding all weekend and placed it on the table in front of her. "Nettie and I found this in the closet in the room where Florence had been sleeping. It was hidden in an opening beneath one of the shelves."

"How did you know it was there?" Idonia asked, and Nettie explained about the hiding place. "It was her secret place," she said. "I'd almost forgotten about it."

Claudia held out her hand for the pin. "It's lovely! Where do you suppose she got it?"

"According to the manager of the residence where Florence was staying, it wasn't among her possessions," Ellis told them. "I spoke with her Friday and she called me back last night. They discourage their guests from keeping valuables on the premises, but she spoke with Leonard Fenwick to get an accounting of any jewelry Florence might have had with her. She had some pearl earrings that had belonged to the woman who raised her, some silver and jade bracelets, and a few other things. He said he'd check and see if anything was missing. Her husband has been keeping her engagement and wedding rings in a safety deposit box."

"Did you ask about the rings she wore?" Zee asked, and Ellis nodded. "The woman I spoke with said they probably came from the dollar store," she said. "Florence loved bright trinkets and she usually bought some whenever they went to the mall."

"Well, bless her heart," Nettie said, shaking her head. "Then somebody even went and took those! What kind of lowlife would do such a thing? Looks like they could've seen what kind of shape she was in. Law, she looked a hundred! I never would've recognized her."

"Beats me," Zee said, passing the pin to Idonia. "People parade in and out of that church all the time with enough diamonds to light up the sky. I think that tacky Arabella Morgan would have them set in her teeth if she could figure out how to do it, and nobody's ever been robbed before."

"I don't believe it was a robbery at all," Lucy said. "I think they just took her things to make it look that way. Somebody lured her over there, I'm almost sure of it. They made a lot of noise knocking over my garbage cans out front, and while Nettie and I were out there cleaning it up, somebody telephoned Florence and told her to come to the church parking lot."

"But how would they know she would answer the phone?" Claudia asked.

"I guess they just let it ring," Lucy said. "There's a phone in the hall just outside the door of the room where she was sleeping and she probably got tired of hearing it ring."

"And don't forget, she thought she was in her own house," Ellis said.

"But who would want to kill her?" Jo Nell said. "And why?"

Ellis gave a halfhearted laugh. "Oh, come on! Everybody knows I'm the most obvious suspect."

"And that's exactly why we're here," Lucy said, making a face at her over her coffee cup.

"I'm betting on Leonard," Nettie said. "I hope the police have had the good sense to find out where he was the night Florence was killed."

Ellis shrugged. "They don't confide in me."

Claudia looked thoughtful. "He could've hired somebody to do it. You know, like a hit man or something."

"Now you're really giving me the creeps," Jo Nell said, setting her coffee cup aside. "Idonia, are you going to hold on to that pin all day?" Impatiently, she held out her hand. "Come on, let me have a look at it."

Idonia waved her hand away. "Wait just a minute. I think I've seen this pin before . . . I'm just trying to remember where."

"It looked familiar to me, too," Ellis said, watching Idonia hold the pin to the light.

"Maybe it belonged to Florence's mother or somebody else in your family," Lucy suggested.

"I don't remember Aunt Eva ever wearing it," Ellis said. "She was more into pearls." She frowned. "No, it was somebody else."

Idonia slammed her palm onto the table so hard, everyone jumped. "I know who it was now! This pin belonged to Calpernia Hemphill."

"Calpernia? Are you sure?" Nettie adjusted her glasses and leaned in for a closer look.

"She wore it to that big gala affair the college held back in September. It was a fund-raiser—remember? One of those things where everybody eats standing up. Somebody bumped into me and I spilled chocolate fondue down the front of my new silk dress."

"I knew I'd seen that pin somewhere before!" Ellis said. "You're right, Idonia. She wore it with a tailored, plum-colored dress—crepe, I think. It had a square neckline and the skirt flared out at the knees. I remember thinking how nice it looked on her, and the pin looked like it was made for it."

"Maybe it was," Claudia said. "That's no bargain-basement jewelry, Lucy Nan."

Jo Nell refilled her coffee cup. "Does Poag make that kind of money?"

"I doubt it," Ellis said, "but I think Calpernia had money of her own. The Folly belonged to her, you know."

"So what was Florence doing with it?" Zee asked.

Lucy stirred sugar into her coffee. "The mud that was on her shoes looked like that clay I saw at the Folly. She must've gotten it there."

"What on God's green earth was that poor addled woman doing out at the Folly?" Zee stood so quickly her chair almost tipped over. "And how did she get here?"

"She must have known Calpernia—or met her somehow," Nettie said. "Was she there when Calpernia fell? I just don't see the connection."

"Who knows? Maybe she pushed her." Idonia shoved the pin away from her.

"For heaven's sake, Idonia," Nettie said. "Why would Florence do that? She could hardly have known her."

"It wouldn't take long," Zee said.

Nobody argued with that.

Clementine wandered over to be petted and Lucy scooped the puppy into her lap. "So here I am with somebody's 'hot' jewelry," she said. "What am I supposed to do with it?"

"You could give it to Poag," Idonia said. "After all, it did belong to his wife."

"Are you absolutely sure about that?" Nettie asked.

"Well, I couldn't swear to it. What do you think, Ellis?"

"Has to be hers. There can't be two like that. Maybe we should let the police decide."

Zee began to collect the empty cups and put them in the sink. "Why don't we wait until we hear from Leonard Fenwick? If the pin turned out to belong to Florence we'd feel pretty stupid. When's he supposed to let us know?"

"The woman I spoke with said he promised to get back to her tomorrow," Ellis said, relinquishing her cup, "so I guess we should just hang on to it until then."

Lucy gave the pin a flip with her finger, sending it skidding across the table. "Why don't one of you hang on to it then? Somebody's already been here twice looking for this thing. It must've been what they were after. I don't like having it around."

"But they've already looked here," Claudia said. "They're not going to come back again. This is the safest place to keep it."

"Will you swear to that in blood?" Lucy met her gaze, unsmiling. She didn't blink.

"*What?* Oh, Lucy Nan, you're teasing, aren't you?" Claudia giggled. "Couldn't you just put it back where it was—in the closet, I mean?"

"I'll think of a place," Lucy said, "but if any of you blab one word of this, just remember—I know where you live!"

After everyone left that morning, Lucy wandered from room to room looking for a place to hide the pin and finally fastened it to the underside of the hem of a formal floor-length gown she hadn't worn in over ten years. The big house echoed silence without Augusta in it but she had left behind a message. Lucy laughed when she saw *Dust me!* written on the tabletop in the upstairs hall.

"Bossy!" she called aloud to nobody in particular, but the house was in need of cleaning and she was in need of something to keep her busy. Lucy hadn't realized how deeply Augusta's absence would affect her. She also knew Augusta's visit to her former apprentice couldn't be put off any longer.

"Is something bothering you?" Lucy had asked the night before when she found the angel pacing from one room to another, pausing only long enough to glance now and again out the living room window. Earlier Augusta had painted her toenails a frosty pink, styled her hair in intricate braids that wound like a golden crown around her head, and polished every piece of silverware in the house, including the set with all the little scrolls and curlicues on it Lucy had inherited from Mimmer. "If you're expecting somebody, maybe I should change my clothes," Lucy said.

Augusta didn't sigh but she looked as if she wanted to. "It's Penelope," she said, straightening the mirror over the living room mantel. Lucy smiled, knowing she did it to sneak a glance at her reflection. "It's her first assignment, you see, and I haven't heard a word."

"Are you supposed to? I mean, wouldn't she let you know if she needed help?"

"You would think so," Augusta said. "And I know she's capable, of course, but she's very young . . . and, I hate to say this . . . a little bit awkward."

"I'm sure she's fine," Lucy said. "Didn't you say she'd been assigned to a new baby?"

Augusta smiled. "Yes, a little girl, but she's quite some distance away. I hope she remembers how to get in touch. It's been some time since I spoke with her."

"If you're concerned about Penelope, why don't you go and see her?" Lucy said.

The sun came out in Augusta's face. "I wouldn't be long—no more than a day or so at the most. I just want to be sure everything's all right."

"You don't have to explain to me," Lucy said. "I'm a mother, you know."

"You will be cautious while I'm gone?" Augusta said upon leaving. "You won't go out to that Folly? I feel uneasy about that place."

"I promise. Don't worry, I'll be fine," Lucy said. She had no intention of going to the Folly, yet she had felt restless since Augusta left. This was one of those times when she missed being behind the counter at Bud's Blooms—missed the interchange with customers dropping by, the constantly ringing telephone, and even the bristly observations of Bud himself.

She spent the afternoon cleaning the house. The furniture shone, the bathrooms sparkled and smelled of lemon and pine. Lucy was even considering tackling the refrigerator when the telephone rang.

"This is Estelle Bivens and I was having my hair done at the Total Perfection the other day when some lady came in with a picture—wanted to know if anybody there had seen her. Said it looked like she'd had her hair done recently and thought maybe Maxine or Evelyn might remember her. Maxine does mine," she added. "Been doing it for close to thirty years now."

"That's nice." Lucy waited. She had been acquainted with many Estelles throughout the years and knew she must have something important to say and would eventually get to the point. This Estelle sounded at least seventy, which was about the average age of that establishment's clientele.

"Anyway, she left this number to call if anybody remembered seeing her and I got to thinking—I believe that's the woman who came in my shop not too long ago. Of course I'm not real sure."

Lucy grabbed a pencil. *Easy now, don't get your hopes up!* she told herself. "What kind of shop?" she asked.

"Oh, I do hair, too. Me and my sister Louise. We got a little place in the back of Louise's house on Red Bud Road. Don't do a lot anymore, just a few regulars, and Louise—she ain't well. Her feet's done swolle plumb up on her."

Lucy said she was sorry to hear that. "Do you remember what this woman looked like?" she asked. "The one who came to your shop?"

"She was about my age—maybe younger. Hard to tell. Medium height and gray hair. Wanted a shampoo and set."

"Would you recognize her if you saw the picture again?" Lucy asked.

"I reckon . . . yeah. I'd have to get another look at it."

Lucy glanced at the clock. It was after four. "I can run it by. Tell me how to find your shop on Red Bud Road."

"Oh, I'm not at the shop. Louise has done gone to the doctor in Rock Hill. I'm at home. It's not too far out on Hatley's Mill Road, just past the old Cantrell home place. You'll need to park at the top of the hill, though. My driveway's been a mess since that last rain. Don't want you gettin' stuck. There's a big old cedar tree at the edge of the road. You can't miss it. Just turn in and park in the drive there."

Lucy wrote down the scanty directions, trying to remember how far out the old Cantrell place was. She used to buy produce from the family that lived there but they had moved a few years ago. Maybe Ellis would remember.

"Wanna take a ride with me?" she asked when her friend answered the phone.

"That depends. Where?"

"Out to Hatley's Mill Road to see Estelle."

"Where's Hatley's Mill Road and who's Estelle?" Ellis sounded suspicious.

"It's where Hatley's Mill is—or was, I guess." Lucy told her about the phone call. "You remember the people who lived in the old Cantrell place, Ellis. We used to get cantaloupes there and those wonderful homegrown tomatoes."

"I sure do miss them," Ellis said. "I forgot that was the name of the road. I've got a casserole ready to put in the oven. We won't be gone long, will we?"

"Be back in less than an hour," Lucy promised.

"Why do you think Lollie was crying when you saw her the other night at the festival?" Lucy asked as they drove out of town. "Could Opal Henshaw have said something to her earlier? Opal's had her drawers in a wad, you know, ever since Lollie refused to let her put a poster advertising her bed-and-breakfast in the window of Do-Lollie's."

"She might've, but I doubt it. It was before they had the drawing. Somebody told me Lollie has a disabled daughter in an institution somewhere and I expect the expense of it pushes her to the limit. Plus, I heard they're raising the rent on the building where she has her shop."

Lucy frowned. "That's a shame. She seems to do a good business, but I guess it's hard to stay ahead. And Opal Henshaw should be forced to iron organdy curtains while watching a table tennis tournament and wearing a turtleneck sweater in July!" It was the closest thing to hell she could think of.

"There's the house where we bought the produce," Ellis said after they had driven a few miles. She pointed to a large Victorian with peeling yellow paint just up ahead.

"And here's the big cedar." Lucy slowed and turned into a rutted driveway on the left. "I'm just going to leave the car right here," she said. "Estelle said she doesn't expect anyone else, so it should be okay." The driveway was of red clay with very little gravel and rocks of assorted sizes scattered about the furrows. Scrub pine and underbrush pushed in from either side and a squirrel chattered at them from a hickory where a few lingering golden leaves shivered.

"She's right," Ellis said as they started down the hill. "You wouldn't want to take your chances getting stuck down here."

"I can't see the house," Lucy said, straining to look around the bend. "Must be behind all these trees."

"She said it was at the bottom of the hill, didn't she?" Ellis asked, then screamed.

They turned at the scrunch of tires on the rough roadbed behind them to see Lucy's car hurtling toward them only a few feet away.

"Jump!" Ellis yelled. "It's gaining speed!"

Lucy stared at the car she had left at the top of the hill, now throwing small rocks, bumping over trenches as it sped closer. She could almost reach out and touch it. Her feet had turned to stone.

"*Move it!*" Ellis yelled again, and pulled her into the ditch as the car plunged past.

Chapter Twenty-one

Lucy came up with a handful of mud and a mouthful of leaves in time to watch her car plow through a fair-sized holly bush and come to a stop in a clump of cedars. Beside her Ellis knelt in the underbrush and plucked blackberry briars from her hair.

"Are you all right?" Lucy stood on wobbly legs and reached out to Ellis with a clay-smeared hand.

"Just hunky-dory. And you?" Ellis spit dirt and began to crawl up the slippery bank, grabbing a clump of weeds for support.

Lucy gave her a shove from behind. "I'm alive . . . I think, thanks to you." She looked at her mud-caked knees, the bleeding scratches on her hands. Her forehead hurt where she had landed in the ditch but everything seemed to work okay. "I don't think anything's broken."

Ellis reached down and gave her a hand up. "Me either. I guess we're lucky." She looked down at a rip in the knee of her jeans where blood was beginning to seep through. Twigs and leaves clung to her soiled jacket. "Can you say *emergency brake?*" she asked as they dusted each other off.

"But I did! I could swear I did. And I left it in park." Lucy looked about her and shivered. Her clothes were damp and muddy and Ellis was limping from the injury to her knee. She couldn't see the main road from here—just a tangle of undergrowth and scrub pine. Even the squirrel had disappeared. "I don't even like to think what would have happened if you hadn't snatched me into that ditch," she said. "My brain wanted me to get out of the way, but my feet weren't listening."

"I noticed." Ellis smiled then. "We must look like scarecrows."

Lucy took her arm. "We need to get warm and call for help. Let's walk on down to Estelle's and use her phone, and we ought to take a look at your knee. Maybe she'll even give us a cup of coffee or something."

"Right now I could use something stronger," Ellis said, "But I'd settle for coffee."

Walking arm in arm, with Ellis favoring her left leg, they stumbled down the gully-washed roadbed trying to avoid the deepest crevices. "How in the world does this woman drive on this thing?" Ellis asked. "She must drive a tank."

"Maybe she doesn't drive." Lucy paused to maneuver around a mud hole. "We're almost there. I think I see the house through the trees."

"This can't be it," Ellis said as they rounded the last curve. "Lucy Nan, nobody's lived in this place for years."

The house—or what was left of the house that greeted them—was entwined in at least a decade's growth of honeysuckle vines whose now-brown tendrils wrapped it from tumbling chimney to gaping windows. The roof of the porch had long since caved in from rot and the weight of debris collected there and a small tree sprouted in the empty doorway.

What else could go wrong? Lucy wanted to sit right there in the weed-choked yard and cry. Instead she laughed. "I don't believe Estelle's at home," she said.

"It's not funny!" Ellis grabbed her arm and started back the way they had come. "Something's wrong! This place gives me the creeps."

"But I followed her directions. It was the driveway next to the big cedar just past the old Cantrell house. Did you see any other big cedars?" Lucy had a stitch in her side, but Ellis wouldn't stop.

"Did you get her number?" Ellis asked. "Maybe later, *if we ever get home*, you can call and find out what went wrong."

"I wrote it down. It's in the car." Lucy started to run. "And so is my cell phone!"

The smell of crushed pine and cedar was a refreshing change from the dank odor of sludge and decaying leaves that had surrounded the abandoned shack and Lucy was relieved to find that other than a few minor scratches and a broken headlight, the car was relatively undamaged. Pushing aside overhanging branches, she managed to open the door on the passenger's side and get the cell phone out of the glove compartment. Ellis, tramping through behind her, wrenched open the opposite door and jammed on the emergency brake.

"I thought you said you left this on," she said.

"I did!" Lucy shook her head. "I must be going crazy."

"Lucy Nan, the gear shift's in drive!" Ellis drew in her breath. "Let's get out of here!"

"Wait, it could've slipped. Just let me call the garage. I'm afraid to try and back this thing out of here."

"Are you kidding? Somebody's trying to kill us. Phone them from the road." Ellis reached for the phone. "Here, let me have that. I'm calling Bennett."

Lucy shivered as they made their way up the hill. It was getting darker and a chill wind rattled the remaining dry leaves on the trees. She paused once to look behind them, dreading to see some dark, threatening shape emerge from the woods, but Ellis urged her on. Bennett was on his way and Lucy had given Ralph Sloan at Super Service directions and left the key under the floor mat.

"What makes you think somebody let the brake off?" Lucy asked as they neared the top of the hill.

"There are too many weird things going on around here lately, in case you haven't noticed. Plus, I thought I heard a car scratch off somewhere close by as we started down the driveway, but I didn't think much about it at the time," Ellis said, scanning the deserted road ahead of them. "There's another house just a little farther down the road and I thought it was probably coming from there."

"If I'd locked the car, this wouldn't have happened. I was in such a hurry to see if this woman recognized Florence's picture."

"You need to get in the habit. You forget to do it half the time—and everybody knows it." Ellis grabbed Lucy's arm and started across the road. "Let's get away from here. I told Bennett we'd wait for him at the Cantrell place."

"Until recently I've always felt safe in my own hometown," Lucy said. "I never used to lock my car in Stone's Throw."

"We're not in Kansas anymore, Toto," Ellis said. "Your car was rolling down that hill at a pretty fast clip. I think somebody gave it a shove."

"There should be tire tracks then." Lucy looked over her shoulder. "Did you think to look?"

Ellis nodded. "Didn't see any. They must've parked on the grass.

"But nobody knew we were coming here—"

"Except Estelle," Ellis said.

No one appeared to be at home at the old Cantrell place, but there was a produce stand near the road that was in use during the summer months that would keep them out of the wind. Lucy found a couple of crates inside and made Ellis sit while she looked at her knee.

"It's a pretty bad gash and it has a lot of dirt in it. You must've hit a rock." She'd been carrying wet wipes in her handbag since Teddy was born and used some to clean around the area. "You'll probably need stitches in this, Ellis. We'll need to go straight to the emergency room."

"Oh, goody! You just want an excuse to postpone calling Roger."

"Who said I was going to call Roger?" Lucy took the phone from her purse and punched in the number the woman had given her.

Ellis frowned, searching the road for Bennett's car. "Who are you calling, then?"

"I'm going to find out right now about this mysterious Estelle," Lucy said, then snapped the cell phone shut and dropped down on the crate beside Ellis.

"What happened? Lucy Nan, if you didn't have mud all over your face, you'd be as white as a ghost. Did anybody answer?"

"Yeah. Evans and Sons Funeral Home." Lucy felt cold through and through. She didn't think she would ever get warm. "Why would somebody want to kill us, Ellis?"

"Are you sure you dialed the right number? Here, let me try." Ellis took the phone and tried again.

"Well?" Lucy asked and her friend gave her back the cell phone without a word.

"Somebody thinks we're getting too close to the truth," Ellis said, hugging herself for warmth. She made a face. "And where's Augusta when we need her? Some guardian angel she turned out to be!"

Lucy had been thinking the same thing, yet she had been the one who suggested Augusta take some time off. "I think you must've been filling in for her today," she said. "Besides, we're *here*, aren't we?" She jumped up as she saw Bennett's car slowing. "And here's your hubby!" She had never been so glad to see any-body in her life.

"You're staying with us tonight, Mom, and that's that." Roger stood in the doorway of the den as if blocking her way. Lucy started to sit, and then thought better of it. If she sat, then Roger would sit, too. It had been like that since he arrived an hour before: When she went into the kitchen, he followed; when she opened the pantry door for a can of soup for supper, he was right behind her, no more than a foot away. A shadow. She worried that he might even try to follow her into the bathroom while she showered and changed. Instead he had stationed himself outside the door.

"What in the world were you and Aunt Ellis doing out there in the middle of nowhere?" Now her son rubbed his forehead and gazed at her with a deeply aggrieved expression, and he did it quite well, Lucy thought. She remembered all the times she had done the same to him. It hadn't worked then and it wasn't working now.

"I've explained the best I can, Roger. And I'll be fine here, really." She glanced at Augusta, who stood by the window looking almost as injured as Roger. The angel had been waiting when Bennett brought her home and had looked on with a bewildered expression while Ellis's husband checked the house before leaving. Although Lucy had tried to downplay the danger while filling her in on what happened, she could tell Augusta was distressed. She had never seen her as subdued.

"Let the police do the investigating," Roger said for about the fifth time. "This is not your business, Mother." He stirred restlessly. "Now, where's your overnight bag? Let's get some things together and go."

So it's *Mother* now, Lucy thought, and it certainly was her business, but her son's patience was wearing thin. And so was hers, but it wasn't worth the hassle. *"All right!"* she said. "Just for tonight." Across the room Augusta nodded with a slight smile and

Lucy knew Clementine would be in good hands while she was gone.

"What happened to that woman who's supposed to be living here?" Roger asked as Lucy threw a few essentials into a bag. "Why is it I never see her?"

"She's rather shy, and of course she travels quite a bit."

Roger muttered something that Lucy couldn't understand, but the very tone of it sent angry darts of frustration smack into the bubble of pent-up emotion that had been building up for so long, and Lucy Nan Pilgrim sat on her bed and cried. She cried until she was good and ready to stop. And then she did.

"Mom, I'm sorry. You know I worry because I love you." Roger knelt beside her, his arms around her, and now and then he patted her shoulder with a clumsy masculine hand. "I didn't mean to make you cry."

Lucy kissed his cheek and reached for the tissues. "It's all right. I'm okay now." Then she noticed that Roger had tears in his eyes, too, and it almost made her weepy all over again.

Earlier she had asked Bennett not to phone Roger. "I'll tell him tomorrow—I promise," she said, but Bennett would hear none of it. Fortunately, Lucy got a brief reprieve as no one had been at home when he first called. He had also telephoned the police from the emergency room where Ellis was having her knee treated, and Elmer Harris, the chief himself, had met them there to get a report of what happened on Hatley's Mill Road.

"You've been through a lot," Roger was now saying, "and I've been so busy at the college, I'm afraid I haven't been around much lately." He grinned. "Hey, you know that soup you ate isn't going to hold you long. Why don't we stop on the way to our place for a couple of burgers and shakes?"

Lucy said that sounded good to her, knowing full well her son would grab any opportunity to eat junk food when Jessica wasn't around.

"Maybe Julie could come for a few days," Roger mused later as they waited for their order. "We haven't seen much of her lately and I think it would do you both good."

"I'd rather you didn't tell Julie about this just yet," Lucy said.

Of course then he wanted to know why and she struggled to explain. "Your sister hasn't been too keen on me since I criticized her choice of boyfriends," she said.

"Oh, that guy? What's his name? Buddy . . . something? He's a jerk! I can't imagine what she sees in him, but she'll outgrow him, Mom. Just give her time."

"I wish she'd hurry," Lucy said.

Now Roger turned to her. "But that's no excuse for keeping her in the dark about what's been going on around here. She's your daughter and a grown woman now. You shelter her too much."

Lucy started to argue with him until she realized he was telling the truth. "It's just that I'd rather have her come home because she wants to rather than because she has to," she said. "And she did say she'd try to be here for Thanksgiving if she can get off. The three of you will be coming, won't you?"

He winked at her. "Are you kidding? I love my wife, but I draw the line at tofu turkey. Of course we'll be there, Mom!"

"What's this I hear about you and Ellis competing in the fifty-yard dash out on Hatley's Mill Road?" Ben Maxwell stood at her door the next morning with a basket of apples and a potted plant. "Christmas cactus," he said, thrusting it into her hands. "They didn't have a wide selection at the grocery store."

"Thanks. I'll look forward to seeing it bloom." Lucy stepped back to let him inside. "And why is it that everybody in town seems to know what happened to us in less than twenty-four hours?"

He set the basket on the kitchen table and looked forlorn. "I'm not everybody in town," he said. "Am I?"

She kissed his cheek which, she noticed, smelled of some sort of spicy soap. "Of course you aren't. I was going to call you this morning anyway."

His eyes brightened. "Is that right?"

"Right. I wanted to invite you to supper tonight."

"Here, you mean?"

"Exactly. A very informal affair. I'm making a big pot of soup, cornbread and a sweet potato pie. What do you say?"

He laughed. "I say just try and keep me away! What can I bring?"

"Just bring yourself. You wouldn't let me help with the picnic at King's Mountain Sunday, remember? Now it's my time."

"Oh, and there's something else I wanted to mention," he said as she walked with him to the door. "You know Patsy Sellers, the young lady who handles the public relations at Bellawood, is expecting a baby in a few weeks?"

Lucy smiled. "Yes, I hope she's doing all right."

"Fine as far as I know, but she asked me to give you a message. Seems they've been having trouble finding someone to fill her position and she thought you might be interested in helping out a few days a week until they can hire someone full-time."

"Really? I did have some experience in that line when Charlie and I were first married, but it's been a long time. I doubt if I'd be of much help."

Her hand seemed lost in his large callused one, but his grip was gentle as he said good-bye. "You might be surprised," he said. "And you did say you'd been kind of at loose ends lately. Just think about it."

She didn't have time to think long because Chief Harris called just then to tell her they had traced the call she'd received from "Estelle" to a public phone booth in the next town.

"I don't suppose you found any tire tracks, either?" Lucy asked.

"If somebody was out there, they parked on the grass verge," he said. "Our men couldn't find any signs of another car."

If? If somebody was out there? Lucy's hand trembled as she hung up the phone. Did the fool man think she and Ellis made the whole thing up? And what about the fake phone call? She could hardly call herself from another town!

Lucy stood by the telephone trying to calm herself before she spoke with Ellis. Her head felt as if it was about to explode. She wondered if the police had told Ellis the same thing.

"Think blue," Augusta said, suddenly standing beside her, and the touch of her hand made Lucy think of summer, a field of daisies ruffling in a light breeze. "What?" she said.

"Close your eyes, take deep breaths and think blue," Augusta said. "It will calm you, add years to your life."

"The police chief doesn't believe us," Lucy said, but she did as the angel directed.

"Then the police chief must be a donkey," Augusta said in that same quiet tone.

"You mean an ass?" Lucy smiled.

"Aren't they the same thing?"

"Not quite," Lucy said.

She was laughing when the telephone rang again.

"I'm calling from Asheville," a woman's voice said. "I saw that woman's picture in the bus station here and I think I sat across from her on the bus not long ago."

"Who is this?" Lucy demanded. She wasn't about to get roped into that little game again.

"This is Juanita Grimble. I work in the Pancake Palace up here and I'm on my break right now. I wonder if you could call me back 'cause this is costing me money."

"Just let me get a pencil" Lucy said. And this time she would get in touch with her roommate as well to see if Juanita Grimble and the Pancake Palace really existed.

CHAPTER TWENTY-TWO

"Well, you can leave me out!" Ellis said. "I can't believe you're going on another wild-goose chase, and all the way to Asheville at that. This time somebody might try to run you down with an eighteen-wheeler on one of those mountain roads up there. And what if this Juanita Grimble turns out to be another Estelle?"

"But she isn't. I called my old roommate. You remember Stella? She was in our wedding. Anyway, she was the one who posted the fliers up there, and the Pancake Palace isn't too far from where she works, so she went there for lunch today and actually *met* this person. She's real, all right. And Augusta's going with me, so I think I'll be okay." Lucy laughed. "After what happened yesterday, she's sticking closer to me than white on rice."

"I don't know, Lucy Nan. I think you're taking a chance. I wish you wouldn't go."

"With all the weird things going on around here, I'll probably be safer up there, and I can't wait to hear what this woman has to say," Lucy said.

Ellis sighed. "Why can't you talk to her over the phone?"

"You know good and well it wouldn't be the same. Maybe this

waitress overheard something, and I want to see if I can find out who Florence sat with, and where she got off the bus. A seventy-year-old woman looking for her mother isn't your run-of-the-mill passenger, Ellis. She must've called attention to herself."

"I guess I should be going with you, except it's been suggested I'm not to leave the county," Ellis said. "You will be careful, won't you?"

"I'll call you when I get back. Ralph said he'd have my car ready early tomorrow, so we'll probably leave soon after breakfast. I wish you could go with us, too, but I don't want the police on my tail," Lucy said. "I think they believe we made up that story about some-body letting the brake off the car." She told Ellis what the chief had said.

"Asshole!" Ellis muttered.

"Augusta says he must be a donkey. By the way, how's your knee?"

"Hurts like the devil but at least I have an excuse not to cook for a while," Ellis said. "And, oh—I almost forgot to tell you I discovered a call on my answering machine this morning from Velda Craig, the lady at the assisted living residence in Illinois. She said Leonard Fenwick has given her a list of his wife's jew-elry. There's nothing on there that fits the description of the pin you found."

"I'm not surprised. As much as I dislike dealing with our doo-fus police chief, I guess I'll have to turn it over to the police, but they'll have to wait until I get back from Asheville. This after-noon I'm cooking supper for Ben."

"Aha! How cozy! First dinner and a concert, then a picnic, and now this! And does Ben know what you plan for tomorrow?"

"No, and I'm not telling him. The fewer people who know about this, the better, so keep it under your hat, okay?"

"My lips are sealed," Ellis said. "Just promise you won't park on a hill!"

That, Lucy discovered would be difficult to do, as there weren't too many level places in Asheville, North Carolina.

It was almost nine-thirty when Ralph brought her car around that morning, so it was close to one o'clock when they stopped at a barbecue place outside of Hendersonville for lunch. Earlier, Lucy had told Roger she would be spending the afternoon with Stella, which was partially true since she planned to drop in on her former roommate while she was in Asheville, and her son had promised to bring Teddy by that afternoon to take Clementine for a run.

"You didn't forget the Brunswick stew, did you?" Augusta asked as Lucy returned to the car after picking up their take-out order.

"Barbecued pork with slaw, Brunswick stew and sweet tea," Lucy said, putting the paper bag containing their meal on the seat beside her.

"Umm!" Augusta peeked inside and sniffed. "A little bit of heaven right here on earth."

"Amen!" Lucy said, laughing. "And speaking of heaven, how was your visit with Penelope? I'll bet she was glad to see you."

Augusta was silent for a minute. "She was of course, and it was wonderful to spend some time with her . . . "

Lucy frowned. "But . . . ?"

"But I needn't have been concerned at all. Turns out she was doing just fine without me."

Lucy laughed. "Welcome to the club, Augusta!"

They found a quiet place to eat on some large rocks beside a clear shallow stream rushing its way through the Blue Ridge Mountains. The rock was warm from the sun and red leaves from a large scarlet oak seesawed from the branches overhead and were carried away by the swirling water. The lulling splash of the stream almost made Lucy forget why they had come.

Augusta spooned up the last of her stew and put the empty

container into the paper bag. "How was your supper last night?" she asked, tossing an acorn into the water.

Lucy smiled. "You should know. You ate some."

"That's not exactly what I meant. How did you enjoy your evening with your guest?"

"You should know that, too," Lucy said. "I saw you lurking on the stairs."

"Angels don't lurk." Augusta rattled her necklace. "I was merely checking the thermostat. It gets a bit warm up there."

"Uh-huh." Lucy concentrated on her barbecue.

"Your privacy was my utmost priority." Augusta's tone bordered on haughty. "If you remember correctly, I made a point to retire to my room soon after you greeted your visitor."

"I know you did, but it wasn't necessary." Lucy laughed. "Hang around as long as you like. It wouldn't bother me."

"It should." Augusta looked at her over her tea.

"What do you mean?"

"Being a chaperone isn't in my job description," Augusta told her. "I don't interfere in affairs of the heart."

Lucy crammed a wad of paper napkins into the bag. "You're being silly."

Now it was the angel's turn to smile. "Just think about it," she said.

"Give me a break!" Lucy said. But she did think about it. She thought about what Augusta had said as they wound their way up I-26 after leaving Hendersonville. Was she using the angel's presence as a buffer to keep from getting too intimate with Ben? She had enjoyed being with him the night before and felt relaxed in his company. In spite of what Ellis had said about Ben's being quiet, Lucy found him to be a good conversationalist and she delighted especially in his dry sense of humor. After supper he had insisted on helping her with the dishes, and they had taken their pie into the small sitting room where they ate it by the fire. Later, Lucy was glad when he suggested a game of checkers, during which the two of them sometimes didn't speak at all, but played in companionable silence. And when he kissed her good night on leaving, she found herself wanting him to kiss her again.

"This woman who called. Is she expecting you?" Augusta asked as they neared the outskirts of Asheville.

"I spoke with her yesterday and we're to meet at the restaurant. She gets off today at three, so we should be just in time."

The Pancake Palace was on the corner of a busy side street and Lucy glanced at the time as she pulled into the parking lot beside it. She had ten minutes to spare. The small restaurant had a sweet, heavy smell, but the white tile floor looked clean and the dark-stained booths lent an air of privacy. There weren't many customers inside and she had no trouble finding an empty booth near the back. The waitress who took her order looked as if she frequently sampled the fare on the menu and she didn't seem happy about having to move from behind the counter to wait on Lucy.

"Whadlyahav?" she mumbled, taking a pad from her pocket.

Lucy smiled. Maybe the woman's feet hurt. "Just a piece of your apple pie and coffee," she said, noticing the name on her uniform: *Gretchen*. She was relieved to see this was not the person she had spoken with on the phone. "I'm to meet Juanita Grimble here when she gets off from work," Lucy told her. "I hope I'm not too late."

"That's her at the cash register," Gretchen said, sighing. "She'll be through in a minute. I'll tell her you're here."

The pie was hot with a tender, flaky crust and tasted of cinnamon and nutmeg. As she ate it, Lucy noticed Augusta eyeing her with a longing expression on her face from the booth across from her. "I'll have another piece to go," she called to Gretchen and was immediately rewarded with an angelic smile.

She was sipping her coffee when the woman slipped into the seat across from her. "You must be Mrs. Pilgrim," she said, holding out her hand. "I'm Juanita Grimble." She looked to be in her mid-thirties and was small—about the same size as her Julie, Lucy thought, with dark curls framing a face that would've been plain if it weren't for her large, expressive brown eyes. Juanita pulled off her apron as she spoke. "I'm afraid I don't have much time. I have to pick up my little boy at day care in about thirty minutes."

Lucy introduced herself. "Would you like something to eat? Coffee?"

"No, thanks!" Juanita laughed. "I've already had so much, I slosh!"

"I know you're wondering what this is all about," Lucy began, and explained as best she could about the elderly woman who had come to her door.

Juanita's large eyes grew even larger. "My gosh, that's like something you'd see in the movies!" she said. She frowned as she examined the photograph Lucy had brought. "Yes, that's the one all right. She sat across from me when I went to see my mother in Greenwood. I remember her because she sort of reminded me of my grandmama—only she kept messing with her purse—opening it and closing it all the time, and she hummed a lot."

"Hummed?"

Juanita nodded. "Yeah. You know, that tuneless kind of humming. I don't think she knew she was doing it."

"Was anyone with her?"

"No. She sat by herself at first, and then this lady who got on when I did moved up into the seat beside her."

"Do you think they knew each other?" Lucy asked, and Juanita shook her head. "I'm pretty sure they didn't. In fact, I wondered why she did that because there were plenty of empty seats. She could've had a whole one to herself." She smiled. "I remember thinking I was glad she didn't sit next to me."

"We're trying to find out where she went before she arrived at my door," Lucy told her. "Do you remember where she got off?"

"Sure do. Got off in Greenville with that woman who was sitting with her. They both must've had tickets to go farther because when the driver got back on the bus after we stopped there, he asked if anybody knew where they were." Juanita leaned forward and frowned. "Oh, lordy, I have a terrible feeling something bad happened to that poor woman! Tell me I'm wrong."

"I wish I could," Lucy said. The young woman's eyes filled with tears when she told her what had happened to Florence.

"Why, I read about her in the paper! There was something on television, too. And to think I sat right there across from her. Bless her heart, I feel just awful about that!"

"I doubt if you could have done anything," Lucy said. "There's no way you could have known.

"This woman she got off with," she continued, "did you say she got on when you did?"

"That's right. Got on here in Asheville. Bought her ticket the same time I did. Had a bunch of packages. I heard her tell the man at the counter her car had broken down."

Lucy glanced at Augusta, who was practically hanging out of her seat. "Do you remember what she looked like?" she asked.

Juanita drummed her fingers on the red Formica table. "Early fifties, I'd say, and you could tell she used to be pretty. Well-dressed, and had her hair done just so."

"Was she tall? Short?" Lucy tried to picture the person she was describing.

"Sort of medium, I guess, and maybe a little on the plump side."

"Did you happen to hear her name? She must've introduced herself."

Juanita stared at her hands, turned her wedding ring on her finger. "Seems she did, but for the life of me, I can't remember it."

"Could you hear what she said? Anything at all?" Lucy asked.

"The old woman—the one you call Florence—well, she didn't do much talking, and she spoke so low I couldn't hear her. Seems like the other one yakked nonstop."

"About what?"

"Questions, mostly. She was asking that old woman all kinds of questions—things like where was she from, and where was she going, and did she have any family . . . that kind of thing."

"And did she get any answers?" Lucy asked.

"Some. I couldn't hear them, though. But I could tell the poor thing was addled. I doubted if she knew the answers herself." Juanita looked at her watch. "Sorry, but I really have to go. Eddie gets upset if I'm late. Hope I've helped a little."

"You've been a tremendous help! I can't thank you enough." Lucy opened her purse to offer a few bills, but Juanita put out a hand to stop her. "Don't you worry about that," she said. "I just hope you find the person who did that to that poor old soul."

"I hope so, too, and I'll be sure to let you know," Lucy told her. "Oh, and one more thing . . . Was the older woman—Florence— wearing much makeup? Do you remember if she looked like she'd just had her hair done?"

Juanita had stood to go, but now she hesitated. "Heaven's no!" she said, shaking her head. "She might have worn a little smear of lipstick, but her hair looked like a rat's nest. I don't think she'd combed it since she left home."

Lucy wrote her phone number on a paper napkin. "If you happen to remember that woman's name, please give me a call— even if it's in the middle of the night!"

"That was enlightening," Augusta said when they got back in the car. "Did her description help at all?"

Lucy nibbled a fingernail as she waited to merge into traffic. "I don't know. I'm so confused, I really don't know what to think. I keep trying to imagine what this woman looked like, and it's making my head spin."

"Then I don't think you should be driving." Augusta darted a look at the four-o'clock traffic.

"Don't worry. I don't mean it literally," Lucy told her. "It's just that . . . well, I don't like what I'm thinking, Augusta."

"And what are you thinking?"

"I believe I know who got off the bus with Florence in Greenville," Lucy said. "But for the life of me, I can't imagine why."

Lucy had phoned her roommate when she left the Pancake Palace and the two met for a brief visit at the insurance firm where Stella worked.

"So tell me about your meeting," Stella whispered, closing the door to her office. "Did you find out anything new?"

Lucy told her about her conversation with Juanita Grimble, but she didn't tell her old friend what she suspected. She had trouble believing it herself. "I believe we're a little closer," she said, "and if you hadn't helped me out by circulating those fliers I sent, we'd still be back at square one."

Stella wove a pencil through her fingers and smiled. "I know you, Lucy Nan Pilgrim. You're holding something back. Come on, give!"

Lucy shrugged. "I can't promise you'll be the first to know, but you're somewhere near the top of the list."

It was well after dark when they finally reached home and the telephone was ringing as they walked into the house. Probably Roger or Ellis wondering where I am, Lucy thought, hurrying to snatch the receiver. "It's okay, I'm home!" she said breathlessly.

"Mrs. Pilgrim, it's me, Juanita," the voice answered. "You wanted me to call when I thought of that woman's name, and it just came to me all of a sudden like. I think her name was Lottie or Laurie. It sounded something like that."

"Could it have been Lollie?" Lucy held her breath.

"*Yes!* She said her name was Lollie. I'm almost sure that's what it was."

CHAPTER TWENTY-THREE

"I don't believe it," Ellis said when Lucy called a few minutes later.

"Ellis, who else could it be? I suspected Lollie from Juanita's description of her even before she thought of the name—but why? What did she want with Florence?"

"From what you've told me, it's obvious Lollie was using her for some reason—don't ask me what! Surely she could see the poor thing was suffering from dementia, yet she made a point to befriend her on the bus and then whisked her off before they even got to Stone's Throw."

"That's the only part I do understand," Lucy said. Naturally Lollie wouldn't want anyone to see her get off the bus with Florence here where everybody knows her."

"So how *did* they get here?"

"Rented a car, I guess. It would be easy enough to check."

"Do you think Lollie knew who Florence really was?" Ellis asked.

"I don't think so. I doubt if Lollie Pate had ever heard of Florence until now. She hasn't lived here but—what? About ten or twelve years. Most people wouldn't know about Florence's disappearance unless their families were here when it happened."

"Maybe she wanted to set her up to steal that pin of Calpernia's," Ellis suggested.

"Get real! It looks like an expensive piece of jewelry, but it's not worth killing for . . . " Lucy paused. "Ellis, I just had the most horrible thought! What if Lollie bribed Florence with that pin in exchange for pushing Calpernia from the Folly?"

"Why would Lollie want her to do that?" Ellis asked.

"Beats me. I've had a headache all afternoon just thinking about it." As she talked, Lucy walked through the house switching on lights, with Clementine frolicking along behind. Augusta stood at the living room window looking out at the dark street and it made her feel better just seeing her there.

She told Ellis what Juanita had said about the condition of Florence's hair.

"Lollie must have been the one who gave her the makeover. That would be right up her alley. I've never seen her that she didn't look like she just stepped out of a bandbox, and I know she styles her own hair." Ellis let out a long breath and groaned. "Damn it, Lucy Nan; do you think she was the one who tried to run us down?"

"I don't know what to think. What should we do, Ellis?"

"I don't know, but I'm scared. What does Augusta say?"

"She thinks we need to talk to the police," Lucy said, glancing at Augusta.

"She's right. This is getting too big for us. Bennett's at a meeting, but he should be here any minute. Let's see what he thinks . . . you do have your doors locked, don't you?"

"Of course. Do you?"

"Double-locked. I think I hear Bennett now. I'll call you back in a few minutes."

"Do you remember that afternoon The Thursdays met here a few days after Florence was killed?" Lucy asked Augusta as she waited for Ellis's call.

Augusta smiled. "Of course. I knew your friend Ellis could see me and that she was having trouble understanding why no one acknowledged my presence."

"After everyone left that day, I discovered that somebody had searched Julie's room, but I never could figure out who it was . . . "

Augusta nodded. "Lollie Pate, of course! She delivered the tarts."

"I completely forgot about Lollie," Lucy said. "I was busy getting ready for the meeting and I didn't see her out. She must have slipped upstairs while I was in the shower."

"She was looking for the pin but she didn't have time to be thorough, so she—or someone—came back while we were at Bellawood with Teddy's class." Augusta stood with her back against the dark window, her upswept hair luminescent around her face. The stones on her necklace, a deep violet now, trailed through her fingers. "It seems, though, that you or someone would have noticed her van in your driveway."

"Not if she parked it on the street," Lucy said. "She does that sometimes if she has to make more than one delivery." She yawned as she glanced at the grandfather clock in the corner. "It's almost ten, Augusta. I wish Ellis would hurry and call. I feel like I've been awake for a week!"

"I'll put on some coffee and there're spice cookies in the jar," Augusta said. "I imagine the others would like some as well."

Lucy had opened her mouth to ask her what others when Ellis phoned to tell her she and Bennett were on their way over. "Bennett thinks you should call the police," Ellis said.

"You mean *tonight?*"

Bennett Saxon had obviously overheard her because he answered, "Yesterday wouldn't have been soon enough!"

"I understand you circulated fliers with Florence Calhoun's photograph." Ed Tillman sat across from Lucy at the kitchen table where, as a boy, he had scarfed down many an after-school snack. Now and then he took a swallow of coffee, so far ignoring the plate of cookies.

Lucy nodded, looking from Ed to his partner, Sheila Eastwood, who sat beside him, notepad in hand. "That's right. We were trying to find someone who might have seen her before she came here."

"And we did." Ellis reached for a second cookie and smiled smugly.

"This woman who phoned you"—Sheila glanced at her notes—"calls herself Juanita Grimble?"

"Because she *is* Juanita Grimble!" Lucy shoved a piece of paper across to them. "You can talk to her yourself. Here's her phone number." She told them about her meeting with the waitress in Asheville. "She remembered Florence as a passenger on a bus trip she took a few weeks ago. It was right before Florence showed up here."

"Only, Florence got off the bus with another passenger in Greenville," Ellis told them.

"And that passenger was Lollie Pate." Lucy watched Ed's face for a reaction.

The young policeman smiled. "You mean she looked like Lollie Pate?"

Lucy shrugged. "From the description Juanita gave me, it was either Lollie or her twin—*and* she overheard the woman introduce herself to Florence as either Lottie or Lollie."

Ed glanced at his partner. "But she wasn't sure?" he asked. He might as well have had DOUBT stamped across his face in big red letters, Lucy thought.

"What would Lollie Pate be doing on a bus in . . . where was it you said?" Sheila frowned.

"Asheville." Lucy frowned back. "And I don't know. That's your job, isn't it?"

"I think I know what she was doing," Ellis chimed in. "She went up there on a buying trip for the gift shop—remember? She told me later the transmission went out on her car and she had to come home in a rental."

"So what was she doing on a bus?" Ed asked.

"I don't know unless she started out that way," Lucy said. "I know Lollie's a little short on money and it would have been less expensive, or maybe she couldn't find a rental car in Asheville." She told them what Juanita had said about Lollie's befriending Florence before getting off the bus together in Greenville. "And apparently both of them had tickets for another destination because the bus driver didn't seem to be aware they weren't going to continue the trip."

Sheila helped herself to a cookie and looked as if she wanted to dip it into her coffee, then apparently thought better of it. "But Lollie Pate wouldn't even have known this Florence. It just doesn't make sense."

Bennett spoke up. "Then I suggest you get Juanita Grimble on the phone and hear what she has to say," he told her. "This has gone on long enough!"

"Don't think Ellis and I aren't aware that some of the people in your department believe we *imagined* that incident with my brakes," Lucy said. She rose to pour more coffee and hesitated with the pot in her hand. "Well, we didn't imagine it and I didn't imagine the woman who phoned me and lured us there, either. Somebody doesn't seem to like our asking questions, and it would be helpful if we could at least have the support of our local police." Steam rose as she poured the hot liquid into Bennett's cup, but Lucy couldn't be sure if it was coming from her or the coffeepot.

Ed Tillman seemed to be studying the design on his coffee mug. It had once held Halloween candy and said *Boo brew for you!* in ghostly letters. "Well, you have it now," he said, standing. "If you'll let me have that number," he said to Sheila, "I'll give Juanita Grimble a call."

"By the way, the clay on those shoes that woman left here turned out to be the same kind as the sample you took from the Folly," Sheila said as Ed used his cell phone to call Asheville. "We even sent somebody out there to check out the place it came from. Looks almost like modeling clay, doesn't it? Peculiar color."

Lucy yawned, nodding. It was a few minutes past eleven o'clock and she was sure Ed's call would get Juanita Grimble out of bed. If the waitress was as tired as she was, Juanita wasn't going to be happy about it. Right now all Lucy wanted to do was close her eyes and fall into bed.

She was close to going to sleep right there at the table when Ed finally got off the phone. "Well, she tells it pretty much the same way you do," he said, reaching for a couple of Augusta's spice cookies. "I'll have to admit, this woman who got off the bus with Florence—if it was Florence—fits Lollie Pate's description, but I just can't figure out the connection."

Bennett helped Ellis into her coat. "So what's the next step?" he asked.

"We'll need to talk with Lollie—see if we can find out what this is all about," Ed said, putting his empty coffee mug in the sink. "And if it turns out she did have something to do with what happened to Florence Calhoun, I'm sure the chief will want an affidavit from the woman in Asheville."

"You will let us know something." It was not a question. Ellis turned to face him on her way out.

Ed Tillman flashed her something akin to a smile. "As soon as the chief says it's okay."

"Chief my ass!" Bennett thundered. "You've practically accused my wife of murdering her own cousin—and God knows what you might suspect in Boyd Henry's death! Seems to me that if these women have done your legwork for you, the least you can do is to keep them informed."

Ed glanced at his partner, who shrugged. "If we learn anything new, I'll be in touch tomorrow," he said, jamming on his hat.

Lucy thought she would fall asleep as soon as her head hit the pillow, but she couldn't stop thinking about Lollie Pate. What possible reason would Lollie have to become involved in the mystery surrounding Florence Calhoun? The clay on Florence's shoes seemed to suggest she had spent some time in or near the Hemphills' cottage at the Folly. Had Lollie been there as well? Lucy flipped her pillow to the cool side. Her eyes burned and her head felt as if it weighed a ton. What connection could these two women have, and what would they be doing together at the Folly?

Lucy was dreaming of Charlie when the ringing of the telephone woke her, and for a minute she thought the alarm clock was waking her husband for work. She rolled over in bed and reached to shut off the alarm on Charlie's bedside table when it hit her with a whammy, as it always did, when she found only an empty space beside her.

"I was about to give up," Ellis said, when Lucy finally answered the phone. "Are you okay?"

Lucy yawned. "Do I have to give you an answer now? What time is it?"

"After nine . . ." Ellis paused and Lucy guessed a big announcement was forthcoming. She was right. "Lollie's flown the coop," she said.

"*What?*"

"I just spoke with Ed Tillman. He and Sheila went to her house to question her early this morning and no one was there."

"She's probably at the shop," Lucy said. "She goes in early on baking days."

"Not there, either. And there's a 'closed' sign on the door."

"Do you think she got wind the police wanted to talk to her?" Lucy followed her nose into the kitchen and poured herself a cup of coffee that smelled of cinnamon. From the window she could see Augusta playing with Clementine on the lawn.

"Maybe. I just wonder where she could be." Lucy heard the rattle of china and the sound of running water and knew her friend was rinsing her breakfast dishes. Ellis refused to put them in the dishwasher with even a crumb on the surface. "Ed told me they were going to search the cottage at the Folly to see if they could turn up anything that might suggest that Florence was there."

"What about that tower? The Folly itself?" Lucy asked.

"They looked there earlier when they found Calpernia's body, but nothing turned up. Ed said there were paving stones all around the foot of it, so they didn't find any footprints."

Lucy waved to Augusta from the window. "I wonder if Poag knows about this. Must be like pouring salt in a wound."

"I just hope they find her soon," Ellis said. "If she's the one responsible for all that's been going on, I won't feel safe until Lollie Pate is locked away in the hoosegow!"

Knowing how much Augusta felt the cold, Lucy guessed that the weather must be mild or the angel wouldn't be outside romping with Clementine. After eating a quick bowl of cereal, she browsed through her closet until she found a pair of jeans that fit and threw on a lightweight sweater. She wanted to see for herself if Do-Lollie's had really been abandoned. And then she remembered the pin. In all the excitement of the last few days, Lucy hadn't thought to check and see if the jeweled iris was still where she had put it. It seemed to take forever to fumble through all the garments she should have long since given away, and she could hear herself breathing when she finally located the formal. *The pin was still there!*

"I should've given it to the police last night. I just wasn't thinking," she told Augusta as they walked with Clementine to town, stopping at every tree and lamppost so the puppy could investigate the smells. It was warm for the first week in November and Lucy was glad for the exercise.

Augusta started to answer, then paused to shade her eyes. "Somebody's waving at you," she said, squinting in the direction of town.

"Why, it's Nettie. Don't tell me you can't recognize her from here!" Lucy waved at her neighbor. "Augusta, you must need glasses."

"Nonsense, I can see perfectly well. The sun was in my eyes." The angel stooped to tickle the puppy's ears.

"Have you heard anything from the fliers we sent out?" Nettie hurried to meet her. She had obviously been to the library, as she had a stack of books under her arm. Lucy noticed one was Patricia Sprinkle's latest mystery.

"How much time do you have?" Lucy started to tell her what had happened when her neighbor interrupted her.

"I was going to stop by Do-Lollie's and pick up some of her

cinnamon buns, but there's a 'closed' sign on the door," she said, seeming alarmingly close to tears. "And my mouth was all set to have one with coffee. I do hope she's not sick."

"I think we'd better call an emergency meeting of The Thursdays this afternoon," Lucy said, with a consoling pat. "There's something you all need to hear."

CHAPTER TWENTY-FOUR

Well, I can tell you why Lollie Pate had it in for Calpernia," Zee announced. "Remember last year when the county celebrated its bicentennial? Calpernia was in charge of casting the pageant, and Lollie didn't get a part."

"That's hardly a reason for murder," Idonia said. "How do you know she wanted one?"

"Because she auditioned—sang, actually." Zee shook her head. "'Chattanooga Choo-Choo.' It was pretty awful, I've heard, but just about everybody else was cast, so it must've been a real slap in the face." She kicked off her shoes and curled up on the leather sofa in Ellis's family room where The Thursdays had gathered around a basket of men's white cotton socks and a large bag of fiber filling. Every Christmas the group made stocking dolls for the children at the local hospital. After the figures were stuffed with the soft fiber, Nettie stitched on the faces, Idonia added yarn hair, and the others made clothes for the sock babies. Today Ellis had decided that since they were going to meet anyway, they might as well get started.

"You had a part in that pageant, didn't you, Ellis?" Jo Nell asked.

"If you could call it a part. Two lines: *I can hardly remember his face*, and *The Yankees are burning the Wilcox place. I can see the smoke from here!*"

"That's three lines," Claudia said, cramming fiberfill into a bulging sock. "I was one of the flappers and we got to dance the Charleston . . . but you're right about Lollie being upset," she added, looking up. "She was after one of the lead roles."

Ellis rolled her eyes. "Calpernia got one, naturally. I thought she looked ridiculous in that *Rosie the Riveter* costume."

"My goodness, that was over a year ago," Nettie said. "Surely she wouldn't hold a grudge that long over something as silly as that!"

She flushed as soon as she said it, and Lucy noticed that everyone tried to avoid looking at Zee.

"Say what you please," Zee said, "but I know for certain that Lollie *did* more than harbor bad feelings over that slight because Poag told me about it himself."

"What do you mean?" Idonia asked.

Zee shrugged. "He said he couldn't prove anything, of course, but somebody poured bleach all over Calpernia's new porch cushions, and one day she found a dead possum in her car."

Lucy laughed. "A dead possum? Where would she get that?"

"Road kill, I reckon," Zee said. "Wish I'd thought of it first." She inspected the lumpy toy she had stuffed, turning it in her hand. "You know what I think?" she asked no one in particular. "I think it's bad enough having to be in the hospital during the holidays without having one of these things thrust upon you!"

"Here, let me have it," Jo Nell said, laughing, and held out her hand for the misshapen doll. She removed some of the stuffing and molded it into shape. "So . . . let's say Lollie *did* have something to do with the two women's deaths . . . why would she kill Boyd Henry?"

"Boyd Henry saw something he shouldn't have," Nettie told her. "I'm convinced of it."

"Heck, she's probably halfway to Mexico by now," Lucy told them. "Her shop was locked up tight, shades were drawn, and a 'closed' sign hung in the door."

"I guess this means we won't be getting any more lemon chess tarts," Nettie said.

"Why, Nettie McGinnis, how could you think of such a thing?" Claudia, who had been sewing stubby arms on her creation, let the doll tumble into her lap.

Jo Nell frowned. "You don't suppose *Poag* had something to do with Calpernia's death, do you?"

"How could he? Poag was on the other side of the ocean when Calpernia died, remember?" Ellis reminded her.

"That's right. She was at that bon voyage concert they gave at the college the night he left," Idonia said. "Even went to the bus to tell him good-bye before they got on the plane. He couldn't have pushed her off that tower unless he can be in two places at once."

"Besides, Poag Hemphill really cared about Calpernia," Nettie said. "Why would he want to kill her?"

Zee stood and stretched. "Don't kid yourself," she said. "Not that the man didn't have feelings for his wife, but Poag will come into a tidy little sum from Calpernia's estate."

"I'm still putting my money on that Jay What's-His-Name," Jo Nell whispered aside to Lucy.

Ellis put a hand on Lucy's arm as the others were leaving to let her know she wanted her to stay. "I didn't want to get into this in front of the others," she told her as they picked up after the stuffing session, "but it looks like Leonard is dropping his suit."

"Really? That's great! What happened? Did old Len get religion?"

Ellis made a face. "Nope, he got a divorce. Our lawyer found out he had filed for a divorce before Florence disappeared, and then, when he learned who she was, he tried to withdraw the suit—"

"Only by that time his wife was dead and the divorce was final," Lucy said. "What a snake!"

"I've been thinking about some kind of fitting memorial in honor of Florence's life," Ellis said, "and Bennett and I have decided to establish a scholarship fund at Sarah Bedford for students from foster families."

"I think Florence would approve," Lucy said, hugging her.

Augusta met her with a smile as soon as she walked in the door.

"What is it?" Lucy tossed her sweater on a chair.

"Your daughter telephoned. There's a message on your machine." Augusta beamed as if she'd invented the device.

"How long ago?" Lucy hurried to check her messages.

"About an hour. She wants you to call."

Lucy punched in Julie's number that was programmed into her phone and listened to her daughter's voice: *Julie and Buddy aren't here right now. Leave a message and we'll get back to you.*

Blah! Lucy thought. Double-blah! But she left a message asking her daughter to call. There was also a panicky-sounding plea from Patsy Sellers at Bellawood begging Lucy to phone her *as soon as possible.* It sounded urgent.

"Thank heavens you got back to me! I was afraid you might be out of town," Patsy said when she called. "Tomorrow is my last day here and I'm afraid we're in a bit of a dilemma. I'm trying to get out a newsletter about the production we're staging here and I could really use some help."

"What production?" Lucy asked, wondering what help she could possibly be after all this time.

"Haven't you heard? The board has decided to present an

annual musical based on the founding of the community. They're calling it *Stone's Throw Remembers*."

"When will all this take place?" Lucy asked.

"Next summer, we hope—as soon as they finish with the barn. They're planning to build a theater in there."

"Sounds exciting," Lucy said, "but Patsy, I don't know how much help I would be. It's been so long since I—"

"I've done most of the layout already and made scads of notes for the lead article if you could put it together for me. The guy who's going to write and direct it is coming here tomorrow if you could just meet him for an interview and maybe take a couple of photographs of the barn. We're trying to raise funds and interest new members, and this would give people an idea of what we have in mind."

When Lucy didn't respond immediately, Patsy jumped in again. "I'll be here, of course, to go over the details with you. I'm sure they'll find somebody to fill my position soon, but this is such an important issue, and you're familiar with the history of the area. Oh, please, Mrs. Pilgrim, you'd be doing me a tremendous favor if you would help out just this once!"

Lucy opened her mouth to say that this was *not* a good time, and then she thought, *Why not?* She had been seeking a new direction in her life, and this was as good a time and as good a direction as any. Besides, it was only temporary, wasn't it?

"What time do you want me?" she asked, then had that stomach-knotting sensation you get when you take the wrong turn on the interstate. What had she gotten herself into?

"I have a feeling I'm going to need an angel looking over my shoulder," Lucy said the next morning as they breakfasted on Augusta's cheese omelet before leaving for Bellawood. She had changed her clothes three times because she wasn't sure what to wear and finally decided on tailored gray slacks with a white blouse and comfortable flats. She felt she looked something like an overgrown pigeon, but it would have to do.

Augusta was looking forward to spending more time at Bellawood because, as she admitted, she felt at home in the past.

"I expect your friend who makes the lovely furniture will be there as well," Augusta said, smoothing the skirt of her tiered georgette dress on which creamy white flowers cascaded against a background of a watercolor blue.

Lucy laughed. "He might. It's a shame he can't see you, Augusta—but then I wouldn't be able to stand up to the competition!"

The angel's cheeks turned almost as pink as her brightly painted toenails. "Good gracious, Lucy Nan, you do make a mound out of an anthill! I only meant the gentleman seems to be pleasant company."

Since Julie hadn't returned her call of the night before, Lucy tried once again to reach her daughter but was greeted with the same recorded message. She was touching up her lipstick when the telephone rang, and Lucy almost collided with the hall table in her rush to answer.

"I've been thinking," Ellis said.

"There's a first time for everything, they say." Lucy ran a comb through her hair as they spoke. "Better tell me quick. I'm heading out the door for Bellawood." She told Ellis about agreeing to help Patsy with the newsletter.

"Bennett found out from somebody he knows at the police department that Lollie Pate did rent a car when she and Florence got off the bus in Greenville that day, and she returned it in Columbia five days later."

"So we were right! That creeps me out, Ellis. I don't suppose she's turned up yet?"

"No, but get this: The car she rented had dents on the front bumper that hadn't been there before."

Lucy looked at her watch. "So she must've hit something. What?"

"Do *garbage cans* ring a bell? Lollie was the one who ran into your cans that night—and probably the one who phoned Florence and told her to meet her in the church parking lot."

"But why? There has to be a reason. And where was Florence all that time?"

"Exactly," Ellis said. "She had to be somewhere before she showed up at your door."

"Her shoes had clay on them like the kind at the Folly. Lollie could've kept her hidden in the cottage—I doubt if it would be all that hard to get in, and Poag wouldn't know. He hardly goes out there anymore, and then he left for that concert tour in Europe."

"Makes sense, except the police didn't find any sign of her when they searched the place yesterday. Poag had somebody come in and clean it after Calpernia died." Ellis hesitated. "That just leaves one place to look—Lollie Pate's."

"I'm sure they've already searched there," Lucy said.

"For Lollie, but not for signs that Florence had been there. I wonder if I could just maybe . . . well . . . peek in a window . . . "

"I don't like where you're headed with this," Lucy told her. "Just let the police take care of it. I gotta go or I'll be late the first day, but promise you won't do anything stupid!"

Ellis laughed. "I promise," she said. Or at least that's what Lucy thought she said.

CHAPTER TWENTY-FIVE

The docents hadn't arrived when Lucy pulled into the parking lot at Bellawood and Augusta took the opportunity to explore the outbuildings while Lucy met with Patsy in her small office off the back porch of the main house.

Patsy, who looked as if she might deliver at any minute, struggled to stand and greet her. "How's the new puppy?" she asked with a welcoming smile.

"Clementine's fine. Nettie's dropping by to let her out while I'm gone." Lucy waved her back into her chair. "Now, please sit down and let me do the legwork today. I might be able to help you with the newsletter, but 'I don't know nothin' 'bout birthin' no babies!'"

Patsy laughed. "Relax! He's not due for another month."

They'd had no trouble finding homes for Clementine's litter mates, Patsy told her, and Shag, the mother dog, had taken up permanent residence in the smokehouse except during holidays when one of the docents claimed her.

The two of them spent more than an hour going over the upcoming edition of *Past Times*, Bellawood's monthly newsletter, and discussing the duties Lucy would be expected to perform if she decided to stay on.

"It doesn't pay much, but I found I could do a lot of the work at home. Sometimes I only come in two or three days a week, and it's never dull," Patsy explained. She looked at her watch. "Jay should be here in a few minutes. I think you'll find him an easy interview, and he certainly seems enthusiastic about this project."

"Jay? Jay Warren-Winslow?" Lucy hoped her astonishment didn't show in her face.

Obviously it did. "Oh, I know, everybody thought he had something to do with Calpernia Hemphill's death, but that's ridiculous!" Patsy shooed the notion away with a wave of her hand. "He's a very talented man: writes, directs, and I think you'll find him a pleasure to work with. We're lucky he agreed to a contract for the little we can afford to pay."

I'll bet! Lucy wanted to ask if they were sure the man hadn't padded his résumé, but this was probably not the time, since she glimpsed the young director approaching from across the yard. She also saw Augusta step from the outside kitchen and follow along behind and had to restrain herself from shouting with relief.

Don't be an idiot, she told herself. *The man has lived in Zee's guest house for almost a month and other than his lack of knowledge about Perry Como, she seemed content with his presence—besides, Bellawood was now swarming with docents and visitors. What could he possibly do?*

"Jay tells me the two of you have met, so I'll skip the introductions," Patsy said as the young man entered and draped himself on a wingback chair across from Patsy's desk. Lucy was happy to see Augusta occupying the other one. The small room was functional yet comfortable with whitewashed walls, narrow recessed windows, and a worn, but still lovely, tapestry rug. Lucy chose to sit on the end of the tufted Victorian chaise which allowed her to speak eye to eye with Jay while being within a few steps of the door. After all, she reminded herself, *someone* was responsible for killing three people and had tried to add Ellis and her to their list. It seemed unlikely that Lollie had done it all alone.

With Patsy's encouraging presence, however, Lucy found herself forgetting her suspicions as she spoke with Jay about his background and experience. The young director had an easy manner and a quick sense of humor and she laughed so much at some of his tales, Lucy had to remind herself to take notes.

"I'll never forget the community production of *The Music Man* that was presented in a large tent during a violent rainstorm," he told them. "So much water had collected the canvas gave way and dumped what looked like about a bathtubful of water on the lead playing Marian the librarian."

"How awful! What did she do?" Lucy asked.

"After the shock wore off, she wrapped herself in a towel and finished her solo," he said. "The audience loved it."

"At least you won't have to worry about that happening here," Patsy told him. "The barn got a new roof just last year."

"About how many do you plan to cast in this production, and does it have a name yet?" Lucy asked.

"Right now we're calling it *Stone's Throw Remembers*, but I'm thinking of holding a contest to name it," Jay said, "and as for the cast—"

The ringing of Lucy's cell phone interrupted his answer and she apologized, excusing herself to take the call. "I can't imagine who would be calling me here," she explained, "unless it's something urgent."

As she stepped onto the porch to answer, Lucy's thoughts went immediately to her family, as they always did when she received an unexpected phone call, and she was comforted to see Augusta beside her.

"Lucy Nan, do you know where Ellis is?" Bennett Saxon sounded almost breathless, which was most unusual for him.

"We were supposed to meet for lunch and I have no idea where to find her."

"Maybe she just forgot," Lucy said, although it would be unusual for Ellis to forget about food, especially food she didn't have to cook. "Have you checked the house?"

"She's not there and her car's gone . . . I thought she might have mentioned her plans to you."

Lucy could sense the panic in his voice and tried to speak calmly. "She probably got in a long checkout line at the grocery store. I'm sure she'll show up. Try not to worry."

"But I do worry. It's not like Ellis to be this late, and with all that's been going on lately, I'm afraid for her safety," Bennett said. "Do you have *any* idea where she might be?"

Lucy took a deep breath. Yes, she did have an idea, but Ellis had *promised*. "Bennett, I don't want to frighten you, but I think you might want to give the police a call." She told him what Ellis had said about looking in the windows of Lollie's house. "I don't think she'd try to go inside, but she was hoping to find some sign Florence might have been staying there," she said. "And it wouldn't be a bad idea to check out at the Folly, too."

"I've got to go!" Lucy told Augusta when she got off the phone. "Ellis has disappeared and Bennett's frantic. I'm afraid she's poking around for signs Florence might have been at Lollie Pate's—or she could've even decided to search out at the Folly. If Lollie turns up at one of those places, Ellis could be in danger."

Augusta spoke softly. "And if you go, you might be in danger, too. It's not a wise idea, Lucy Nan."

"But what if she's in trouble? What if she needs help?"

"Then her husband and the police should be able to take care of it." Augusta came close to sighing. "I hope you can understand just how very frustrating it is when someone you care about ignores your advice," she said. "I'm asking you not to go."

If they had been in a different situation, Lucy would have laughed. "How could I *not* understand? I'm a *mother!*"

And if Ellis hadn't ignored *her* advice, she wouldn't be in this quandary, she thought. "All right, since you put it that way, I won't go—but on one condition."

A wind blew across the porch where they stood and Augusta pulled her cape more closely about her. "And that is . . . ?"

"You go in my place." Lucy could see the angel was about to refuse. "Look around you, Augusta. There are people all over the place, Patsy's right inside, and Ben is probably somewhere close by. I'll be perfectly all right."

"Just see that you stay that way," Augusta said finally. "I won't be long."

"Please look after Ellis!" Lucy whispered to her as she stepped back inside.

"Is anything wrong?" Patsy Sellers asked as Lucy closed the door behind her. "I hope no one's sick."

Lucy forced a smile. "A friend of mine got her lines crossed. Nothing serious." *I hope.*

"It's the strangest thing," Jay said suddenly, "but I've been smelling strawberries all morning. Tell me I'm imagining it."

Patsy laughed. "So have I! Maybe it's because we're hungry. I didn't realize it was after one. Why don't we stop for a lunch break? You can buy snacks and drinks here, but there's no place close by for lunch, so I took the liberty of bringing soup and sandwiches from home. Hope everybody likes ham."

Everybody did like ham, it seemed, as the three of them quickly put away the sandwiches and homemade vegetable soup. Lucy was pleased when Patsy pointed out a small refrigerator and microwave in a recessed area disguised as a cupboard.

"I hope you two won't mind if I bow out a little early," Patsy told them as they finished their dessert of oatmeal cookies. "Have to collect our twins for a dental appointment and I don't want to be late."

"I think a few more questions should cover it," Lucy said quickly. As entertaining as Jay was, she still didn't relish the idea of being alone with him.

"Jay, why don't you show Mrs. Pilgrim the changes we plan to make in the barn?" Patsy suggested. "And we'll need several photos, too." She took a camera from her desk drawer. "This makes pretty good pictures and it's not too complicated," she said, showing Lucy how to operate it.

"I'll try my best," Lucy promised, "but only if you'll stop calling me Mrs. *Pilgrim!*"

Patsy laughed, "I'll try to remember, *Lucy*," she said on her way out.

"By the way," Lucy called to her, "is Ben Maxwell in his shop? I thought I'd stop in and say hello."

"He was here yesterday, but I think he went to a sawmill somewhere in North Carolina to see about ordering wood," Patsy said.

"I'll talk to you later," she said to Lucy. "Call me if you have a problem."

God forbid! Lucy thought, hearing the other woman's footsteps cross the porch and fade away. Looking at Jay, she tried to imagine him laughing as he charmed Calpernia Hemphill to the top of the Folly before shoving her to her death. "Okay," she said, grabbing her notepad, "before you shove—I mean, show me the barn, let's talk about your writing background, Jay. Have there been other plays?"

"A few—mostly light comedies, and a couple of one-act dramas. This will be my first experience with a production based on history and I'm going to have to depend on a lot of help from Stone's Throw's longtime citizens." He glanced at his watch. "In fact, I have an interview this afternoon with a neighbor of yours.

Zee tells me Nettie McGinnis is a descendant of one of the town's founders."

"You're right, and you'd better take a thick notepad and a lot of pencils," Lucy told him, laughing. She grabbed the camera. "Now, let's go see what they plan to do to that barn."

It was almost three o'clock when the two of them circled around the back of the kitchen and hurried past the small stone building where the springhouse once kept milk and butter cool. Lucy called to Shag, who perked up briefly from her nap on the smoke-house steps, then went back to sleep. As they passed through the gate where the puppies had escaped, Lucy noticed the locked door on Ben's woodworking shop. The schoolchildren had gone home now, and only a few curious visitors remained. Bellawood would soon be closing for the day and the place seemed lonely and silent. A narrow, dusty path led to the weathered old barn which was located at least a football field away from the house. It was unlocked, Lucy noticed, when Jay pulled open one of the huge double doors—probably because there was nothing of value inside to steal. The barn still smelled of the livestock that had once been kept there, and hay littered the floor in stalls now empty of horses. In a narrow tackroom to the side, a few harnesses and bridles—even an ancient yoke—hung from the walls and the burlap sacks used for picking cotton had been tossed in a pile in the corner.

Jay stood for a minute looking about as he drank from a bottle of water, then, putting the bottle aside, wandered about the vast building with long, loping steps. Lucy took a deep breath. If she closed her eyes she could almost imagine she was back on her un-cle's farm, where she and her brother took turns riding an old dappled mare named Sugar who always went at the same plodding pace. She stopped to take a couple of photos of the main part of the barn where a collection of primitive tools lined the rough-hewn walls and a ladder led to the loft.

It seemed Augusta should have been back by now and Lucy tried not to think of what might have happened if Ellis had run into Lollie Pate. *Where was she, and why hadn't someone called?* Lucy checked the cell phone in her purse to be sure the power was still on.

"Lucy?" Jay must have been trying to get her attention because he was looking at her quizzically. "Here's where we plan to build the stage," he said, pacing off an area at one end of the large room. "We'll only be using a portion of the building," he told her. "The dressing rooms will be backstage, of course, and there'll be a concessions area and rest rooms near the entrance, leaving the rest of the building in its original state."

"What about the loft?" Lucy asked as he posed in a comic stance while she snapped his picture.

He looked up at the wide boards, now gray with grime and time, where remnants of straw sifted through the cracks in the wind from the open door. "It'll need reinforcing, but it should give us just enough room for the flies—that's the space where scenery and equipment are raised and lowered. The floor of the auditorium will slope up, allowing room for docks beneath the stage." Jay laughed at Lucy's blank expression. "That's just a fancy name for storage space."

"It's hard to believe they could turn this creaky old place into a fancy theater," Lucy said, shaking her head. "It's going to cost a fortune!"

Jay stepped back and looked around him. "It won't be fancy, but it's not going to be cheap, either," he said. "That'll be your job, I guess, if you decide to take it on. We'll have to get everybody so excited about this project they'll be standing in line to donate their money!" He groaned as he looked at his watch. "Oh, crap! I'm late already! Do you mind seeing yourself out? Just pull the door shut behind you."

Lucy checked the film in her camera. "I won't be far behind, but I do want to get a few shots from another angle. Now, where did you say the dressing rooms will be?"

Feeling a little guilty and a lot silly for having suspected Jay, Lucy quickly took the photographs she wanted and sat on a wobbly bench to jot down a few technical terms before she forgot them. No wonder Zee enjoyed the young man's company! His enthusiasm was contagious, and Lucy was becoming more and more captivated by the lure of Bellawood.

She wasn't even aware that Lollie Pate stood behind her until she heard the creaking of the ancient floor timbers.

CHAPTER TWENTY-SIX

Whatever you do, don't show fear!

Lucy stood, measuring the distance to the door. Unfortunately, Lollie stood in the way. "Lollie. I didn't know you were here." Lucy spoke as if she had just come upon her at a reception, a backyard barbecue. *Take a deep breath. Act natural.* She took a step forward. "It's chilly in here, don't you think? Let's go where it's warm."

Lollie blocked her way. "I want the pin," she said.

Lucy's smile felt as if it had been plastered on her face with mucilage. "I don't know what you mean."

"Yes, you do. You may as well admit you have it. I know she left it there." The woman's usually neatly styled hair hung in limp strands about her face. She wore no makeup and her beige slacks were smeared with dirt.

Lollie Pate was probably a few pounds heavier than she was, but Lucy had it over her in height, and although Lollie didn't seem to have a weapon, one could easily be concealed in the pocket of her coat. Lucy thought of the cell phone tucked in her purse she had left on the floor behind her. If she could just get her hands on it, it would only take a few seconds to summon help. "Who?" she asked. "What pin, Lollie?"

"Shirley, of course! Or Florence—whatever her name was! Don't pretend with me. She left it with you, didn't she? Where have you hidden it?"

Lucy inched backward toward the purse. "Tell me about the pin, Lollie. Why do you want it?"

"I *must* have it! You don't understand. She took it, you see, and I have to get it back. My *life* depends on it." Lollie's voice rose and her hand trembled as she shoved the hair from her face. "Look, I don't want to hurt you, Lucy. Just give me the pin. *Please!*"

The purse was only a few inches away. "Nothing will happen to you if you only turn yourself in," Lucy said, keeping an eye on the other woman's face. "Just tell them the truth. They've been looking for you, Lollie. They want to help."

"Bullshit! You must think I'm a total fool. They want to lock me away—blame me for everything. Do you know what it's like to be afraid to go home? To have to live out of your car?" Lollie thrust her hands in her pockets and moved closer. "I've been watching you, you know. Waiting. I followed you here today."

Lucy drew herself up and stood her ground. One good smack would send this rotten little twit right into next week. *If she didn't have a gun, that is!* "What's so important about that pin?" she asked. "Why do you think Florence had it?"

"It belonged to that bitch Calpernia. Shirley—that little thief—took it from the cottage, must've sneaked it into her pocket when I wasn't looking." Lollie held out a hand—empty, Lucy noticed thankfully. "Why won't you just give it to me? The pin is all I'm after. You don't need it, but I do. It's my insurance, my only chance!"

"Your only chance for what? You're not making any sense,"

Lucy said. "And do you honestly think I would carry expensive jewelry around with me?"

"My only chance for life. He's after me now, too. I'm next, don't you see? But as long as I have the pin, he won't dare do anything!"

"He?"

"Poag. Poag Hemphill, that lying low-life slime, and who knows where he is now? He could be here at any minute." Lollie's mouth quivered. "Just take me to your house, please," she begged. "You can have my shop, my house—anything, if you'll let me have that pin."

"That was you at the Folly, wasn't it, that afternoon I was out there gathering cornstalks? You were looking for that pin." Lucy remembered the eerie feeling of being watched.

"Poag was furious when he discovered it missing. If Shirley had taken it, everyone would know where it came from, and he couldn't afford that. I was hoping it might've fallen behind something, but now I know better. What have you done with it, Lucy?"

"Oh, for heaven's sake, Lollie, I don't even have the pin. I turned it into the police yesterday."

"I don't believe you." Lollie dabbed at her eyes with a crumpled handkerchief.

"I don't care if you do or not, it's true," Lucy told her. "And why should I believe those lies about Poag?" she asked. "You were the one who lured Florence off that bus in Greenville and brought her here to Stone's Throw. Surely you could see the woman wasn't quite right—but that just suited your purpose, didn't it?" Lucy slid her foot to the side and felt her heel come in contact with the purse. "Why did you kill her, Lollie?" she asked softly.

"It was an accident! I didn't mean to. I called your house and told her that her mother was waiting for her in the church parking lot—she kept talking about her mother, you know. She got frightened when she saw me there and ran away when I tried to get her back into the car. She *fell* down those steps—I'll swear to God!" Lollie wiped away a tear . "I wouldn't have hurt that poor soul for the world! I'll tell you, it's just about torn me up inside—and how was I to know she was the little girl who used to live in your house? You could've knocked me over with a feather when she jumped from the car at that stop sign and ran up on your porch like a crazy person."

"Just what *did* you intend to do with Florence?" Lucy asked.

"It was all *his* idea. He lied to me—told me he loved me, that we'd be together. But all he wanted was that land—Calpernia's land. Poag planned it all."

Lucy spoke softly. "You look like you could use a tissue . . . and do you know you have dirt on your pants?" When Lollie looked down to brush off her slacks, Lucy picked up her purse and opened it, scooping up the cell phone with one hand as she gave the packet of tissues to Lollie. "What on earth would Poag Hemphill want with Florence?" she asked.

Lollie almost smiled. "Didn't you notice? She looked like her."

Lucy frowned. "Like who?"

"Why, Calpernia, of course! I noticed it as soon as I saw her sitting on that bus, and then, when I had a chance to talk with her, I could see she was—well, a few pickles shy of a quart. Why, she couldn't even remember where she lived. All she could talk about was going back to find her mother. With a different hairdo and makeup, I knew I could make her look enough like Calpernia Hemphill to fool everybody. After all, she would only be seen from a distance."

That's why Nettie had said that Florence looked familiar. She had been made up to look like Calpernia! Lucy swallowed. "I see," she said. And regrettably she did. "So Calpernia Hemphill was already dead when her husband left with the chorus for Europe? Did you push her from the Folly?"

"No! *No!*" Lollie Pate screamed, her face red and contorted. "I never touched her! I never killed anybody."

"You just helped to plan it."

"I did it for him! Poag and I . . . well, we had something special, or at least I thought we did, but after Calpernia died he didn't even want to be in the same room with me. Told me it was a safety precaution, that we'd get together later, but I could see it was over—and after all I did!"

Lucy's fingers closed around the phone, counted the buttons . . .

"Nobody was supposed to *die*," Lollie whined.

"Except Calpernia."

Lollie nodded. "Right, except Calpernia, and Poag took care of that. Took her out to the Folly on a hike the afternoon before he left on that tour."

"But Calpernia was afraid of heights."

Lollie smiled. "Too bad she wasn't afraid of Poag! He got her up in that tower by telling her he wanted to get a better view so she could explain how she planned to develop her precious theater workshop." Her laugh sounded more like a groan. "Poag wasn't about to let valuable land go to waste like that when a developer was willing to pay big bucks to build a fancy golf course out there."

"What did you plan to do about Florence? Weren't you afraid she would give you away?" It was difficult to use a cell phone when you couldn't see what you were doing and Lucy hoped she was pressing the right buttons for 911. She tried to hold Lollie's attention so she wouldn't notice.

"Not from L.A.!" Lollie reached for her arm. "Come on, let's go to your place. I know you have that pin somewhere."

Lucy had almost completed the call, all she had to do was send it. "L.A.? You mean Los Angeles?"

"I was going to put Shirley on a plane to California. It was far enough away so she'd never find her way back, and once they discovered her wandering around the airport out there, it wouldn't take them long to realize she belonged in some kind of institution." Lollie shrugged. "I told her her mother was out there . . . hey, what're you doing?"

"Get out of my way! I've had just about enough of you." Lucy pushed her aside. The phone was dialing the number.

"Well, well, well, if it isn't two of my favorite people! How nice to find you together." Poag Hemphill stood only a few feet behind them and held out his hand. "I'll take that cell phone, please." In his other hand he held a gun and it was pointed right at Lucy.

Was this the man who not so very long ago had taught her to rumba at one of the many parties he and Calpernia hosted? The man she always enjoyed playing bridge with because he knew such great jokes?

He wasn't joking now. Lucy felt as if an empty cast of herself were standing there. The hand holding the cell phone seemed to be frozen in place. Words formed in her head but she couldn't get them out of her mouth. Would she ever see her family again?

"The phone," Poag repeated. "Give me the cell phone, Lucy Nan."

Someone answered at the other end of the line. She could hear a voice, but couldn't make out the words. "The barn at Bellawood!" Lucy shouted. "Hurry!" And she threw the phone as hard as she could at Poag Hemphill's face.

It missed him by inches as he stepped quickly to the side. "Nice try, but no cigar," he said, kicking the phone out of reach. The hand with the gun remained steady. "If anyone heard you—which I doubt—they'll never get here in time. Too bad, because I've always been fond of you, Lucy Nan. It's not a good idea, you know, to probe about in affairs that don't concern you. It does seem a shame, though, to do away with this venerable old building."

For the first time Lucy noticed the kerosene lantern he had set on the floor behind him. She could smell the acrid scent as she watched the lighted wick flicker blue in the wind. "Why?" When Lucy spoke, it sounded like somebody else's voice.

His laughter had no sound. "Can you really see all that beautiful land at the Folly turned into some kind of *theater colony?* Now I support the arts as much as the next person, but that's going to the extreme. Why, if Calpernia had her way, they would have started on the amphitheater by Christmas!"

"You're crazy! I'm sorry I ever had anything to do with this!" Lollie tried to run past, but he pivoted like a dancer, swung her about, and threw her in Lucy's direction where she stumbled and fell to the floor. "I'd rather not put a bullet in your head, Lollie dear. It would just ricochet in your empty little skull," he told her.

Lucy kept her eyes on the lantern. "Why did you have to kill Boyd Henry? He was never a threat to you."

"Lollie seemed to think he was. Ask her." He glanced briefly at the woman who now crouched crying at Lucy's feet. "I'm afraid he made the mistake of *approaching Lollie* about the night that Shirley woman was killed. Said he saw her leaving the parking lot at the Methodist Church when he was out planting tulips that night. It's as bright as day in front of that church with all the lights they have out there, and old Boyd Henry, bless his heart, never missed a thing. Wanted to know if she noticed anything unusual going on."

Lollie Pate, still sobbing, crawled to her feet. "He wouldn't leave me alone! Every time I turned around, there was Boyd Henry Goodwin wantin' to know if that wasn't a new car I'd been driving that night, and was I *sure* I hadn't seen anything. I could tell he didn't believe me. Something was bothering him, he said, and I knew it was only a matter of time before he told somebody else. He just about drove me crazy!"

"So you came to me, and of course I had to get him out of the way," Poag said. "Just what did you expect me to do?" He looked at Lucy with a smug smile. "The Saxons' pool was a clever touch, don't you agree? I called and told him Ellis and I were as concerned as he was about what was going on, and asked him to meet us there. Couldn't swim a lick—can you believe it?"

Lucy watched in horror as he picked up the lantern, motioning to them with the gun. "As much as I'm enjoying this little chat, *tempus fugit*, as they say, and I think it's time for a tour of the tackroom—a brief tour, in your case." Swinging the lantern, he urged them in front of him. "I wouldn't try running if I were you. I may not be much of a shot, but I can hardly miss at this distance."

"I can't believe you're doing this after all we had between us," Lollie said, reaching out to him. "You know I care about you, Poag! I'll never tell a soul—I promise! We can go somewhere together— someplace where nobody knows us."

"I'll admit I found you enticing—even amusing—for a period, and I do thank you for your part in helping to arrange for Calpernia's last bow—so to speak, but I'm afraid your services are no longer required, my dear girl." Poag Hemphill held the lantern in front of him. "Step lively, now, ladies," he said, raising his voice. "My patience is wearing thin."

Lucy's patience was wearing thin as well, and she had no intention of allowing that fool to lock her in the tackroom. *I'd rather be shot than burned to death,* she thought, but would prefer to avoid either. And what was taking Augusta so long? If this was how she watched over her charges, she needed to get her angel status upgraded to *dependable.* She should have been back by now.

Should she run now and take a chance on being shot, or wait for a better opportunity? Lucy wondered. She was running out of time and the tackroom was only a few feet away when the light scent of strawberries told her Augusta was near. And there she stood directly in front of them, her hand resting on a shelf beside the tackroom door.

Fear and anger simmered to the boiling point inside her. If she opened her mouth she would spew lava, Lucy thought. Here she was about to become barbecue and Augusta Goodnight stood before her as relaxed and unconcerned as if they were waiting in line for a movie. The angel's fingers drummed a light tattoo next to the half-filled bottle of water Jay had left behind.

Bottle of water! Poag was so concerned about getting them inside the narrow room, he didn't see Lucy snatch up the bottle, and when he set down the lantern to herd them inside, she threw its contents over the wick of the kerosene lantern and watched the flame sputter into smoke.

"In the corner! Quickly!" Augusta directed, following them into the straw-littered room. *The corner? Does she think Poag won't notice me in the corner?* Lucy looked where Augusta pointed. *Where the burlap sacks were piled.*

Lollie's screaming distracted Poag for only a few seconds, but it was long enough for Lucy to snatch up one of the rough brown sacks and throw it over his head, then, giving him a swift kick in the place where she thought it would hurt the most, she tackled him and threw Poag Hemphill to the floor. In all the confusion, she didn't notice he had dropped the gun until Lollie picked it up.

"Help me, Lollie!" Lucy sat on Poag's struggling form. "I know I saw some rope hanging out there somewhere. Help me tie him up!"

But Lollie just stood there and for a few seconds looked from the gun in her hand to the two people on the floor, and then she turned and ran. Unfortunately for her, she tripped over a bale of straw that hadn't been there before.

"Lucy Nan, are you all right?" Ellis raced to a stop in the doorway. "And who's that you're sitting on?"

"Poag Hemphill, and I'm getting tired of it." Lucy gave her a brief rundown of what had happened. "Do you think you could give me a hand?"

Ellis grinned. "Love to!" She plopped down on the moaning form with a thump. "Bennett's outside with the police. They got your call and were just in time to greet our friend Lollie."

"But she has a gun!" Lucy said.

"Turned out to be a prop gun," Ellis said. "All it does is make a loud noise."

Lucy, who had been binding her prisoner mummy-style, pulled the rope a little tighter.

"Where were you?" Lucy asked as the two of them walked back to the main house, leaving the police in charge of Poag. "Bennett was worried to death."

"I did go out to Lollie's, but not by myself," Ellis said. "I took your advice and let the police handle it." She grinned. "Talked Ed and Sheila into meeting me there. Guess I clean forgot the time."

"Did you find anything?"

"Zilch! But Ed says they've been talking to this woman who runs one of those little dinky motels a few miles outside of town, and it sounds like Lollie and Florence might've been staying there."

"They're a pair, aren't they—Lollie and Poag? They deserve each other!" Lucy walked a little faster. She was dying for a cup of coffee and a bathroom—not necessarily in that order.

"Augusta had a feeling something was wrong out here," Ellis said. "She caught up with us at Lollie's and couldn't get back fast enough. Heck, I reckon I made Bennett break every speed record getting here to see if you were okay. If the police hadn't been so eager to catch Lollie, they'd probably put both of us under the jail."

"At least you're not a suspect anymore," Lucy said. "You ought to make that Elmer Harris eat crow!"

"Thanks to you and Augusta—and The Thursdays, of course. Guess it doesn't hurt to have an angel on your side!" Ellis looked about. "Say, where is Augusta? I know I saw her a few minutes ago."

"Probably gone back to the house where it's warm. You know how cold-natured she is."

Ellis frowned. "You mean your house in town? How does she *do* that?"

Lucy shrugged. "Beats me. I don't care how she does it as long as she sticks around. That house is too big for one person."

Ellis glanced at the woodworking shop as they paused at the gate. "What about Ben?" she asked, giving Lucy a slight jab with her elbow.

Lucy jabbed back. "Don't rush me. Besides, if Ben could see Augusta, I'd have tough competition. I think she has a crush on him." She quickened her pace as they approached the main house. "I hope the police will make their questions short. I'm ready for a long, hot soak in the tub and maybe some of Augusta's soup."

"Better tell her to make enough for three," Ellis said, stopping her with a hand on her arm. "I almost forgot—you have company! When I called your house earlier to see if you'd gotten home from Bellawood, Julie answered the phone."

CHAPTER TWENTY-SEVEN

*I*f you run out of directing jobs, you can always get hired as a cook," Ellis told Jay as The Thursdays sat around the dining room table at Zee's. Jay had made a big pot of clam chowder to thank them for their part of clearing his name in the murder of Calpernia Hemphill. Claudia had brought her favorite green salad tossed with walnuts and apple slices, Lucy contributed some of Augusta's bacon-cheese muffins, and Ellis, her usual funeral cake. "I don't know how many times I've made it, and I never get to eat any," she told them.

Nettie provided the wine. Now she refilled Jay's glass and her own. "What a shock that must've been, finding Calpernia like that at the foot of that tower!" she said.

He helped himself to another muffin and nodded. "Not something I'm likely to forget. Her car was parked at the cottage and I could hear the two dogs yapping inside, but nobody came to the door, so I thought I'd find her strolling about the property. Cal liked to be outdoors, but if you'll remember, it was cold as a witches' t—— uh, a banker's heart that week."

"Unusual for that early in October," Jo Nell said. "Went down to freezing that night. And that poor woman was lying out in the cold while Lollie was right there in the cottage making up Florence to look like Calpernia."

"I doubt if she noticed it, Jo Nell, since she was dead," Zee reminded her. "I heard that Lollie Pate told the police Poag brought some of Calpernia's clothing out earlier for Florence to wear. And then of course he had a fit later when he learned Florence had taken that pin because it connected her to the Folly. What a cold-blooded monster he is!"

Idonia shuddered. "And to think we invited him to our Christmas drop-in last year! He and Lollie have been planning to do away with Calpernia for some time, I hear."

"Since Calpernia started making serious plans for that theater workshop," Lucy told them. "Lollie says he wanted her to push Calpernia from the tower but she refused. Actually, they didn't have a definite plan in mind until Lollie met Florence on the bus—"

Nettie stabbed the air with her salad fork. "I *told* you she reminded me of somebody!"

"Poag strung Lollie along by telling her they would go somewhere together and live off the money he'd make on the sale of the land," Lucy continued. "I understand they had been lovers— if you can call it that—for a year or so, but toward the last, he was just biding his time until the occasion was right. He couldn't pull this off alone. He had to have Lollie's help."

"And somewhere down the road, he would've probably managed to get rid of her as well," Nettie said, shaking her head. "But why did Lollie take Florence to the cottage? She could've dressed her just as well at the motel, couldn't she?"

Ellis refilled her bowl from the tureen in the center of the table. "Don't forget Calpernia's makeup was there, and the dress she was to wear. Plus, somebody had to feed the dogs. They had to make it look like Calpernia spent the night there, you see, then fell from the tower when she went for a walk the next morning. Lollie even went so far as to make the bed look like it had been slept in and cooked a breakfast meal that afternoon of eggs and toast, then left the dishes in the sink."

"And that's when Florence took the pin," Nettie said. "Just think, if it hadn't been for that pin, we probably wouldn't have realized the link between Florence's death and what happened to Calpernia."

"Except for the shoes," Lucy said. "When Florence left her shoes in my closet she didn't realize she would be helping to solve her own murder. *And she told me she had eaten two breakfasts!* At the time, I just dismissed it as rambling, but now that we know more or less what happened, I see she was telling the truth. She ate the eggs Lollie cooked at the cottage, and had breakfast again the next morning."

"What happened to those rings Florence was wearing?" Nettie asked. "Remember, Lucy Nan? That young policeman spent most of a day searching our backyards."

"Lollie took them—*and* her money to make it look like a mugging after Florence fell down the steps," Ellis told them. "Probably got rid of them somewhere. I hear Calpernia's sister will be getting the pin."

"She could use a little sparkle in her life," Idonia said. "But who's taking care of her two little dogs?"

"One of her students at the college is adopting them, I believe," Claudia said. "She lives here in town and used to look after them when Calpernia was away—seems to be fond of them."

Everyone agreed that was a sensible solution, and silence reigned while they concentrated on their food. Lucy eyed Jo Nell's attempt at an arrangement (Ellis called them 'derangements') in the center of the table. It was her contribution to the meal and since it was the first week in December, consisted of a couple of silk poinsettias pointing cockeyed in different directions and a mound of Styrofoam balls shedding glitter, interspersed with sprigs of pine. Lucy found it beautiful, just as she found beautiful the friends gathered around it. How lucky she was to be among them!

"What I don't understand is how Lollie managed to get Florence to the concert that night without anybody suspecting anything," Jay said, ladling chowder into Zee's empty bowl.

"Oh, you know how Calpernia liked to put on the dog," Ellis told him. "It wasn't unusual for her to rent a chauffeured limousine if she wanted to make a splash, and don't forget, Poag had access to the wardrobe room at the college. Lollie simply dressed as a chauffeur and escorted Florence to Calpernia's usual box. It's practically inaccessible to the other seats in the balcony, and they got there after the lights went down, then left just before the concert ended. Nobody got close to her except Poag, who made a point to lean in the window and kiss his 'wife' good-bye."

"And the college newspaper even got a photo," Lucy said.

Nettie lifted her wineglass. "To Florence Calhoun, my old playmate. If she hadn't been who she was, he might have gotten away with it."

"Do you think it was Poag who called pretending to be Estelle?" Ellis asked Lucy as the two drove home together.

"Lollie denies it, and I believe her. She claims she was catering some kind of function at the college that afternoon, and Poag can sound just like a woman. Remember how funny he was in that womanless wedding?" Lucy made a face. "*He* should have been in the drama department!"

"He could've fooled me," Ellis said. "I thought he and Calpernia were as close as Siamese twins."

"You know, in a weird way, I think he really did care for her.

Calpernia was a good bit older than Poag, but they always seemed to get on well together. I ran into him out walking the dogs not long after she died, and I could swear he was heartbroken—it's just that he loved her money more."

"How was your visit with Julie and her boyfriend at Thanksgiving?" Ellis asked as she turned into Heritage Avenue. "I haven't had a chance to talk with you since she left."

Lucy smiled. "Actually, it went very well. You won't believe how tactful I was—although I'll admit I had to bite my tongue a couple of times. I heard Julie remind him more than once to take off his hat in the house and keep his feet off the furniture, so maybe the relationship's wearing thin. And remember, she was here for the weekend back in October—because she was worried about me, she said, but I think she needed a break from Buddy, too."

Ellis laughed. "Sounds like progress to me. Do you think she'll be home for Christmas?"

"I'm hoping. Ben and his son are joining us for Christmas dinner."

"The one who's a doctor?" Ellis asked.

"And good-looking, too," Lucy said, as Ellis pulled to a stop behind her house.

"You *are* wicked, Lucy Nan Pilgrim!" Ellis laughed as she drove away.

Lucy laughed, too, but she hesitated before going inside. Something was on her mind—something she needed to ask Augusta, and she wasn't sure she was going to like the answer.

"Who's wicked?" Augusta stood in the kitchen doorway with a quizzical smile on her face. Her long necklace sparkled amber and green against a soft sweater that might have been knitted from the twilight sky. From behind her came the piquant aroma of her savory vegetable casserole and . . . Lucy sniffed . . . yes . . . buttery garlic twists.

"Somebody phoned from Bellawood today," Augusta said. "They want to know if you plan to stay on after the holidays."

Lucy paused at the top of the steps. "Do you think I should?"

Augusta shook her head. "I'm not here to make decisions for you, Lucy Nan. As you know, life is made of choices, and this choice has to be yours." She followed her inside and took bread from the oven. "It might be a pleasant experience, however, with that nice man working nearby," she added in a soft voice.

Lucy turned from hanging her wrap on a hook by the door. "And what about your choice?" she asked, almost dreading the answer. Augusta had been unusually busy about the house lately: cleaning, baking, straightening things here and there. Was the angel putting things in order before moving on?

Setting the bread aside, Augusta tossed her apron over a chair. "My choice?"

"Your choice to stay here in Stone's Throw. Now that we know what happened to Florence and Calpernia, and Ellis isn't a suspect anymore, I thought you might be assigned elsewhere." Lucy swallowed, keeping her eyes on the purple-flowered apron. Its colors swam in a mist of tears. "And what's with all the constant cleaning and cooking? There's not an inch of room left in the freezer."

Augusta spoke softly. "My dear child, Christmas is less than three weeks away. I want us to be prepared." Gossamer skirt swirling, she whirled to the window and drew aside the curtain. "And haven't you noticed the weather lately?"

"The weather?" Lucy frowned. "What about it?"

"Why, everything is as it should be. I hear we might even have snow for Christmas—which means Sharon must be doing her job right." Augusta laughed at Lucy's puzzled expression. "*Sharon*, your former guardian angel. I hear she's been permanently assigned to the Heavenly Weather Department, so it seems you're stuck with me."

For a moment her smile faded. "And I have a feeling there are other secrets here in Stone's Throw that could use my attention as well."

"What secrets? Now you have me worried!" Lucy was torn between relief and apprehension.

"A wise man once said there are two days in the week about which one should never worry. One is yesterday and the other, tomorrow." Clapping her hands for Clementine, Augusta tossed her cape about her and took the puppy's leash from its hook. "Now, how about a quick stroll before supper? Race you around the block!"

Since readers have been asking for recipes for some of Augusta's specialties, here are a few. . . .

Stone's Throw Delicacies

Augusta's Heavenly Strawberry Muffins

1 (10 oz) package frozen strawberries, thawed and put through food processor (or $^1/_2$ pint of fresh berries, chopped and sweetened with about 2 tablespoons of sugar)

$^3/_4$ cup sugar

$^2/_3$ cup cooking oil

2 eggs

1$^1/_2$ cup all purpose flour

1 teaspoon soda

$^1/_2$ teaspoon salt

$^1/_2$ teaspoon cinnamon

Glaze:

$^3/_4$ cup confectioners' sugar

1 tablespoon or more of strawberry juice or milk

Heat oven to 350 degrees. Grease and flour muffin tins. (Augusta likes the baking spray.) Combine berries, sugar, oil, and eggs. Beat 2 minutes and add flour, soda, salt, and cinnamon. Add nuts if desired. Bake about 18 minutes. Cool and glaze. Store in tightly covered container in refrigerator. Makes about 12 or 14.

A favorite with children. To make a loaf, bake in loaf pan at 350 degrees for 50 to 60 minutes.

Lucy Nan's Cheese Straws

1 pound sharp Cheddar, grated

2 cups all purpose flour

1 stick butter, softened

1 teaspoon baking powder

salt to taste

$^1/_2$ teaspoon red pepper

$^1/_8$ teaspoon paprika

Preheat oven to 375 degrees. Grate cheese; add other ingredients and mix well. Run through cookie press in "straw" shapes about 2 or 3 inches long. Bake on ungreased cookie sheet until light brown or about 10 minutes. If you like them richer, add another $^1/_4$ cup butter. For those who don't have a cookie press, the dough can be refrigerated in a long roll until firm, then sliced and baked cookie style. Chopped pecans can also be added if you're making them this way.

(Served at most Stone's Throw social functions)

Ellis Saxon's "Funeral" Cake

(A cake to die for!)

2 cups all purpose flour

2 cups sugar

2 sticks butter or margarine

1 cup water or cold coffee

3 or 4 tablespoons cocoa

$^1/_2$ cup buttermilk

2 eggs

$^1/_2$ teaspoon cinnamon

pinch of salt

1 teaspoon soda

1 teaspoon vanilla

Mix flour and sugar in bowl. In saucepan, bring butter, water (or coffee), and cocoa to a boil. Pour over sugar and flour and blend. Add rest of ingredients and beat until smooth. Pour into greased 9 x 13 inch pan and bake 20 to 25 minutes at 400 degrees or until done.

Frosting:

1 stick butter or margarine

3 tablespoons cocoa

6 tablespoons milk or coffee

1 teaspoon vanilla

$^1/_2$ teaspoon almond extract

1 cup chopped pecans

$^1/_2$ cup grated coconut (optional—the frozen kind is fine)

Mix icing while cake is baking. Heat butter or margarine, cocoa, and milk until it boils. Add all other ingredients and stir until well mixed. Pour over hot cake when it is taken from the oven. Serve from pan.

Augusta's Raisin Nut Sandwich Filling

Cook in double boiler until thick:

1 cup sugar

1 beaten egg

grated rind of two lemons

1 tablespoon butter

juice of 2 lemons

Add while hot:

Enough mayonnaise or salad dressing to spread (about $^1/_2$ cup or less)

1 cup pecans, chopped or ground

1 cup raisins, chopped or ground

Remove crusts from bread and cut into shapes. Spread filling on bread for sandwiches, or refrigerate until ready for use.

(The Thursdays LOVE this!)

Frogmore Stew

Crab boil mix (comes in a small bag)

1 (12 oz) beer (optional)

juice of 1 lemon

1 large onion, quartered

Worchestershire sauce to taste

A couple of dashes of hot sauce

3 or 4 small red potatoes per person

1 ear of corn per person

$^1/_8$ to $^1/_4$ pound of kielbasa sausage per person

$^1/_3$ to $^1/_2$ pound of shrimp per person

Fill large pot about $^3/_4$ full of water. Add first six ingredients and bring to a rolling boil. Add potatoes and cook until tender. Remove potatoes, reserving boiling liquid. Put the potatoes in a large pot with a lid to retain heat. Add the corn to the boiling mixture and cook for about 5 to 10 minutes or until done. Remove corn and place in pot with potatoes. Add sausage to boiling mixture and cook about 5 minutes; remove and add to corn and potatoes. Lastly, add shrimp to the boiling mixture. As soon as they are pink, remove from water. (Overcooking makes them tough.) Add to pot with other ingredients and serve with cocktail sauce.

(This is a recipe from Frogmore, South Carolina. Some recipes include crab and others omit the potatoes.)